Other Books by Steve Brown

Black Fire
Radio Secrets
The Belles of Charleston

The Myrtle Beach Mysteries

Color Her Dead
Stripped To Kill
Dead Kids Tell No Tales
When Dead Is Not Enough
Hurricane Party
Sanctuary of Evil

Carolina Girls

Carolina Girls

Steve Brown

Chick Springs Publishing
Taylors, SC

First published in the USA in 2006 by
Chick Springs Publishing
PO Box 1130, Taylors, SC 29687
E-mail: ChickSprgs@aol.com
Web site: www.chicksprings.com

Library of Congress Control Number: 2006901920
Library of Congress Data Available

ISBN: 0-9712521-7-3

10   9   8   7   6   5   4   3   2

Author's Note

Acknowledgments

My thanks to the Carolina girls and boys for their assistance in preparing this story: Susie Brown Bunch, Mark Brown, Sonya Caldwell, Carla Griffin, Jennifer Guerette, Sally Heineman, Missy Johnson, Kate Lehman, Walter McGee, Kimberly Medgyesy, Mary Jo Moore, Ann Patterson, Stacey Randall, Linda Walker-Smith, Susan Snowden, Dwight Watt, and, of course, Mary Ella.

Dedication

This book is dedicated to all the people who believe that Pawleys Island is a very special place and still remember how it used to be.

Cast of Characters

Kate Youngblood—from Judson Mill
Johnny Youngblood—her uncle
Raymond Youngblood—Kate's father

Melanie Durant—tobacco heiress from Durham
Carolynn Hamby—Melanie's mother
Lee Hamby—Carolynn's husband & Melanie's stepfather

Virginia Lynne (Ginny) Belle—High Battery, Charleston
Mrs. Adelaide (Addy) Belle—grandmother to Ginny
Simms Belle—Ginny's father
Franklin Belle—Simms's uncle & brother of Adelaide
Augustus—creekman

Bailey Gillespie—political heiress from Fraser County
Irene Gillespie—Bailey's mother
Walter Gillespie—Bailey's father & United States senator
Arlie—Senator Gillespie's chief of staff
Alice Frey—maid
Wilma—Alice Frey's daughter
Marybeth—new wife of Senator Gillespie

Others
Jeb Stuart—Kate's boyfriend
James Stuart—Jeb's younger brother
Preston Winthrop—Bailey's boyfriend
Melvin Ott—private investigator

"One friend in a lifetime is much;
two are many; three are hardly possible."
—Henry Adams

Readers' Note

This is a story about going to the beach in the mid-sixties, the beach along the Carolina Coast. For those unfamiliar with the area, there is only one USC, the University of South Carolina, and the only real dispute between North and South Carolina is which school is the real "Carolina." But on one point there is no disagreement and that is that Carolina girls are the best in the world!

Before Pawleys . . .

Kate Youngblood was using a straw from her grandmother's broom to tempt a doodlebug from its lair when her uncle walked out of the back of her grandmother's house, down the steps, and into the backyard. A red-headed girl with a peach tone to her skin, Kate lay on the ground, her back to the house and her body curled around the hole of her prey.

Long-limbed and agile, Kate had just turned seventeen and wasn't oblivious to boys, just disinterested. While most of her friends spent their time tying up the party line, Kate had other interests, such as doodlebugs. This amused her uncle, and he stopped several feet away and listened to his niece as Kate tried to coax the bug from a hole not much larger than an eraser head and surrounded with loose sand.

"Doodle, doodle, come and get some bread and butter; doodle, doodle, come and get a barrel of sugar."

The teenager paused.

"Doodlebug, doodlebug, come up and get a grain of corn. Your house is burning up."

The broom straw did not move, and Kate's voice became more strident. "Doodlebug, doodlebug, come out of your hole; your house is on fire, and your children will burn up."

Kate jiggled the twig. Her impatience was showing, and to Uncle Johnny, that wasn't all on display. Besides the long limbs and curly red hair, his niece's wiry frame had produced an eye-catching chest and nicely rounded bottom; but that delicious-looking figure had never been seen outside Greenville County and very few times in a bathing suit. His niece spent too much time on her studies, and as anyone knew, too much book learning could scare off any beau.

"Doodlebug, doodlebug, come out of your house," his niece went on. "It's burning up with your wife and all your children, except Mary—she's under the dishpan."

The Youngbloods were descendants of Cherokees who'd escaped into the mountains of North Carolina and then interbred with the whites to such an extent that all *their* descendants wanted was a decent job, which could only be found in one of the textile mills in South Carolina.

The family now lived in Judson Mill. Kate's uncle sported a ducktail, blue jeans and a fresh T-shirt, a pack of cigarettes rolled in one sleeve. He stood patiently behind his niece, listening and smiling, perhaps remembering a time when he, too, had been able to enjoy the simpler pleasures of life.

"Doodlebug, doodlebug," called out his niece, who was now hunched over the tiny hole, "come out of your hole; if you don't, I'll beat you black as a mole."

2

Johnny couldn't help but laugh. "Kate, you won't have any friends if you treat them all that way."

His niece whipped around, saw who it was, and dropped the straw. "Uncle Johnny!" By the time she was on her feet, apprehension had gripped her face. "Did Grandma finally make up her mind?"

"Such a beautiful girl you are," continued her uncle with an even larger smile. "You must have a pack of boyfriends, and I doubt you'd want to leave them for a trip to the beach."

The girl's eyes widened, came alive with excitement, and she glanced past him. "Grandma said I could go? She really did?"

Johnny Youngblood thought that when his niece smiled she was a dead ringer for her mother, and perhaps that's why Kate's father never came round.

"Yes," said Johnny, "she really did. Now go pack your suitcase."

Kate threw her arms around him and gave him a big hug. "Oh, Uncle Johnny, I've had my bag packed for weeks and I've been saying my prayers."

Uncle Johnny returned her hug, and then held her out where he could see her. His niece was tall enough to meet him eye to eye, another attribute of his long dead sister-in-law. "You've been praying to go to Pawleys Island?" he asked with another smile.

"Uncle Johnny, I've never been to the beach." And Kate pulled out of his arms and raced off toward the house.

As he watched her go, Johnny couldn't forget the impression his niece had made on him when they had hugged, and if he hadn't missed it, his guess was the boys at the beach wouldn't miss it either.

DURHAM, NORTH CAROLINA

"Mel?"

The teenager looked up from where she sat on the edge of her bed in the shallow light from the lamp on her nightstand. Though the girl was all the way across the room, her mother could see the bruise on the side of her daughter's face.

"Stand up," said her mother, crossing the room.

The teenager turned away and her brown hair fell across her face. She stared at the coverlet on the bed as if deciding whether or not to sleep in her own bed.

"Melanie, I said for you to stand up."

The woman took her daughter's hand and gently pulled the teenager to her feet. The bedroom was spacious, well-appointed, and deathly quiet. None of that vulgar rock and roll played in these quarters as it had in the other bedrooms in this house. But all those other children were gone, and that might be the problem.

After examining her daughter's injury, she said, "Take off your top."

Melanie looked away but did as her mother said. Once the top was removed, the girl held it tight to her chest. Melanie was a small young woman, who, since her siblings had left home, had learned no matter how much money your family had, you could still end up all alone in the world.

"Turn around," ordered her mother.

She did, and her mother gasped at the bluish-black marks across her daughter's back. The imprints looked like a giant's fingers had gripped her back there.

"Pull down your bottoms."

4

The teenager shuddered and began to sob. When she wouldn't pull down the pajamas, her mother gripped the bottoms and jerked them down.

Bruises down there, too, and Carolynn Hamby bore similar marks, the mark of a man who takes what he wants, and the marks of a man who had finally gone too far.

"Put on your clothes."

Her daughter pulled up her pajama bottoms.

"No," said Carolynn Hamby, gripping the girl's top. "Put on some clothes. Get dressed. We're leaving."

Melanie appeared puzzled, but only for a moment, and then her eyes widened and she gaped over her mother's shoulder. She gasped and jerked the pajama top from her mother.

Her mother turned around in time to take the hand across the face. The blow snapped Carolynn's head around and she went down, hitting the bed, bouncing off the side, and sliding to the floor. Tears appeared before the stars disappeared, and Carolynn instinctively pulled her housecoat tight. Her daughter backed into the nightstand, collided with the lamp, and knocked it over. The lamp fell to the floor, and despite the thickness of the carpet, a crack appeared in its side.

"Carolynn, what the hell's going on up here?"

Her husband was a thickset man, as broad across the shoulders as any laborer, but he wore a business suit, shirt open at the collar, and tie loosened. "I come up to kiss my stepchild good night and find you two playing some sort of striptease." His words slurred, as if he'd had one too many drinks.

When Carolynn wiped her mouth, she saw the blood.

Very quickly she ran her tongue around her mouth, and as she did, noticed the cracked lip. Still, her teeth were intact. If there was anything she hated, it would be another trip to the dentist.

"This is the last straw, Lee," said Carolynn, looking up from the floor. "I want you out of this house, and I want you out tonight. I'll help you pack."

She gripped the bed, pulled herself to her feet, and tried to stand. Again her husband slapped her, and she thudded to the carpeted floor. Her daughter burst into tears and huddled against the wall, trapped between the bed and nightstand.

"Shut up, Melanie." To his wife, he said, "Don't tell me what to do in my own house."

Gripping the bed to keep the room from spinning, his wife couldn't stop her tears. "This isn't your house, Lee. It's my family's . . . and you're to leave immediately. We're finished. Our marriage is finished."

Her husband leaned down, and Carolynn flinched and turned away. That's where her husband's hand found her, and, once again, her daughter gasped. Through the tears, pain, blood, and mostly the humiliation, Carolynn fumbled with a pocket of her housecoat.

Her husband didn't appear to notice. "And who's going to throw me out?" Straightening up, he gestured at the bedroom door. "One of the servants? They're too old. That's what's wrong with this family, and that's why your father hired me. To rejuvenate the bloodline." He glanced at his stepdaughter hiding behind her mother, pajama top clutched to her chest, brown hair in disarray. "And that requires someone to report for duty in

6

my bedroom. Now!"

Carolynn had her hand in the pocket of her house-coat. "This is your last chance, Lee. I'm warning you."

Her husband put a foot on his wife's ankle, turning the foot and flattening the ankle against the thickly car-peted floor. Carolynn cried out and her hand came out of the pocket. She gripped her husband's foot but found it impossible to ease the pressure from his shoe.

"Lee, please . . . you're hurting me."

Melanie began another bout of tears.

Lee ignored them both. "I'm not leaving, and if you decide to go, Melanie stays. Got that?"

His wife knew what that meant, so she took her hands off her husband's shoe and dug into the pocket of her housecoat again. This time she found the weapon, her father's target pistol.

"Do you understand, Carolynn? Answer me!"

Her husband ground his heel into her ankle again and his wife screamed. The pistol fell from her hand, hit the floor, and tumbled under the dust ruffle.

"Lee!" she was barely able to get out. "Please stop!"

He only ground his foot harder.

Now she was shrieking and so was her daughter, jumping up and down but with nowhere to go, trapped behind her mother and between the bed and the night-stand. When Carolynn looked up and saw the terror on her daughter's face, she gritted her teeth, took her hands off her husband's shoe, and reached for the pistol again.

The pain in her ankle was horrendous, her hands shook even when she found the weapon, and they continued to shake as she leveled the pistol at him. Still, she forced herself to aim as her father had taught her, and pulled the trigger.

At the sound of the gunshot, her daughter screamed again.

HIGH BATTERY, CHARLESTON

"I'm not going with you."

Her father ignored her, as did the Negro servant. Two large suitcases lay on the teenager's bed and her clothing was being packed, though in a rather unorthodox manner. Her father was taking his daughter's clothing from closet, dresser, and highboy, and tossing whatever he thought suitable into one of the two large suitcases lying on the bed, making it impossible for the servant to make heads or tails of the packing, or be able to keep up.

Her father, a heavy man who had accumulated most of his pounds during a successful career as an attorney, gathered up a dresser drawer of scarves, along with handfuls of underwear, quickly tossing the latter on the bed. The Negro buried these intimate things in one of the suitcases, knowing how little contact her employer wished to have with these garments.

"Daddy, you're not listening to me."

The chunky teenager shared her father's physical characteristics: black hair, pale skin, and striking blue eyes. They were Belles of Charleston, French Huguenots who'd lived in the Low Country for thirteen generations. The girl wore navy walking shorts, sandals, and a white sleeveless top. Her face, usually pale, had reddened from her outburst and the unorthodox way her clothes were being packed.

Her father went to the vanity dresser where his daughter's jewelry lay in a tray or hung on silver towers. Without comment, he picked up both tray and towers, stepped over to the bed, and unceremoniously dumped the jewelry into one of the suitcases.

"Daddy, what are you doing?"

"You had your chance. The twins are already packed. You're going to Pawleys whether you want to or not."

"Daddy, Pawleys is out in the middle of nowhere."

"I'm sorry, dear, but you must go."

"But I need to stay in Charleston this summer."

"Yes, and I know who you want to stay for."

He pulled open more drawers, found bathing suits of all sizes, shapes, and very little fabric, and his nose wrinkled as, by the handful, he began tossing what passed for bathing suits into the suitcases.

"Your grandmother's ill, so you'll probably have to spend most of the summer there."

"She's just on another bender, that's all."

Her father glanced at the servant, but the woman was so busy packing she appeared not to have heard.

"Why not send her to the sanitarium? If Mother were here, that's what she'd do."

Finally, the father faced his daughter. "But your mother's not here, is she, Virginia Lynne, and *you* chose not to move to San Francisco, so you're stuck with us."

"I still might move there. Girls have a lot more freedom in California."

Yes, they do, thought her father, and it had been a seri-

9

ous error in judgment to believe any California girl could settle down in Charleston, certainly not his former wife. But that union had produced Virginia Lynne, and the daughter was worth ten of the mother. And he suspected that Virginia Lynne, and even the twin boys, knew just how wicked their mother could be, or why had none of them followed her to San Francisco? Well, not yet.

Simms Belle glanced out the window overlooking the Battery. What kind of woman abandons such a view? Certainly not a Carolina girl.

"Well," said his daughter from behind him, "you'll have to hire a sitter because I'm not babysitting all summer."

And that's when he knew he still had her. For how long he had her, he didn't know, but for some reason he still had her, and facing the window overlooking that majestic harbor, he uttered a small sigh of relief.

FRASER COUNTY, SOUTH CAROLINA

The couple watched from the stone patio as their daughter made the jump, reined in her horse, and turned around for another run. The girl was a lithe, blond figure, striking-looking, and she knew it. Filled with a fierce self-confidence, Bailey Gillespie knew what she wanted and where she was going in life. She would follow in her father's footsteps and be elected governor; later on, United States senator.

Well, thought her father, she'd better damn well be certain of who she was because when *The State* ran the story of her parents' impending divorce, it'd be enough to rattle anyone's self-confidence, even a girl with such a sense of destiny.

"When are you going to tell her?" asked the girl's mother. Between the couple was a table with an umbrella and more than one chair.

You could see the resemblance between mother and child: blond hair, blue eyes, and the same tanned, athletic figure. And since Irene Gillespie worked very hard at keeping her figure, it made her detest her husband that much more. Still, up to this moment, she had worked very hard to save her marriage. Today she wore a blue sundress with a smattering of yellow flowers—colors Walter liked on her—and around her neck and on her ears, jewelry given to her on the occasion of their fifteenth wedding anniversary, not to mention a thin watch with a single diamond mounted in the face; a gift for their twentieth.

"If you can't tell her yourself, turn it over to your chief of staff. He'll put it on his to-do list."

The senator, a distinguished-looking man, his temples already graying, looked at her. "Don't be like that, Irene. You promised you weren't going to be that way, for Bailey's sake."

"Maybe I won't be able to keep my word." Irene Gillespie looked over a backyard that included not only the jump but a swimming pool and tennis court. "Just as some men can't keep their pants zipped."

Her husband sighed. "We've been through all this before. Why must you bring it up again?"

"Maybe because I'm not the one who took up with some floozy."

"My dear, Marybeth was Miss South Carolina and runner-up for Miss America. I hardly think she'll be considered a floozy in Washington."

"They'll talk behind your back. They'll make fun of you."

"If I'd worried about what people said about me, I never would've run for public office in the first place."

"Which is why you seduced all those girls on the sly, isn't it? You wanted to be a United States senator, and now that you've been reelected for a second six-year term, you're feeling pretty invincible, aren't you?"

"And you put up with my philandering because you wanted to be the wife of a United States senator."

Irene sat up. "What a rotten thing to say. Despite your philandering, I promised to go as far as you wanted."

"Well, now, my dear," said her husband, smiling, "there are places I'd rather not take you."

For a second his wife stared at him, and then she picked up her cocktail glass and threw it at him. Her husband merely leaned back and watched the glass fly by.

Once it had shattered on the patio's surface, he got to his feet. "Well, it appears this conversation is over."

"And so is this marriage," said his wife, standing. "I'm starting our new life on Pawleys. Bailey and I'll spend the summer there. Hopefully she'll be able to get her wheels under her before returning to school. You know how much she looked up to her father," she added rather sarcastically.

The senator seemed to consider this. "Then I'll tell her now."

"Not while she's on her jumps. It might upset her."

"Nothing upsets Bailey. She takes after my side of the family."

"Yes, the Gillespies have always been known as the icebergs of Fraser County."

Walter glanced at his wife as he stepped off the patio and almost missed his step. Once he recovered, he said, "That's the pot calling the kettle black. Did you ever ask yourself why we only had one child?" And he headed toward the jump.

"Walter," said his wife, following him, "please don't do this. I beg you, not while she's on horseback."

The senator continued toward the jump. "Oh, come on, Irene. Remember that summer when Bailey fell in love with modern dance and walked everywhere on her toes. She was in her own world then"—he gestured at the blond girl on horseback—"just as she is now. Like me, Bailey can focus on the task at hand. Besides, I have to be getting back to Washington."

"And to a woman half your age. What is she, some sort of trophy?"

He smiled. "Yes, my dear, as you were in your day."

Irene stopped and stared at the bastard. An only child, Bailey was sure to be devastated. Certainly, there had been fights, some more awful than others, but Irene had always been able to make peace with her husband, and hold her head up. And she wondered if her father's death, less than a year ago, had contributed to her husband's decision to abandon his family and take up with a younger woman.

Irene had no brothers, just a drunken uncle, so there was no one to speak up for her, no one to fight for her as there had been in the past when the Gillespies and the Baileys fought tooth and nail for control of Fraser County and later for control of the political machinery of South Carolina. The marriage between a Bailey and a Gillespie supposedly ended such ruinous divisions, and a child named for each family should've buried the hatchet. But her husband had found that hatchet and used it on their marriage.

Irene watched as her daughter reined in her mount and cantered over to where her father stood. Their daughter's Tennessee Walker was solid black with a white blaze, and the girl could get the most out of the animal whether competing in English or model events.

The senator gripped the harness and smiled up at his daughter's sunburned face, a face dominated by a set of piercing blue eyes. Bailey took off her riding helmet and shook out her golden hair. She was a gorgeous creature, thought her father, and one who in the future would break many a boy's heart. His daughter *could* aspire to be governor, though that office was certainly out of reach for a girl. But there was always secretary of education, perhaps lieutenant governor, especially if her father put in a good word for her. The only question was: would Bailey want him to speak up for her after today?

"Can't wait to see you in the fall shows," he said, smiling.

"Will you be here?" His daughter did not return his smile, only looked down at him with those blue eyes.

"I can't plan that far ahead, but all you have to do is call my office and they'll pencil you in."

"I'd rather be written in in ink."

The senator stopped smiling. "Listen, Bailey, you and I need to talk. Would you please dismount?"

Bailey glanced at her mother standing between the

14

jump and the patio. Her mother had somehow found a cigarette and now lit up. Bailey ignored her. It was the cigar smokers you had to watch out for.

"I know what you're going to tell me, Daddy. You're going back to Washington and I'll never see you again."

Her father's grip on the reins loosened. "What? What do you mean?"

"You wanted sons and Mother didn't give you one. That's why you're leaving." The girl's head rose and her cold blue eyes surveyed the countryside. "You don't have to live in horse country long to learn what people think of its women. You can look perfect on horseback, or standing beside your husband, but if you don't produce sons, as far as the other sires are concerned, you're sterile."

The senator was taken aback. Who was this child, and had he ever really known her? Walter cleared his throat to speak, something that rarely happened to such a seasoned politician. "I'm sorry things didn't work out with your . . . how long have you known?"

"If the rumors are to be believed I've known for over a year. If the other rumor's true, it's been true longer than I've been your daughter."

The senator stood there, not knowing what to say. He, too, knew the other rumor, the one that would never go away, but since no rumor had yet to destroy him . . .

He released the reins. "Well, stay in touch, Bailey. You have the number of my private line." And he hurried away, hurried past the girl's mother, and hurried toward his new life. Still, he couldn't put his daughter's words out of his mind. "If the other rumor is true, it's been true longer than I've been your daughter."

In front of the four-car garage, a black man in a dark

suit opened the door of a black Cadillac. The senator nodded his thanks and slid into the backseat where an overweight man in a rumpled suit waited for him.

"Everything go well, Senator?" asked his chief of staff.

"I believe so."

"You believe so?"

The senator turned to this man who'd pulled his bacon out of the fire so many times and said, "Everything's going to be all right, Arlie."

"You told Bailey you're leaving her mother?"

"I didn't have to."

The driver got in behind the wheel, started the engine, and pulled out onto the dirt road, and as the Cadillac passed under the pecan trees lining both sides of the road, the senator turned and watched his old life disappear behind him.

He said, "I do believe Bailey's a bit farther down the road on this issue than either her mother or me."

"She knows . . . everything?"

"Yes," said the senator, glancing at the driver. "It appears she does."

The overweight man shifted around in the backseat and looked out the window. When he faced forward again, he said, "Well, I hope she knows to keep her mouth shut. Women do the craziest things when they get angry."

The first summer

THE NEW GIRL

"**W**hat are you doing here?"

Kate Youngblood stood in the middle of the kitchen, cabinets empty and pieces of wood lying on the floor, linoleum ripped back, and the stove and sink missing. She stopped thumbing through the Betty Crocker cookbook lying on the stove and looked up. It would appear that there was more to cooking than her grandmother had taught her. Her grandmother cooked from memory and cooked a small selection of meals. Kate had never seen a cookbook in her grandmother's kitchen, or any of her friends' mothers' kitchens.

Standing next to the refrigerator, which was now attached to the wall by an extension cord and shoved into the hallway, was a girl her own age and height, but this blonde wore different clothing. Where Kate wore dungarees, dirty Keds, and a man's shirt tied at the waist, this girl wore culottes and a sleeveless blouse. And where Kate's red hair was irrepressibly curly, the blonde's hair had been shaped into a flip. The blonde's eyes were red and puffy. Plainly this girl had been crying.

19

"I said what are you doing here?'"

Kate smiled. "I'm the gofer."

"What?"

"I run errands," explained Kate.

"Run errands . . . for who?"

"For my uncle." Kate pointed at the back door. "He's gone to the lumberyard."

"Then why didn't you go with him?"

"I was reading this here book." Kate gestured at the barely used cookbook, which, to Kate, appeared rather odd. Rows and rows of books, mostly thick paperbacks, lined the shelves of the living room in this house, and it appeared that all those books had been read more than once, especially a well-worn copy of Grace Metalious's *Peyton Place.* But this cookbook had hardly been used, and it made Kate wonder what kind of a renovation job her uncle had come up with down here at the beach.

She added, "I already know how to size lumber, so I didn't go along."

"Well, you shouldn't be inside the house."

"You want me to wait outside?"

"Well, you can't stay in here."

Kate closed the cookbook and started for the screened door. The day was warm and muggy, not exactly hot, but Kate was being sent to stand off the property—she'd been made to do that last time she'd gone to see her father—and this time without the benefit of shade.

The blonde followed her. "And next time don't let me find you going through our things."

With the screened door still in her hand, and standing amid the appliances on the back porch, Kate faced the girl. "I ain't no thief."

But the blonde was staring at a swarm of children being herded up the stairs behind Kate, and the teenager doing the herding appeared to be their age. This girl, and for that matter a couple of twin boys, who had to be the girl's brothers, shared similar characteristics: black hair, blue eyes, and pale skin already sunburned. An assortment of children followed the twins, and with Kate holding the screened door open, they hurried inside. Still, the clamor wasn't loud enough to cover a moan from the blonde.

"Hello, there," said the brunette, smiling at Kate as she finished the stairs. "Sorry for the mob scene." Her face lost its smile when she saw the look on the blond girl's face. "Bailey?"

But the blonde had disappeared into the interior of the house.

In the kitchen the children stopped and looked around. With the kitchen torn apart, the room was in a state they found fascinating, and disorienting.

The brunette returned her attention to Kate. "I'm Ginny Belle, and you are . . . ?" There were always new people on the island this time of year and you never could know them all.

The redhead didn't reply but hurried down the steps and across the crushed shell parking area, which was hidden from the road behind wax myrtles, cedars, and the occasional palmetto tree.

Ginny Belle's attention was drawn back to the children begging for their lunch. Very quickly she closed the screened door, told the children to watch where they put their feet, and to watch out for nails!

She looked around. It was highly unusual for anyone

to remodel on Pawleys. "Arrogantly shabby" was how the island billed itself, and Pawleys remained one of the few noncommercial communities along the East Coast, filled with plenty of creaky old beach houses.

After shooing her brothers and the other children into the dining room, she told everyone to take a seat and to stay put or they wouldn't be fed. Ginny figured that was good for about five minutes, and then she went upstairs to Bailey's room and tapped on her friend's bedroom door.

Hearing sobbing, Ginny opened the door and peered inside. The blond girl lay across the bed.

"Bailey, what's wrong?"

At the head of the bed stood a pile of stuffed animals, the windows were open to catch any breeze, and the walls were covered with teenage heartthrobs: James Dean, Richard Chamberlain, and Tab Hunter.

When her friend didn't answer, Ginny went over to the bed. "Bailey, are you all right?"

The blonde rolled over and wiped away the tears. "I went downstairs and found that . . . that creature in my house."

"Creature?" asked Melanie Durant, coming through the bedroom door. Melanie was a tobacco heiress from Durham and her family owned the house between Ginny's and Bailey's. Today she wore a jumper and blouse; she was the same age as the other two but shorter and exceedingly thin, with only a hint of bust-line or bottom. Her chestnut brown hair had just come out from under her Lady Norelco home hair dryer and she was proud to show off her curls. Freckles ran across the bridge of her nose.

"You must be referring to those creatures dow
stairs," she went on to say. "They are literally tearing
the house apart. There's lumber everywhere."

"I don't care," said Bailey, and she rolled over on the
bed again. What did it matter what happened to the
house, to her, to anyone? Her father had abandoned her,
and worst of all, everyone in South Carolina knew it!

"What's wrong?" Melanie asked Ginny.

"I don't know. Bailey, tell us what's going on."

From the bed came a muffled reply. "That redhead
was in the house when I went downstairs. She frightened me."

"Frightened you? Nothing ever—"

"Melanie, I don't think this is the time or the
place . . ."

The thin girl shrugged. "Okay, but she's the one
always calling me a scaredy-cat."

Bailey rolled over, propping herself up on her elbows.
"You wouldn't be so flip if you'd been here when I went
downstairs and found that—"

"Creature," furnished Melanie.

"She was in my kitchen, Mel!"

Ginny nodded, finally understanding. Each summer
the visitors became bolder. "Melanie, would you take
care of the children while I call the sheriff? She couldn't
have gone far."

"Sure, but . . ." Melanie's voice trailed off when she
saw Bailey's eyes flicker with fear.

Her friend turned away, burying her face into the
pillows again. Bailey Gillespie afraid? Not the girl who'd
chided them into climbing the water tower or led them
on a shoplifting foray through the Gay Dolphin.

On the way downstairs Melanie passed Ginny talking on the phone on the hallway table. In the kitchen she found peanut butter smeared on white bread and red faces and glasses of Kool-Aid lying on their sides, dripping cherry liquid on the floor. One of the twins seemed intent on plugging the electric drill into the wall but was being foiled by the unfamiliar three-pronged plug.

By the time they had the children seated around the dining room table there came a knock at the back door. Standing beside a big-bellied deputy in a brown uniform and a Smokey Bear hat was a red-headed girl wearing dungarees and a man's shirt; she was in tears, and the deputy had a smug look on his face.

"She didn't get far," said the deputy, who took off his sunglasses. The Georgetown County deputies were always on their best behavior whenever dealing with the residents. You never knew who was related to whom. Or how.

"I found her hiding in the bushes."

"I—I weren't hiding," stammered the redhead. "I was getting out of the sun."

The deputy turned on her. "You'd better watch what you say, young lady. This is Miss Belle you're talking to."

"Melanie, make sure nobody leaves their chair while I talk with this girl." Ginny walked over and opened the screened door.

Melanie stood in the hallway, ostensibly watching the children in the dining room, but fascinated by the girl at the back door. Where did this girl find the nerve to walk into a stranger's house? Melanie could never do such a thing.

Ginny identified herself as the one who'd called and asked if the deputy knew this girl. When he answered in the negative, Ginny quizzed the redhead herself.

"What house are you from?"

Tears streamed down the girl's cheeks. She was having a hard time speaking, and she repeatedly looked over her shoulder as if expecting someone to ride to her rescue.

Fat chance, thought Melanie, she's been caught, you might say, red-handed.

The deputy took the girl's arm and shook it. "Young lady, you'd better answer Miss Belle's questions."

Instead, the girl squealed and burst into tears. Behind Melanie, Bailey came downstairs, saw who was at the back door, and muttered, "Oh, my God!" and raced back upstairs.

"Bailey," called out Melanie, following her friend to the base of the stairs, "aren't you going to press charges?"

"No, no. I don't want anything to do with that girl."

Which was also strange, thought Melanie. Bailey Gillespie would cajole, coddle, or curse anyone who wouldn't do her bidding, and this redhead had broken into Bailey's house. The whole scene just didn't make sense.

At the door Ginny continued to lecture the redhead. "Listen, young lady, I don't know who you are, but you can't be walking into people's homes."

Nothing but tears from the redhead.

"Where are you from?"

More tears; the girl's hands fluttered around, and Melanie thought she heard "Greenville."

"I meant where are you staying on the island?"

Melanie glanced in the dining room, saw all was quiet on that particular front, and edged her way into the kitchen in time to hear the girl say, "I . . . I don't live . . . on Pawleys Island."

Ginny pressed on. "We know you don't live here, but what house did your family rent?"

"It ain't no house. It's a trailer."

Wrong answer, thought Melanie. There were no trailers on Pawleys Island.

"Well," said Ginny with a shrug, "I guess she's one of the locals, so I'll turn her over to you."

"You won't have to worry about her again, Miss Belle," said the deputy, hitching up his Sam Browne belt. He looked at Melanie. "Neither does Miss Durant or the senator's family. And this girl will spend the night in jail if she doesn't tell the sheriff what he wants to know."

"Jail?" wailed the redhead, and she burst into tears again as the deputy led her away.

That was too much for Melanie and she crossed the kitchen and pushed back the screened door. "I know this girl," she found herself saying.

The redhead was brought up short when the deputy jerked her back up the stairs. He stared at Melanie.

"What are you talking about?" asked Ginny, joining her friend at the door.

"She was to meet me here. I'm sorry. I forgot."

And that was as far as Melanie got before her hands began to tremble. Very quickly she grabbed the redhead's arm and led her down the steps. Dumbly, the redhead followed. As they started across the parking lot Melanie could see the confusion in the redhead's eyes. But how could she explain what she was doing? She didn't understand herself.

"Come on. We'll go over to my house."

The snuffling stopped, the redhead nodded, and the two of them crossed the parking lot. The deputy made no effort to stop them. If this was a quarrel between a couple of rich bitches, what did he care.

"But who is she?" asked Ginny, stepping out on the porch.

"Ask Bailey. She should know."

FAST FRIENDS

"I have to go back," said the redhead, giving a final snuffle and wiping away the last of her tears.

"And why's that?" asked Melanie as they walked down creek road.

"My uncle . . . he'll miss me."

"Your uncle? The one who owns the trailer?"

"No," said Kate, shaking her head. "We just rent it."

"Oh, and why's that?" asked Melanie, whose family fortune made it possible for her to purchase anything her heart desired, whether it brought her satisfaction or not.

"We're just here for the job, so we're renting."

"Remodeling the Gillespies' kitchen?"

"Yes, ma'am, and if Mrs. Gillespie likes our work, she might refer us to other jobs."

"Oh, no," said Melanie, laughing, "that won't do."

"But my uncle's a good carpenter. He done work for the Gillespies over in Fraser County."

"What I mean is, people don't fix up their homes on

Pawleys. You should've heard the flak we got when we put in air conditioning."

"Flak?"

Melanie held out both hands, curled her fingers, and shook her hands, making the sound from the often-repeated documentary, *Victory at Sea.* "Ack-ack! You know, like from antiaircraft guns."

But Kate didn't understand, and Melanie had to remind herself that some Americans didn't own television sets. "Don't worry about it." She took Kate's arm again.

Reluctantly, Kate allowed herself to be pulled along, all the time wondering how much work could be found on this island if nobody wanted to fix up their house. It was true she lived in a mill village, but people there owned their homes, and those proud of them kept them up. If there was one thing Kate had learned after only a few days on Pawleys, there were plenty of proud people living here, so why didn't they want to fix up their houses? At least slap on a quick coat of paint.

"Where are you from?" asked Melanie.

"Greenville."

"North or South Carolina?"

"I didn't know there were a Greenville, North Carolina."

"There's a Greenville in about every state in the Union, but only one Pawleys Island."

This appeared to puzzle the redhead even more.

Melanie released her grip on the taller girl's arm. "I'm Melanie Durant from Durham. Durham, North Carolina," she added and stuck out her hand.

Not in the habit of shaking hands with women, Kate did, and rather lamely. "Pleased to meet you, ma'am.

I'm Kate Youngblood."

"I'm not a ma'am, and before you ask, yes, I was named for Melanie Wilkes. My mother is a big fan of *Gone With the Wind*."

"I—er, I weren't going to ask."

They passed through another break in the wax myrtles and entered another crushed shell parking lot.

The Durant beach house had been destroyed by Hurricane Hazel and had been rebuilt as a majestic but rustic-looking clapboard house with three bedrooms on the second floor, an attic bedroom Melanie didn't have the nerve to sleep in, and plenty of parking under the ground floor. All bedrooms had their own window air conditioning unit.

Kate glanced back at the Gillespie house. "What if my uncle comes back and finds I'm not there?"

"I'm sure they'll tell him where you went."

Kate stopped in the middle of this new driveway. "You have to believe me, Miss Durant. I didn't steal nothing."

"Melanie. You're to call me 'Melanie.'" She tugged Kate toward the screened-in back porch. Under this house was parked a Lincoln Town Car, identifiable by a unique padded vinyl top, and a T-bird convertible, the first car with a "swing away" steering column and dashboard ends that blended in well with the door panels.

"I know you're no thief. I figured that out all by my-self."

Kate stopped again, pulling Melanie up short. "Are you making fun of me?"

"No. Why should I?"

29

"I was told to watch out for your type."

"I have a type?" asked Melanie, smiling.

"You're doing it again."

"Now you're mocking me."

"No, ma'am. I'm minding my manners like my grandma told me, just like back there at the Gillespies'."

"Kate, you're going to have to cut Bailey some slack. She's going through a rather bad patch."

"That's no reason to be calling me a thief."

"No, it's not." And, once again, Melanie tugged her new friend toward the stairs. "But we have to make allowances this summer. Bailey's father abandoned the family before the end of the school year and she really looked up to him."

Now Kate understood the blond girl's anger. The very same thing had happened to her, but much earlier in life.

Leading Kate up the steps, Melanie asked, "You say your grandmother told you to mind your manners, not your mother?"

"My mother's dead. She died of tuberculosis."

"Really? I didn't think anyone died of TB these days."

Kate stopped on the steps. "I ain't no liar. I told you that once before."

"Well," said Melanie, smiling down at her from the porch, "we've established that you're no thief, nor a liar, but are you hungry?"

Kate looked back at the Gillespie house. Her uncle would be returning with lunch after finishing at the lumberyard, and she was hungry, but she sure as the devil didn't want to go back to that house.

"Thank you. I do believe I'm hungry."

"Well, come on up. I'm sure we'll find something inside."

Kate followed Melanie to the back door of the wrap-around porch where her new friend whispered, "And try not to use the word 'ain't' around my mother. She's a frustrated English teacher."

"I don't know what that means."

"All the Durants are English teachers. That's the way we come into our majority."

Misunderstanding Kate's puzzled look, Melanie sought to explain. "Look, you're on Pawleys, right?"

"I know where I am."

"Kate, don't be so prickly. This is your first visit to Pawleys, isn't it?"

Kate nodded.

"And including Bailey, you've met some rather strange characters, haven't you?"

Kate had to agree. There were some queer customers on this island.

"You have to understand that those who come to Pawleys aren't regular folks. Some are eccentrics like Ginny's grandmother who lives next door, but even Mrs. Belle is well educated, articulate, and refined. So mind your p's and q's."

Kate knew what that meant, but still, nothing could prepare her for the Durant kitchen, generally considered one of the best kitchens on Pawleys Island, at least when the Durants brought their cook down from Durham.

Inside, a Negro in a maid's uniform was slicing tomatoes on a table in the middle of a huge room of cabinets and appliances, the major ones on the floor, the smaller appliances on the counters.

Kate had never seen such a place, and she turned around, taking it all in. It appeared someone, and that someone must enjoy their food, had knocked out the wall between the original kitchen and a small bedroom or storage area. The kitchen had a side-by-side refrigerator, a self-cleaning oven, and even a dishwasher!

Without missing a beat, the cook continued to slice the tomatoes and told them lunch would be ready in a few minutes and asked why didn't Miss Melanie and her friend wait on the front porch; she would bring out some iced tea. Melanie thanked her and motioned for Kate to follow her.

But Kate couldn't stop looking. Could there be any way she could get her uncle to see this place? The cabinets were dull with age, the linoleum worn in places, and the floor sagged, but the room had such potential, if only for its size. And that table in the middle where the cook stood, it'd make a neat—what were they called in homes up north? She'd seen them in a magazine at the newsstand, an expensive and slick-to-the-touch magazine.

Islands! Yes. Tables set into kitchen floors were called islands. Maybe if . . .

Melanie took Kate's arm again and tugged her down the hallway. "You act like you've never seen a kitchen before."

"Not one this big."

Going down the hall they passed a sewing room/laundry room and a study opposite it. In the laundry room another Negro ironed blouses with what appeared to be one of those new steam/dry irons, and Melanie spoke to the woman quite cheerily. It would be some time before Kate learned that her new friend was not at all like the confident and well-informed teen she'd just met. When Melanie was outside her circle, she clammed up, and sometimes Melanie would become so agitated that her mother would find her in a ladies' room stall with her feet up on the toilet seat, hugging her knees to her chest. Telephone booths would do in a pinch.

"Uh-huh," said Melanie, with another smile, "and maybe you were thinking you'd found more work for your uncle."

"Yes," said Kate, returning the smile, "I'd love for my uncle to see your kitchen."

"If he's as good as you say, he will. My mom knows Bailey's mom, and there's sure to be a party once your uncle's finished remodeling."

Going down the hall Kate got a quick look upstairs to the second floor and a glance into the dining room, one end of its table covered with a monstrous puzzle. Opposite the dining room was a spacious living room where an elderly woman sat on a sofa, and across from her, an attractive middle-aged woman sat in a director's chair.

The elderly woman was silver-haired, thin, and tanned to a bronze finish. She used a cigarette holder to make her points. "I have no idea why the Negroes are so upset. It must be Northern agitators, but I doubt if this civil rights legislation will change anything. You can't force people to associate with those they don't care to be around."

"Oops!" muttered Melanie. Trying to retrace her

steps, she ran into Kate, who, mesmerized by the house, squealed in surprise when Melanie's feet came down on her toes.

"Melanie," called one of the women from the living room, "is that you, dear? Come in here and speak with Mrs. Belle."

Melanie made a face at Kate and then plastered on a smile before pulling the redhead into the living room.

The room overlooked a screened-in porch with a view of the beach. The huge room had a stone fireplace and was filled with rough-and-ready furniture complementing the unfinished look. Behind the sofa where the elderly woman sat was a large picture window, and since Kate's uncle had warned her not to stray too far from where they were working, Kate couldn't help but gape through that glass at the waves washing ashore. In side windows, air conditioners hummed away, and on a table-size phonograph Doris Day sang "Sentimental Journey."

Mrs. Hamby had Grace Kelly looks, wore a tan sundress, and her arms and legs were still winter-white. "Oh, I didn't know you had someone with you." Mrs. Hamby extended a hand from her director's chair. "I'm Carolynn Hamby, Melanie's mother."

Shaking hands with women seemed to be a big deal on this island so Kate took Carolynn's hand and shook it, this time with more vigor. And remembering her manners drummed into her by her grandmother, she said, "I'm Kate Youngblood." Then she skirted the coffee table, on which lay a copy of *Rabbit, Run* by John Updike. She shook the older woman's hand—the one using the cigarette holder—and introduced herself again.

"Adelaide Belle," said the bronze woman on the sofa, "but you may call me 'Mrs. Belle.' I live next door, and all the brats you run into on this beach will probably be my grandchildren. I didn't raise them. Their mother left them, and about this time each summer I remember just how much I didn't like that little tramp."

"Addy, please . . ." said Melanie's mom.

"I mean every word." And the elderly woman set her jaw.

Adelaide Belle had been coming to Pawleys since you had to ferry up the Waccamaw to Waverly Mills Landing, and if you ever sat next to her at a dinner party, you were going to get an earful. Today she wore a long-sleeved blouse and pants she called trousers.

Kate was staring over the older woman's head and out the huge picture window. "It's beautiful."

Melanie's mother looked around. "Well, the room does need a bit of straightening . . ."

Adelaide said, "I think she means the beach, Carolynn."

"Oh, yes." Mrs. Hamby glanced out the enormous window. "This house, or one like it, has been in my family for several generations. I suppose I take it for granted; the view, that is."

"And where are you from, Kate?" asked Mrs. Belle.

"Greenville." Kate glanced at Melanie. "South Carolina."

Finishing a drag off her cigarette, Addy winked at her. "We both know there's only one real Greenville, just as there's only one Carolina, right?"

"Oh, no, Addy," said Carolynn Hamby, smiling broadly, "you're not going to draw me into that hoary argument."

Kate wasn't sure what she'd just heard. Had Melanie's mom just use the word "whore" in polite conversation?

"Well, you did attend the *other* Carolina, didn't you?" Adelaide Belle looked up at Kate again. "And where is your family staying on Pawleys, my dear?"

Melanie saved the day by asking, "May Kate stay for lunch?"

"Of course. I'll have Hazel set another place." She looked at the redhead. "That way we can get to know your new friend."

"Actually, Kate and I might eat on the porch."

"Really, my dear, that's what dining rooms are for."

"If I didn't eat on my porch," said Adelaide, "I wouldn't know where to eat." And she took another drag off her cigarette.

"I promised Kate we'd look for sand dollars."

"Really, Melanie, aren't you a bit old for beachcombing?"

"They're not actually dollars," blurted out Kate, "but sea urchins, Order *Clypeasteroida.*"

All three women looked at her and Kate flushed. "I—I read it in a book."

"And pronounced it properly," said Adelaide. "Would you happen to know the Alester Furmans or the Charles Daniel family of Greenville?" The Furmans owned a good chunk of Greenville, and Charles Daniel had built the tallest building in the state—at twenty-five stories.

"Well," said Carolynn Hamby, smiling at her daughter, "you just might improve your science grades if you hang around Kate."

"We'll be back for lunch." And Melanie took Kate's

hand and pulled her out of the living room and in the direction of the front door. "Nice to see you again, Mrs. Belle."

"Don't be gone long, dear. Lunch is about ready."

As the girls went out the door, Adelaide called after them. "Melanie, I thought you were helping my granddaughter babysit."

If the girls heard her, they didn't reply but continued across a porch filled with wicker furniture and down the stairs. Glancing up the beach, they saw Ginny Belle and Bailey Gillespie staring at them from the front porch of the Gillespie house.

Kate and Melanie went in the opposite direction down the beach. Ahead of them children chased each other in and out of the surf and a young man was having a hard time keeping a kite in the air. Everyone was still pale from a long, harsh winter, that, to those living in the Carolinas, meant the temperature had occasionally dropped below freezing.

"I don't know if I should go too far. My uncle's sure to be back from the lumberyard, and I'm his gofer."

"Gopher?"

"I fetch things for him."

"Oh, 'go for.' Sounds more like being a slave."

"Oh, no, he's teaching me stuff."

"Like what?"

"Well, like how to use a plane."

"A plane?" Now it was Melanie's turn to be mystified.

"It's a tool for smoothing or shaping wood. You use it like so." And Kate held her fists side by side and moved them back and forth in a straight line in front of her waist as they continued down the beach.

Melanie nodded, but in truth, she had no idea what the girl was talking about. Planes flew to Paris or London, and the new Pan Am jets were the best. No more long hours in the air, and the new jets were *sooo* quiet.

"And those," said Kate, gesturing at the huge pieces of wood lying on their sides and anchored into the beach by short pilings, "are called groins."

Melanie laughed as she stepped up on the barrier that disappeared into the surf and kept the beach from washing away. "That doesn't sound at all polite. Call it a jetty."

Kate stared up at her. The jetty, or groin, made her new friend slightly taller than her.

"How do you know all this?" asked Melanie, leaping to the other side.

"Know what?" asked Kate, following her.

"The Latin name for a sand dollar or what a plane is? Or a groin?"

"Books. Well, I didn't read in the book how to use a plane, my uncle showed me. He said I had to make myself useful."

"Useful? Why would you need to learn how to use tools? I can understand you might need to know about flora and fauna, that's for school, but carpenter's tools?"

"I want to be a cabinetmaker when I grow up."

"A cabinetmaker? Why in the world would you want to be a carpenter?"

"It kinda comes natural. Everybody in my family is good with their hands." From her jeans pocket Kate pulled a new pack of Dentyne. After pulling the string on the pack, she offered it to her new friend. "Gum?"

"No, thank you. I don't chew gum in public."

Kate stared at the pack, and then returned it to her jeans. She looked over her shoulder and saw the other two girls and a gaggle of children following them down the beach. "Those are your friends, aren't they?" she asked.

Melanie glanced over her shoulder. "Sometimes."

When Kate looked at her, Melanie explained, "We've been friends since elementary school."

"You went to the same grammar school together?"

"What I meant to say was that we've met on Pawleys ever since we were children. Bailey's from Fraser County, Ginny's from Charleston, and like I said, I'm from Durham."

They continued down the beach, stepping up on and leaping from groins—it was impossible to get into a rhythm walking—and they passed more bathers and families strolling on the beach, many of whom Melanie seemed to know. She nodded or spoke to them all.

"Why did you do it?" asked Kate.

"What?"

"Why'd you take up for me? You don't even know me."

"I know Bailey." Melanie glanced over her shoulder again. Ahead of them was land's end, and the other two girls, even with the children in tow, would soon catch up with them. "You heard about Bailey's father running off with that beauty queen?"

Kate shook her head. "Don't know her. I just work there."

"Senator Gillespie. He's divorcing Bailey's mom."

Kate didn't seem to understand.

"You *do* know your senators, the ones from South Carolina? Gillespie and Billings?"

"I don't pay much attention to that stuff."

"Politics?"

Kate nodded before stepping up on the next groin, the last one before an area referred to as the Bird's Nest—that is, until all the trees were cut down and the birds had to find other places to nest.

Melanie followed her to the other side. "You know how to plane furniture and the Latin name for a sand dollar, but you don't know the names of your own senators?"

Kate shrugged. Where she came from, it wasn't good to advertise your book learning, and she had to admit, because she'd been nervous, she'd been showing off back at Melanie's house.

"You do know that your uncle is remodeling the senator's beach house, don't you?" asked Melanie.

"I know Uncle Johnny knows some folks who have places along the coast, and they want the remodeling done when they're down here, probably to keep an eye on the work. This year I was lucky to be brought along."

"So," asked Melanie, stopping, "you don't know who Bailey Gillespie is?"

"Not really."

"And you didn't know anything about her father?"

Kate hunched her shoulders and continued down the beach. It was a moment before she realized her new friend wasn't following her. Instead, Melanie had turned around and was calling to the other two girls. Kate turned around and looked, horrified.

"Hey, you two, come on! I want you to meet some-one."

The other two girls stopped and put their heads to-gether, but the twin boys took this opportunity to race toward Melanie and Kate. Soon the other children were following, and that meant that soon Ginny and Bailey were following them.

When Melanie turned around she saw that Kate had taken off, racing toward land's end. "No! Stop!"

She tried to catch up, but it was no use. She stopped, bent over, huffing and puffing as Bailey reached her.

"What did she do?" demanded the blond girl.

Melanie tried to speak, but it was all she could do to catch her breath. She couldn't even straighten up. "She didn't . . . she didn't . . ."

"Just leave her to me." And Bailey raced off.

Ginny reached Melanie about the same time her friend was able to catch her breath.

"What happened?" asked Ginny.

The younger children raced ahead, in and out of the surf, screaming and hollering. Overhead, the sun be-gan to burn into the girls' skin, and they had no lotion on.

"Nothing," said Melanie.

"Then why is Bailey chasing her?"

"Nothing," repeated Melanie, wheezing. "Really, she did nothing."

"Mel, I think you need to sit down."

"No," said Melanie trudging off after the other two. "We have to catch them."

Ginny looked to where the redhead had disappeared. It wouldn't be long before Bailey ran her down. Bailey rode, danced, and even played basketball. And the rules of girls' basketball had recently changed. Now the girls played with two roving forwards, racing up and down the court. It wasn't at all ladylike.

But Bailey didn't catch the redhead and she returned to where Ginny was rounding up the children and shooing them in the general direction of their homes.

"That bitch! I almost had her."

The children turned around and stared.

"Bailey, watch your language."

"You're not my mother."

"Yes, but I am responsible for these children."

"Where did Kate go?" asked Melanie.

"Kate?" Bailey stared at her. When Melanie didn't reply, she added, "She looped the island. She's fast as blazes."

"Thieves usually are." Ginny was busy making sure the children kept moving when all her brothers wanted to do was cut figure eights.

"I've told you, Kate's no thief."

"And how do you know that?" asked Ginny, looking back at Melanie.

"Tell her, Bailey," said Melanie.

The blond girl stared at the sand as they walked along.

Melanie explained. "Kate's with her uncle. He's—"

"Remodeling our kitchen," finished Bailey, not making eye contact with either friend. Absentmindedly, she rubbed her skin where it was drying out.

Ginny looked from Bailey to Melanie and back to Bailey. "You mean—"

"I mean," said Melanie, "that Kate took off before I was able to explain that she doesn't know the senators from her own state."

"What?" asked Bailey, looking at her.

"Which means," said Ginny, "that she doesn't know anything about your father and his girlfriend."

"And if you don't apologize," added Melanie, "you'll spend the whole summer babysitting with Ginny."

"Ugh!" Bailey watched the twins getting in their last licks before naptime. Several girls tumbled to the sand as the boys tagged them viciously.

After screaming to leave the girls alone, Ginny said, "Then apologize, Bailey. I'd rather slit my wrists than spend my whole summer with Nana."

"I'm going to tell Grandma," said one of her brothers as they ran circles around the three teenagers.

"And," said Ginny, shaking a finger him, "next time a storm comes up, I'll throw you to the Gray Man."

The twins squealed in horror and raced away. Legend had it that the Gray Man only appeared when a storm had the capacity to flatten buildings, and little boys. The other neighborhood ghost was Alice Flagg, a society maiden forbidden to marry a woodcutter. Alice died of a broken heart and was buried, sans engagement ring, and cursed to forever haunt her home, The Hermitage, in search of that ring.

"And with Kate's uncle remodeling Bailey's kitchen," said Melanie, giving both friends a smug little smile, "it goes without saying that I have the only safe house."

"Well, Bailey?" asked Ginny. She'd need some friends to talk things out this summer, and she sure didn't want to do that with those Converse girls.

"You know," said Bailey, rubbing her skin, "I really need to put some lotion on."

"Well?" demanded Ginny.

The three girls were silent as they approached the houses. From one came the sound of an electric saw; from another the Negro maid was shouting it was time for the younger children to come inside and take a nap.

When Ginny saw that all the children had ended up at the correct houses, she turned to her friend. "Well, what's it going to be?"

"Okay," said Bailey. "Let's go find the little twit and get this over with."

Boy Meets Girl

One evening when Kate had received permission from her uncle to sleep over at the Durants', the girls were gathered around a huge piece of driftwood that had washed ashore after a brief but violent storm had pounded Pawleys Island. Kate and Bailey were balancing at opposite ends of the log, actually a palmetto tree, while Melanie and Ginny sat in the middle and looked out to sea.

It was a glorious night with long, thick, horizontal clouds refracting the setting sun into rich yellows, reds, and oranges. The girls had been told to stay within range of Mrs. Belle's voice for some imagined slight committed by Ginny earlier in the day. When one of them mentioned that this piece of wood had ended up "on the beach," Melanie asked if the girls had read the book. Melanie was the big reader in the group.

"My mother took me to see *On the Beach*," said Bailey jumping down from the log. She wore short-shorts and a halter top, and couldn't wait for some boys to come along. She was in a traffic-stopping mood. "I hated that movie, but my mother said I had to learn about the realities of living in the Atomic Age."

"Oh, yes," said Ginny, "warfare that ends all life; that's reality enough to make a girl go all the way."

The girls laughed, if somewhat nervously. All of them wanted to go all the way but still remain virgins. The trick was how to do it. So far, they hadn't come up with an answer.

"The realities of life are brought home when we crawl under our desks at school," said Ginny, who wore a tank top and a pair of bell-bottoms.

"Yeah, like duck and cover could save our butts."

"Watch your language," said Ginny.

"Yeah," said Bailey, smiling, "like duck and cover could save our asses."

Ginny shook her head. Kate said nothing but continued to walk back and forth. If it was true that "duck and cover" couldn't protect you, then why did her school insist on them doing it?

Melanie stood, brushed off her bottom, and let out a sigh. "I just wish I had more butt to cover." Below a long-sleeved blouse tied under her small bosom she wore a pair of cuffed shorts.

"Did you see that movie, Kate?" asked Ginny, trying to include the newcomer in the conversation.

Kate shook her head and continued to walk back and forth on the dead tree. She wore a pair of hip-huggers with a short-sleeved "boy" top borrowed from Melanie.

Around her waist was a wide leather belt.

"She probably only goes to see beach movies," said Bailey, who took a seat on the end of the log and stuck her legs toward the ocean. The evening was pleasant, the mugginess of the day having been blown inland.

"Oh, yeah," said Ginny, "like you'd turn down a chance to go to a drive-in movie."

"You know," said Melanie, "Frankie Avalon is kind of cute."

"Aren't we getting off the subject?" asked Bailey, canting her head around. "We were talking about *On the Beach.*"

"*You* were talking about *On the Beach,*" said Melanie. "I read the book so I didn't have to go see the movie. The book was bad enough. Imagine having to kill your own baby."

"The mother didn't kill anyone," said Bailey. "She made the father do it."

"She did no such thing."

"Aw, you've got a crush on Anthony Perkins. You can't see him as a killer because he's so cute."

"I *have* seen him as a killer. I saw *Psycho.*"

Bailey turned a wicked eye on Kate. "I'll bet even Gopher has seen *Psycho.*"

The other three looked at the redhead teetering on the log in the growing darkness. Kate had tried a new maneuver, whirling around on the soles of a pair of borrowed loafers. Melanie Durant had more clothes than most department stores.

"Hey," taunted Bailey, sticking her face up and yelling in the redhead's face, "don't fall!"

Kate did, landing on her feet. "My grandmother

wouldn't let me see *Psycho*." By now everyone knew that Kate's mother had died of tuberculosis and that she was being raised by her grandmother. Well, it wasn't like anyone else had an Ozzie and Harriet family.

From down the beach three young men appeared out of the darkness. Other people had passed by, strolling up or down the beach, but these three boys were definitely headed for the dead tree. Hair was brushed back, blouses and spines straightened, and Melanie stepped over the log, positioning herself between it and the approaching boys.

Two of the young men smiled, and one of the smilers was blond; the other wore a gray fedora. The third, slightly taller than the other two and sporting a pair of wide shoulders, had the same features as the boy wearing the fedora: dark hair, dark eyes, and a rich tan. All three wore Ban-Lon shirts, walking shorts, and were barefoot. They joined the girls at the same moment that Kate involuntarily trembled at the thought of going to see the movie *Psycho*.

Bailey saw this and played to the new crowd. "Oh, look," she said, pointing at Kate, "Gopher's scared."

The blond boy laughed, but not the two dark-haired ones, who began to evaluate Kate in what little light there was from the beach houses. Floating down to them on a breeze came the sound of Rick Nelson singing "Fools Rush In."

"Who's this?" asked Jeb Stuart, the taller of the three. Beside him stood his younger brother, James, the one wearing the fedora. The blond was Preston Winthrop, whose father was deeply involved in the preservation of the Ansonborough area of Charleston. They were, like

Ginny Belle, from Charleston and lived in the historic district. James Stuart and Preston Winthrop had flat-tops, but Jeb's hair was cropped short. Next year would be his senior year at the Citadel.

Before Bailey could say something really mean, Ginny introduced Kate as Melanie's houseguest, and then looked hard at the blond girl.

"I'm not scared," said Kate, wondering what her hair looked like, not to mention it had been pretty dumb to break a sweat showing off just before these boys arrived. Thankfully, Melanie had let her borrow a pair of hip-huggers and a new top. Otherwise, she would've looked pretty square.

"It's just the breeze," said Kate.

Preston sidled over and tried to put his arm around her. "I'll keep you warm, baby."

Kate jerked away, stumbling, and Jeb Stuart caught her.

"Watch what you're doing." Jeb righted Kate. "You okay?" he asked.

She nodded and broke out of his grasp.

"Yeah," said brother James, pushing back the fedora, "give her a little more time to learn what a huge Romeo you are."

Preston shrugged and took a seat on the log next to Bailey. Out came a pack of cigarettes, and he passed them around. Melanie and Kate demurred, along with the Stuart boys. A Zippo lighter followed, and soon the cigarettes were going, albeit held down low behind the driftwood and out of sight of the houses. The younger Stuart pulled some Dubble Bubble from his walking shorts and offered it to the nonsmokers. Kate almost took the gum, thought better of it, and shook her head. She failed to notice the interest that Jeb Stuart had taken in her.

Lost in her own thoughts, Kate stared out to sea and listened to the waves breaking on the shore. It was beautiful here, but that didn't mean Pawleys was worth it. Kate couldn't wait until she and her uncle finished the kitchen so they could get back to Greenville. She was sick and tired of being picked on by Bailey Gillespie.

But for tonight she was stuck here. Sure, she could use the Durants' phone, but what if she called the trailer park and the manager said her uncle wasn't there? What if Uncle Johnny *was* there and drinking again? She couldn't ask him to come fetch her, not after the row they'd had last time he'd driven home drunk from that bar outside Georgetown.

Kate hated it when her uncle drank, because more than likely he'd leave her all alone, and some of the men in the park had begun knocking on her door. That's why she'd endure about anything from her new "friends." But enough was enough, and now these boys were here. Still, the boy who'd caught her when she'd stumbled was kind of cute, even without any hair. Why did Citadel boys always cut their hair so short?

"If you aren't afraid," said Bailey, "then prove it."

"What?" asked Kate, interrupted in sneaking a look at Jeb Stuart.

"Prove you aren't afraid."

"Prove it how?"

Preston grinned from where he sat on the log. "Oh, I don't know, maybe ring Old Leatherface's doorbell."

"I don't know who Old Leatherface is."

Bailey took a drag off her cigarette and tossed it into the incoming tide. "Give me a hand, Preston."

And he tossed away his cigarette, leaped to his feet, and helped the blond girl to her feet.

"No problem," said Bailey, brushing off her bottom and stepping over the log. "I'll show you his house. And his doorbell."

"You can't do that," said Melanie, backing away as everyone crossed the log in her direction.

"You want her to be part of the group or not?" asked Bailey. "Everyone's done it, or something just as bad. Why not her?"

"You're just picking on her again."

"Am not!" It was almost a shout.

Melanie turned to Ginny. "Isn't she?"

"Sorry, Mel, but I agree with Bailey. Kate has to prove she belongs." Ginny tossed her cigarette in the water. Smoking made her sick. She definitely needed more practice.

"But this isn't fair."

"Life isn't fair," said Bailey, rather bitterly.

"Yeah, and we all know who you think it's not fair to. Just because—"

"Melanie!" This from Ginny, and it *was* a shout.

"I'll do it," said Kate.

Everyone looked at her, including the boys who had sensibly remained quiet during the argument.

"You don't have to do this," said Melanie.

"What's the big deal? I've rung doorbells before."

"Yeah," said Bailey, putting her arm around Kate and walking her down the beach, "but Old Leatherface has a dog, a real mean one."

"I'm not going to let you do this," said Melanie, and she followed them down the beach.

"Sorry, Mel," said Ginny, "but you have no say in the matter."

The three young men trailed along, knowing something was about to happen, something very exciting, and that something might lead to even more excitement later that night. Anxious to ingratiate themselves with these girls, the boys gave each and every one of them a hand over the groins as they moved down the beach. Jeb elbowed his brother out of the way to assist Kate, and that caused a good number of bubbles to be blown and popped in quick succession.

Melanie glanced at her house. "I just might tell."

"You wouldn't dare," said Ginny, when she really meant "that's no fair." No way she'd miss this. She'd even risk more restrictions.

Noticing Melanie had stopped, Bailey said, "You need to grow a backbone, Mel."

"And I need to use the bathroom," said Kate, heading toward the Durant beach house.

"You going to tell?" asked Ginny, glancing at her grandmother's house again.

"Nope. I just want to use the bathroom before you girls scare the pee out of me."

INITIATION RITES

Old Leatherface was one of the original residents of Pawleys, another eccentric who had been able to hold onto his house despite an increase in property taxes and the occasional hurricane. A wooden fence ran

51

around his bungalow, and his dog was chained to one of the pilings. The dog slept under the porch and legend had it that the dog always slept with one eye open.

At least, that's what small children believed, and anyone who crossed the fence was fair game. Even the Georgetown County sheriff backed up Old Leatherface in this matter, much to the chagrin of the summer residents; so the gauntlet had been established, and only the bravest would dare make the dash for the porch, much less ring the bell. In the collective memory of those who had spent their summers on Pawleys, no girl had ever made the dash, which was why Melanie Durant continued to berate Bailey and Ginny as they moved down the beach, gathering up even more kids as they went along.

"And I so wanted to go to the pavilion Saturday night," whined Melanie. "But with Kate going to the hospital—"

"Don't be so melodramatic," shot back Ginny.

"Yeah," said Bailey as she guided Kate down the shoreline. "You're in this, too."

"How's that?"

"Because your houseguest said she'd do it."

"But nobody's ever done this before."

"Hey," said Preston, indignantly, "we've all done it."

"That's different. You're boys." Melanie tried a new tack. "Kate, your family will have to pay for your hospital bills. Do they have the money to pay for shots?"

Kate forced a smile. "Don't worry, I've had my shots."

Ginny and Bailey laughed, as did the others, which

by now had grown to almost fifteen people, young kids and teenagers.

"Oh, that's right, laugh it off." Melanie stopped.

Up and down the beach, houselights broke the darkness, and the sound of the ocean was joined by the murmur of people sitting on porches and enjoying the night air. From one house came the champagne music of Lawrence Welk; at the next house someone hollered for them to turn it up.

"I'll be here if you need a doctor," said Melanie.

Many of them clucked at her. "Chick . . . chick . . . chicken."

Melanie jerked a thumb toward the houses behind her. "No, you dummies! This is Doctor Rose's house." Dr. Rose, or someone in his family, had been ministering to prominent families since, well, before medical doctors were thought much of.

Bailey gestured at the bungalow. "You don't mind a little dog bite, do you, Gopher?"

"Why does she call you that?" asked Jeb.

"He's not going to bite me," said Kate.

"Oh," said Ginny, "another soldier pressed into the army of positive thinking."

"I don't know what that means," said Kate, her eyes focused on the bungalow with the fence.

"It means you believe you can do this."

"Well, we'll soon find out, won't we?"

After clambering over the next jetty, everyone stopped and stared at the darkness under the wooden porch.

"I see his eyes," said someone.

And that might be true as there were few lights at this end of the beach, and Old Leatherface's porch was certainly not lit up. Any light came from a waxing moon.

"He's under there," said someone.

"Fang," said another.

"Fang?" asked a young girl.

"That's what we call him," said one of the teenage boys. "He'll chew you a new asshole."

"Would you please watch your language?" said Ginny. "There are small children here."

"Oh, don't be such a fuddy-duddy," said someone from the interior of the group.

Bailey grinned at Kate. "Ready?"

"I'm—I'm ready," stammered Kate, her hands becoming small fists at her sides.

One of the boys saw this. "For cripes sake, you're not going to knock him out. Just ring the doorbell and run."

"Run for your life," said another.

"Yeah, it's your only chance."

"Kate," said Ginny, suddenly losing her taste for all this, "you don't have to do this if you don't want to."

"What you talking about?" demanded Preston. The blond young man glanced at everyone above the high-tide line. "She'd damn well better. We came here for a show."

Ginny sighed. There was no way she was going to be able to stop these boys from cussing, and really, what was about to happen was much more serious.

"Sure you want to do this?" asked Jeb Stuart. "There's no shame in changing your mind."

"Not for a girl," said his younger brother, who had a look of awe on his face. James Stuart had never seen a girl do anything this remotely dangerous, not even Bailey Gillespie.

"I can do this." Kate looked around. "Anyone got a straight pin?"

There was a quick discussion and a hairpin was produced.

"I'll need it back," said the girl who provided the pin.

Everyone laughed, and from under the porch came the sound of growling. Or was that the surf? From an open window of another house, Roy Orbison sang "Only the Lonely."

Jeb leaned over and whispered to Kate. "What I think you should do is rush the porch, ring the bell, and then wait for the animal to make his move. That's called holding the high ground and it affords you the opportunity to choose your path off the porch, away from the dog and out of the yard." Their eyes met and Jeb smiled down at her. "Remember, the dog has to bring along his chain and he knows a piling or a post can hold him up."

"Th—thanks." Kate didn't know if her stammering was caused by looking into this boy's eyes or because she was scared to death.

Kate left the high-tide line, and the gasps from the younger children followed her as she headed toward the house. Smaller children turned away and thrust their faces between the legs of their babysitters, and James Stuart popped his bubblegum until his older brother told him to knock it off.

Kate couldn't see the dog, but what did that matter? If the dog didn't exist, then another cruel joke had been played on her, and what else was new? Still, if the dog was there, no one could alert him to her presence, or she'd have reason to turn tail and run, and hopefully, someone else would become the butt of their jokes. Melanie Durant received a taste of this when she rejoined the group.

"You know, Mel, you make any noise and Billy and I are going to pick you up and toss you over that fence ourselves."

"Yeah," said Billy, "it'd be a shame for such a pretty face to get chewed up by a dog."

"Is she really going do it?" asked one of the younger kids.

"I don't know. She's just standing there."

Jeb Stuart told them all to shut up. When they did, they thought they could make out the sound of a growling dog, and as they watched, Kate vaulted the fence and made for the porch. In an instant she was up the stairs, and at the same time, from under the porch, a dark form emerged, dragging a chain behind him. Gasps came from the high-tide line and Jeb Stuart stepped forward.

"No," said Bailey, seizing his arm, "this is Gopher's show."

Jeb glanced at the blond girl's hand on his arm. "And maybe that's why I've never liked you, Bailey."

When they looked again they saw Kate bent over and working on the doorbell. Suddenly, the bell began to bong, and the growling became louder as the dog took up a position on the walkway. And just as Jeb had told her, the animal knew there was little to be gained by rushing the porch and having the intruder leap off in another direction. So the dog simply waited. Still, the animal did appear puzzled by the constant bonging, and the intensity of his growling increased as he heard his master's footsteps approaching. Kate had returned to the head of the stairs, but she just stood there.

She froze, thought Jeb. He shook off Bailey's hand, and giving a rebel yell, rushed the fence. The dog looked around, and when he did, more teenagers broke into a run, screaming and hollering and rushing the fence. The doorbell continued to bong, and behind her Kate heard a lock thrown.

Kate whistled, using two fingers and causing the dog's attention to return to her. Then she was down the steps and moving toward the animal. Jeb stopped, stunned at what he was seeing. He, too, had heard Kate whistle, and now watched as she waved to get the animal's attention.

What was going on?

But, instead of leaping for the girl, the dog yelped, threw itself on the walkway, and started pawing its snout.

Behind Kate the porch lights came on, and then Kate really froze, but only for an instant; when the door squeaked open, she raced for the fence, leaping it but catching her trailing foot. When she came down it was Jeb she landed on.

They fell to the sand, and when she rose up on both arms, straddling Jeb, she smiled down into his face and said, "Well, hello there."

By the time Kate scrambled to her feet, Stuart had taken her hand and started pulling her down the beach. Behind them Old Leatherface stomped down the steps, glanced at the whining animal rolling around on the walkway, and began hollering at the kids scattering up and down the shoreline.

"What'd you do back there?" asked Stuart as they raced down the beach.

"Threw a handful of black pepper in the dog's face."

"You didn't!"

"I did! I got it from Melanie's kitchen."

And, laughing, they disappeared in the darkness together.

LEARNING TO SHAG

Melanie was called downstairs and met her mother at the foot of the stairs where Carolynn Hamby spoke to her daughter in hushed tones. "Melanie, I'm concerned about that girl."

Her daughter glanced in the living room where Kate Youngblood sat on the sofa, head down. Anyone with half a brain could see she was upset.

But when Melanie tried to go to her, her mother held her up. "I'm not sure this will work out. Kate comes from a different world."

"It wasn't but a few weeks ago you said it would be a good idea if I palled around with Kate. You said it might help with my grades."

"Yes, but she's crying and won't tell me why."

"Mother, even I don't tell you all my problems."

Melanie shook off her mother's hand and went to her friend, taking tentative steps toward the sofa. Finally, she sat down.

Carolynn Hamby bit her lip and took up a position near the doorway but out of sight of the two girls in the living room.

"What's the problem, Kate? Bailey been giving you a hard time again?"

"No, no. It's not that."

Melanie leaned over and gave her friend a one-armed hug. "Well, I'm sure whatever it is, we can work it out."

"It's Jeb."

"What about him?" asked Melanie, releasing her friend, anxious to hear more.

"He's asked me to go to the pavilion Friday night."

Melanie gripped both of Kate's hands and turned the redhead to face her. "That's great! Jeb's a real gentleman, not like some of the boys who're always trying to cop a feel."

Kate shook her head. "I—I can't go."

"Your uncle KO'd the idea?"

"I—I haven't told him, but I think he'll be okay with the idea. He's pretty tired of babysitting me."

Melanie looked her friend over. The girl could use some help with her makeup, but she was pretty enough; kind of tomboyish with those shoulders, but she did have a figure. It was the jeans and the man's shirt. She'd never seen Kate actually dressed up. "Did you bring a dress to the beach?"

"I have one for church. I go every Sunday."

Uh-huh. So that's why they never saw Kate on Sundays. It wasn't because she couldn't catch a ride over to the island. "Well, then, you're set." Melanie suddenly had second thoughts. "Er—maybe you should bring the dress over and let me take a look." She hoped it wasn't one of those frilly, but tacky things she'd seen on hillbillies when they came to town on Saturdays.

Kate pulled her hands away. "It doesn't matter if I have a dress. I can't dance."

"You . . . can't . . . dance?"

Kate nodded and stared into her lap again. There her hands found each other and held on tight.

"Well, you can slow dance. All you do is slide around the floor and hold onto your partner."

Kate shook her head but did not look up.

"Wait a minute, you've never danced, square danced, line danced, anything?"

"I'm Baptist," said Kate, finally looking up. "No drinking, smoking, cussing, or card playing, and absolutely no dancing."

"I know Baptists who dance."

"Not in my family they don't."

Melanie leaned back on the sofa. A smile began at the corners of her mouth, and out in the hallway Carolynn Hamby had to cover her mouth and hurry down the hall, through the kitchen, and out the back door. Only when Carolynn had reached the back porch did she give in to her laughter.

Kate must've heard something because she scrambled to her feet and started out of the room. "I'm sure this is funny to people like you, but I was taught that dancing is a sin."

"Well, there goes Jeb then."

The redhead turned around and faced her.

"Kate, you'll have to learn how to dance, and perhaps even hold your liquor, if you want to catch a boy like Jeb Stuart."

Kate said nothing, only stared at her.

"What I'm trying to say is boys like Jeb Stuart don't

come along every day and girls have to make sacrifices to land them. What you're missing here is that military academies expect their graduates to be officers and gentlemen, and that means they must be able to dance. Now I don't mind teaching you, but I don't want to contribute to your going to hell."

"That's blasphemy!"

"Not if I'm taking you seriously."

Kate considered this, and as she did, looked over Melanie's shoulder and out the large picture window where the waves washed ashore. It was July now, the heat was fierce, and the air conditioning was turned up high. The only other air conditioning Kate had seen, well, she hadn't actually seen it, but movie houses had air conditioning, and people flocked to the movies to escape the heat. Wags said before the advent of air conditioning nobody really knew they were hot, and that movies were ruining the good character of Southerners, and they didn't mean when theaters showed *And God Created Woman,* starring Brigitte Bardot.

Kate had seen her friend moving to music played on her record player, but that was different. All Melanie had been doing was . . . well, to be frank, she'd been shaking her bottom, which had been drummed into Kate as a mortal sin, especially if you shook your bottom in public. It wasn't something nice girls did.

"I know it's a sin to cuss and drink and take up with women, and my uncle does all those things, and I pray he'll find his way off such a path of wickedness . . ." Still Jeb Stuart was *sooo* cute. He had dark eyes, dark hair, a tan that wouldn't quit, and shoulders even a tall girl like Kate could call home.

"You really think your uncle's going to hell?" asked Mel.

"Gosh, I hope not. He takes me to the state fair every fall. What I'm saying is I think God forgives us for crossing lines, if we hurry back to the right side. I don't think God would mind if I did this one thing. I mean, I'm not going to be kissing and all that other stuff . . ." Kate turned red and stared at the floor. It was a moment before she could speak. "I've already done the kissing part and it weren't so bad."

Melanie came off the sofa and across the room. "Jeb's kissed you and you never told me?" She pulled her friend back across the room and down on the sofa. "Where? When? Did he use his tongue?"

"No, no," said Kate, looking away again. "It weren't anything like that. The night I rang the doorbell at Old Leatherface's . . . after that, we were walking and talking, and it seemed he really liked me . . . even if I do talk funny and don't know all the stuff he knows. You know, Jeb Stuart's real smart."

"Kate, you're really smart."

"Thank you . . . anyway, I think Uncle Johnny will let me go to the pavilion, or even the roller rink. I done that when I was a GA, that's Girls Auxiliary, but what if he asks me to dance?"

Melanie couldn't care less about the dancing. She wanted the inside scoop on the smooching. Lowering her voice and leaning forward, she asked, "Kate, what about the kissing?"

"Well, it were before we came back to that log that was hauled away for the bonfire—"

"Yes, yes, the palmetto tree. I noticed you two were

holding hands. I didn't know it went any further."

"It really didn't. He . . . he took me in his arms and hugged me and told me he thought I was really brave, you know, for ringing that doorbell."

"And then?"

"It just happened."

"Oh, how cool!" said Melanie, clapping her hands. "I'm so happy for you."

"Er—thank you." She looked hard at her friend. "You didn't think I could have a boyfriend like him, did you?"

"That's not so." Actually, Melanie was wondering how long this summer romance could last.

"Because of the way I talk, right?"

"There's nothing wrong with the way you talk . . ."

The redhead straightened up. "I thought you were my friend. Does this mean you're going to tell Bailey and Ginny that Jeb kissed me?"

"Oh, no, I wouldn't do such a thing."

"Cross your heart and hope to die."

Melanie did so, slashing across her heart both ways and promising not to tell. "But if you don't want people talking about you, you're going to have to make a few changes."

"What do you mean?"

"All I've ever seen you in is those jeans, and nobody wears dungarees to the pavilion or the skating rink."

"Well, beside a couple of dresses and other jeans, they're all I've got. Uncle Johnny said he'd take me to the dry goods store in Georgetown, but so far he hasn't had time."

Dry goods store! "What about those hip-huggers I loaned you?"

"Oh, I meant to wash them out. You know I spilled Coke on them when the boys brought the cooler out to the log."

Melanie smiled. "Or did you think you might hold onto them for your date with Jeb?"

Kate stared at the sofa between them.

"Stealing, isn't that breaking one of the commandments?"

Kate's head jerked up. "No, no. I can bring them back."

"Keep them," said Melanie, pushing her friend's hands away. "You looked great in them."

"And I love them, I really do."

"You should wear short-shorts," said Melanie, standing and modeling the pair she had on. Her top was a sleeveless blouse.

Kate fell back in her seat. "Oh, I wouldn't dare."

"I'm sorry, Kate, but that's one of the changes you're going to have to make. Nobody but old people wear Bermuda shorts. Who wants boys looking at your knees when there's more to a girl's legs?"

This appeared to put her friend in real agony. Kate swallowed hard, her face twisting up in pain. "I don't know . . . I don't know . . ."

"Look, Kate, I haven't pushed you on this, and I was happy to loan you the hip-huggers, but if you don't get into something a bit more fashionable, they're going to make fun of more than your accent."

"I've tried to change . . ."

"And you're doing great, but Jeb won't be the only boy who'll want to take you dancing."

The redhead straightened up. "You think so?"

"Well, strutting *is* part of life at the beach."

"Strutting?"

"Sashaying down Ocean Boulevard at Myrtle Beach. It's a way to attract the boys. We all do it."

"I don't know about that . . ." The way her friend put it made it sound, well, kind of dirty.

"You'll learn when we go to Myrtle. That's where all the boys are, not Pawleys. It's also where the local girls go. Girls from Georgetown can't compete with the girls who come to Pawleys from Greenville and Spartanburg."

"I wasn't looking for another boyfriend."

"Oh, you've settled on Jeb, have you?"

"Well, he is kinda cute."

"But there are plenty of boys, and they all come to Myrtle. That's where we meet them."

"Not Pawleys?"

"Oh, Pawleys is okay but Myrtle is where the action is." Melanie pulled her new friend to her feet. "You're taller than me. Want to try on a pair of my mother's walking shorts?"

Kate grimaced. "Maybe . . . I don't know."

"Your church is that strict?"

Kate nodded.

Melanie pursed her lips. "But what I don't understand is why you think you have your uncle's permission to go on a date but don't have his permission to simply go dancing."

"Oh, he served in the Marines, and that's what Jeb's joining when he graduates. Uncle Johnny thinks it's really neat that I've made some new friends down here at the beach."

"Kate, please, 'cool,' not 'neat,' and 'boss' if it's even better."

"Oh, yes, cool. Uncle Johnny thinks it's really cool that I have friends here, or he'd have to spend all his time watching out for me."

Melanie glanced into the hallway. "May I ask where Jeb's going to pick you up for your date?"

"Well, sure, at the trailer park. He knows where it is."

"Jeb's not going to think you're cool if he keeps picking you up at any trailer park. Eventually he'll have to explain to his friends why he picks you up there. Why not have him pick you up here? He knows you sometimes spend the night, even work at Bailey's, right?"

"Yes, and he thinks it's . . . cool that I'm learning a trade."

Melanie smiled. "And I'll have a pair of walking shorts waiting for you."

"I don't know if I can go that far."

"Speaking of how far you're willing to go . . . you'll tell me if he tries anything, won't you? Ginny'll speak to his mother. The Stuart and Belle families have known each other ever since there was a Charleston."

Kate nodded.

"Then go out and have fun!"

"What—what about the dancing?"

"Sure you want to learn?"

"I—I think so."

"It won't get you in trouble?"

Kate set her jaw. "I'm willing to risk it."

Melanie threw her voice down the hall. "Mother, are you there?"

66

Her mother appeared at the door. "I was just passing by . . ."

"Yes, yes. Can you help me teach Kate how to shag?" To Kate, she said, "My mom's one of the best dancers on the whole island." Melanie began tying her long brown hair into a ponytail as she crossed the room to the phonograph.

"I don't know about that . . ." Mrs. Hamby studied the redhead as she came in the room. "You don't know how to dance, my dear?"

"No, ma'am, I'm Baptist."

"Really? I know some very nice families who are Baptist, and they all dance."

"Mother, I didn't ask you in here to discuss your Baptist friends."

Mrs. Hamby followed her daughter to the phonograph where she picked up several LPs protected by their cardboard sleeves. "I think I have something that will pass for shag music, maybe Les Paul and Mary Ford."

Her daughter lifted the lid and picked up a smaller record. "I've got that forty-five by the Tams."

"Yes, my dear, but those boys are colored and it's not appropriate for nice girls to be dancing to their music."

"You don't mind if I dance to Johnny Mathis."

"Yes, I do," said her mother, turning on the machine, "and for a completely different reason."

Still, Carolynn let her daughter put the forty-five on the turntable and place the needle on the edge. Soon the sound of "What Kind of Fool Do You Think I Am?" filled the room. Carolynn shook her head but called for the maid to roll back the oval rug and help them move the coffee table.

Once that was done, and the maid had returned to her duties, Melanie and her mother moved into the middle of the floor, took each other's hands, and began to dance. When the song ended Kate was totally discouraged. She couldn't see how she could ever learn all those steps, certainly not by Friday night.

"No, it's easy," said Melanie, pulling her into the middle of the room. "If we have to, we'll tie a rope to a door so you can practice."

Kate had no idea what that meant.

"All you have to do is listen for the beat."

Melanie had left the record player's changer pulled back, and when the Tams sang again, Kate listened closely but had no idea what her friend was talking about.

Mrs. Hamby snapped her fingers. "You hear that, Kate? It's just a lazy jitterbug."

"Mother, you aren't teaching this to a bunch of your Yankee friends down here for the summer. If Kate doesn't know how to dance, then how would she know the jitterbug?"

"What kind of music do you listen to? You do listen to music, don't you?"

"Yes, ma'am. I listen to Elvis." And watch *American Bandstand* when she could sneak a peek. But shagging was nothing like *American Bandstand*. On *American Bandstand* the kids jumped around like water bugs, or did the twist.

"Elvis Presley," said Carolynn. "No wonder your church doesn't want you dancing."

"Mother, please! All the preachers are men, and they're the ones who don't like Elvis."

Still, Kate began to snap her fingers, and by the end of the second playing, she'd discovered the beat. "I've got it, I've got it." And she did, snapping her fingers when the song played a third time.

So the three women stood in the middle of the living room, leaning forward slightly and snapping their fingers in time with the music. In the kitchen, and upstairs, the Negro servants stopped what they were doing and began to dance. They all knew how to shag. As old timers said: "The shag is a warm night with a cold beer and a hot date."

During the 1940s, white teenagers had been allowed to attend Negro nightclubs along the Carolina coast where they watched the dancing from the balcony, a sort of reverse segregation called "jumping the Jim Crow rope." From there, it was only a matter of talking the jukebox owners into installing some of the "colored" songs in jukeboxes and the rest was history. Actually, the shag was history; it had a good twenty-year run and was killed off by a younger generation doing the twist, the mashed potato, or the Freddy, and other ungraceful lunges, leaps, and stomps across the dance floor—the worst of them being disco.

Melanie took Kate's right hand and held it out. "Now, I'll be your date. We face each other."

This time Kate's nod was barely perceptible.

"Bend your arm at the elbow," said Carolynn. "You'll be moving forward and backward like you saw us do."

Kate bent her elbow and Melanie continued with the

lesson. "The guy leads with his left hand, so you'll respond with your right. You move from the knees down, so your hips don't sway." Melanie smiled. "That should keep you from going to hell."

"Melanie!" said her mother.

"And your shoulders always face your partner."

Kate nodded.

"Just watch my feet."

Melanie listened to the music for a moment and began to step toward Kate, and then back, right, and left; then she repeated the motion. Up, back, right and left, repeated again and again. She said it was called "the basic," and that some folks called it dancing like a Southerner.

"Up-two-three. Back-two-three, right, left. Up-two-three. Back-two-three, right, left."

Kate watched and held onto her friend's hand, but without an inkling of what her friend was doing.

Carolynn Hamby saw her dismay. "No, no," she said, and taking Kate by the hips she turned the redhead around so that Kate stood beside her daughter. "Now she can see."

Mrs. Hamby took a position on the other side of Kate, and at that moment the song stopped and they waited for the replay.

"Really, I have some LPs that would work just as well."

"Mother, you don't have anything like this music."

"And I know why. Whatever happened to the big bands?"

"They all died during the war."

"Melanie, be civil!"

But by then the Tams were singing again, and this time Kate began to move her feet like the other two women.

"That's right, Kate," said Mrs. Hamby, nodding. "Bend your knees and relax your shoulders. Yes, yes, that's good, and learn to slide across the floor. Never be caught flat-footed. That's why you never take drinks on the floor. Show respect for the dance floor. After all, they're usually made of wood."

And being a quick learner, by the time the song ended Kate had the basic step down pat.

During a pause in the music Carolynn left the room and returned with her Instamatic and snapped a few shots of the two girls dancing. Still, when the Tams finished singing, she asked, "Don't you have another song?"

"Mother, there is no other song this summer. Besides, when Jeb asks Kate to dance—"

"Jeb?" Carolynn looked at Kate with raised eyebrows as the music continued to play. "Jeb Stuart asked you out?"

"Yes, Mother, and if I don't miss my guess, they'll end up at the pavilion."

"Have you discussed this with your uncle?"

"It'll be okay. My Uncle Johnny was a Marine, too."

"Well, I'm not sure being a Marine is the sort of recommendation I'd want for a young man taking my daughter dancing."

"Kate's not your daughter, Mother."

"Yes, my dear, but Kate understands that I'm her chaperone while she's at the beach, don't you, my dear?"

Kate nodded. "Yes, ma'am, I do."

"And for that reason I'm not sure I want you going out with any Marine."

"Jeb's not a Marine yet," broke in Melanie. "He's from a nice family in Charleston, and a boy you've always wanted me to date."

"Yes," said her mother, placing the Instamatic on the fireplace mantel, "but there's always James, his younger brother."

"Mother!"

"You could do much worse."

"I'm not going out with James Stuart. He's the same age as Kate and me."

"And the problem with that is?"

"He's too immature. He puts on that stupid hat and sneaks up on children at night, making them think he's the Gray Man."

"I'm sure James is only trying to keep up with his older brother. After all, it's Jeb who catches all the girls' eyes."

And right then and there Kate knew she was going to learn how to dance and even how to drink. As for the other stuff, the stuff that made her shiver all the way to her gut, well, maybe, but she wasn't going to lose Jeb Stuart to any girl from Georgetown, Greenville, or even Spartanburg.

"I figure if Jeb asks Kate to dance, she can always put him off until the DJ plays 'What Kind of Fool Do You Think I Am?' and she'll be more comfortable. That song is getting a lot of air play, so why wouldn't the band at the pavilion know it? It's already on the jukebox."

Mrs. Hamby stared at her daughter. If she could only get Melanie to act like this around strangers, but

Melanie couldn't. Wouldn't. And having a mother who had shot her stepfather hadn't driven Melanie into her shell. She'd always been a wallflower, not at all like her older siblings. You'd never find them spending a summer at Pawleys, not once they were old enough to drive.

Carolynn had no idea why Kate had brought her daughter out of her shell, but for that reason she tolerated this girl from the wrong side of the tracks, the one who spoke through her nose and wore dungarees and men's shirts. Even her neighbors, meaning Bailey's mother and Ginny's grandmother, had inquired as to what "that strange creature" was doing hanging around. And Addy Belle had wondered out loud whether Kate Youngblood was a bad influence on the girls.

But not on Melanie, and no longer did Carolynn find Melanie sleeping in her closet, something her daughter had regularly done until Kate Youngblood came along. Father dead, stepfather shot; if this hillbilly could help her daughter survive the summer, who was she to complain?

The judge had said, "Mister Hamby, you understand the terms of this divorce?"

Carolynn's husband fidgeted in his wheelchair. "What are you talking about, your honor? I'm the one who was shot." He gestured at his leg in the cast. "I'm the aggrieved party."

"Mister Hamby," said the judge from his bench, "we are keeping this incident out of the papers and you, sir, out of jail. No husband can be considered the aggrieved party when the family doctor swears to the number of bruises found on your wife and your daughter."

At this remark Carolynn only stared at the table in front of her. Her attorney put an arm around her, and the court reporter glanced up from her shorthand machine and flashed a look of sympathy. She'd heard it all before.

From his wheelchair her husband pleaded, "You don't think people don't know who shot me?"

"If they do, sir, it's because you've opened your big, fat mouth."

"Your honor, you can't speak to me like that."

"Son," said the judge, peering down at the man in the wheelchair, "this is my courtroom and I'll speak to you any way I like. Now tell me, son, isn't it true the sheriff has answered domestic disturbance calls at Mrs. Hamby's house in the past?"

"My house, your honor! I run the Durant Tobacco Company. Why, old man Durant personally selected me for the job."

"And look how you've repaid him." The judge glanced at Carolynn. It wasn't lost on him that the woman sat on the far side of her attorney, as far away as she could sit from her husband.

"I don't see where it's the court's business how I run my business, or my family."

"Sir, you've lived among us for some time now, but you still haven't learned that we don't like to have our women used as punching bags. Compared to you, General Sherman was a gentleman."

"Why can't you Southerners forget that damn war? We have."

"Probably because of the number of Yankees making their homes down here. You people should remember you're guests in our part of the country."

"You're only siding with her because of where I come from."

"No, sir, I'm trying to teach you some manners." The judge glanced at the cast on the man's leg. "But it appears I'm too late. Your wife has already done that."

"Yes, sir. I was assaulted, and I insist—"

"And to protect you from further assaults, I'm granting her request for a divorce. That should keep you out of harm's way."

As the man in the wheelchair sputtered, the judge turned his attention to the woman, a fine-looking woman, a charitable woman, and a church-going woman. Granted, this woman's father had seduced more women and had created more jobs than either the Dukes or the Reynolds, but some of the best businessmen couldn't keep their peckers in their britches.

"Mrs. Hamby, I believe it'd be best if you spent the next few weeks in Vegas."

"Yes, sir, but would you consider Pawleys Island? I still have a child at home, and we have a summer place there."

"Very well, Pawleys it is." And the judge brought down the gavel, ending the session, which had been held behind closed doors.

During a pause between songs came a knock at the front door. The sound startled Carolynn and both girls noticed this.

"Mother?"

Melanie placed a hand on her mother's shoulder. Both were of one thought: Had their husband/stepfather followed them to the beach? Was he out there standing on the porch and hammering on the front door?

"Would you like me to get it?" asked Kate.

But no one was hammering. It was simply someone knocking at the front door.

"I'll get it," said Carolynn, shrugging off her case of nerves and went to the door. You had to face your fears. That would be the example she would set for her daughter.

Bailey Gillespie and Ginny Belle were at the door and they were hard to make out because of the glare off the ocean—that is, until someone moved behind them. That was Wilma, the Gillespie's light-skinned servant, and in her hands was a paper sack from the A&P. The Negro had the same brilliant blue eyes as Bailey, but that was a skeleton hanging in someone else's closet.

"It's Bailey and Ginny," announced Carolynn from the hallway. "Come on in, girls."

The three girls came into the house, and when Bailey saw Kate Youngblood, she made a face and stopped in the hall. As for Kate, she backed away.

Carolynn Hamby was having none of that. "Have you met Melanie's new friend?" she asked.

"Yes, we have," said Ginny, forcing a smile.

Bailey said nothing, well, nothing about that. "Mother sent this over for tonight. It's a chicken casserole. Alice Frey made it." Bailey looked Kate in the eye when she added, "Though I don't think we'll have enough for Melanie's friend." In the background the Tams began to sing again.

"I'm sure there'll be plenty to go round. And your

mother didn't have to go to this much trouble with her kitchen in such a state. Wilma, would you please take the casserole to the kitchen?"

"Yes, ma, am." And the light-skinned girl disappeared into the rear of the house.

"Will you be inviting Kate to dinner?" asked Carolynn, glancing at her daughter. "The Gillespies are eating here because their kitchen is such a mess."

"Yes," said Bailey, still standing in the hallway, "I think Melanie's friend had something to do with that."

"What y'all doing?" asked Ginny, leaving Bailey and entering the living room.

"Teaching Kate how to shag," said Carolynn, happy to have the distraction. She remembered how it'd been when she was young, and how the sudden infusion of another personality into the group had altered the group's dynamics.

Kate said nothing, only stood on the far side of the room with the oversized air-conditioning unit blowing against her back. She had perspired during the dancing; now she felt chilled and began to tremble. The phonograph stopped playing and a hiss came from its speakers before the song started again.

Melanie looked at Bailey, still in the hall. "I thought about having Bailey and Wilma give Kate a few lessons."

Ginny joined Mrs. Hamby in trying to broker an uneasy peace. "Why not? Bailey's the best dancer in our group."

"I'm really not in the mood," said Bailey.

"I'm not sure about Wilma dancing with you girls," said Melanie's mom.

But Melanie brushed past Bailey and hollered down the hall. "Wilma, would you come out here, please?"

"My goodness, dear," said her mother with a nervous smile, "there's no reason to shout."

Wilma pushed her way through the swinging door from the kitchen and saw who was calling. "Yes, Miss Melanie, what can I do for you?"

Melanie met her coming down the hall and took her hand. "Come on in here. There's someone I want you to meet."

The servant girl did not come easily, and kept glancing at Bailey.

"Wilma, this is Kate and she doesn't know how to dance. She's a Baptist."

"I'm a Baptist," said the blue-eyed Negro.

"Well, Kate's from one of those sects that doesn't dance, play cards, or go to the movies."

"I've been to movies before," said Kate, rather lamely.

"Anyway," said Melanie, letting Wilma's hand go, "I wanted you to show Kate some of your dance moves."

Wilma looked at Bailey, who stood stone-faced in the hallway.

The black girl looked to Carolynn Hamby for support. "I really need to be getting back to the house."

On the phonograph the Tams finished singing "What Kind of Fool Do You Think I Am?" once again.

"Don't be silly. There's nothing for you to do with the kitchen all torn up."

"Melanie, I don't think it's your place to determine the usefulness of the Gillespie family help."

But her daughter had taken Wilma's hand and pulled her into the center of the room. "Come on."

Wilma went into the larger room, all the time staring at Carolynn Hamby.

"Here," said Bailey, sighing, "let me do it." And she took Wilma's hand, and when the Tams sang again, the two girls began to dance.

Kate's mouth fell open. She'd never seen a white person dance with a Negro before, and no wonder the preacher didn't want young people dancing. Bailey and this girl were doing all manner of twirls, one where they twirled each other, the other where they twirled together. Then they promenaded down the middle of the living room, only to turn around and head in her direction. When they reached where Kate stood, they turned and returned to the center of the room, but not before Kate could see that beads of sweat had broken out on the foreheads of both girls despite the air conditioning.

Melanie and Ginny took turns calling out different steps.

"Belly roll!"

"Duck walk!"

"Prissy!"

"Sugarfoot!"

And no matter what was called out the two girls moved effortlessly together, the huge room suddenly made small by their presence.

They were really going at it, thought Kate, like two warriors, and when the song ended the girls released each other and backed away, both winded. Kate had heard Negroes could really dance, but this was more than she could have imagined. And Bailey Gillespie had matched her servant step for step.

Ginny and Melanie were clapping, but Carolynn Hamby appeared ill at ease. So did Wilma.

"Well," said Wilma, "I really should be getting back to the house." And she was out the door, across the screened-in porch, and down the steps before anyone could say a word.

As Kate looked out the window over the air conditioner, she saw Wilma plodding through the sand, a wild, angry look on her face, and for that reason it was a moment before Kate remembered to compliment Bailey on her dancing.

"Dancing with girls is nothing," said the blond-headed girl, touching up her flip in a mirror over a narrow table. "What you need to do is go to the pavilion . . ." Bailey turned away from the mirror. "The Myrtle Beach pavilion is where the real dancing is. I go up there each summer; otherwise, you never know how good you are, or what the new steps are."

"I don't think I can . . ."

"Oh," said Bailey, putting an arm around Kate and turning her so they faced the others, "but that's just where we're going. If this girl wants to learn to dance, she needs to go up to Myrtle."

"I don't know about that . . ." said Carolynn Hamby.

"Sure," said Bailey, her arm still around Kate, "there's no better place than The Attic to learn how to dance."

Ginny jumped right in. Only a month on this island and her brothers were already driving her nuts. "Yes, The Attic! You have to be a kid to get in there."

"Yes, yes," said Bailey. "Fresh meat!"

"Pardon me?" asked Carolynn. "What did you say?"

Bailey looked at Mrs. Hamby again. "I said 'it'd be real neat.'"

Steve Brown

Kate tried to put an end to this before someone let it slip that she had a date with Jeb Stuart. "I don't think my uncle would dare let me go out at night, and certainly not all the way up to Myrtle Beach."

"Oh, sure he will," said Bailey, in a sugary tone, "as long as you have three chaperones who know their way around."

Turned out Uncle Johnny thought Kate going dancing was a dandy idea, because Johnny Youngblood, like Ginny Belle, had had enough of babysitting and wanted to go out and kick up *his* heels.

But later, when Mrs. Gillespie was peeling off her girdle, she said to Bailey, "I spoke with Melanie's mother and we're not sure about you four girls going up to Myrtle."

Her daughter sat on a stool in front of a vanity dresser and brushed her blond hair its nightly one hundred strokes, though she didn't know why. Who cared what happened this summer?

"What's the problem? We've done it before, even last year when we were only sixteen."

"Yes, yes, I know, but this summer's different." Irene finally got the girdle off and let out a sigh of relief. Over her panties relaxed a roll of fat. "I'm worried about you, Bailey."

"And I'm worried about you, Mother, but I don't poke my nose into your business."

"Bailey," said her mother, reaching over her daughter's shoulder and picking up her cigarettes, "I'm your mother, and it's my job to 'poke my nose into your business,' as you say."

Bailey put down the brush and whirled around on the stool. "And what do you accomplish with all that worry? I've put Daddy in the past. That's where he's chosen to be, not a part of my future."

Her mother shook out a cigarette and tossed the pack on the dresser. Prying open a matchbook she took out a match and struck it. Talking around the cigarette in her mouth, she said, "I just don't want you to make the same mistakes I made."

"Don't worry. I intend to make my own mistakes."

Her mother lit up and let out a smoke-filled breath as she shook out the match and placed it in an overflowing ashtray on the dresser. "The pavilion and the skating rink have always been good enough for you girls in the past."

Bailey was on her feet now, hands on hips. "Contrary to what you think, Mother, I'm no hellion."

To this Irene Gillespie had to agree. Her daughter was strong-willed and determined but certainly couldn't be considered wild. Even before that bastard of a husband had made up his mind about running for governor, Bailey had marched into the study one afternoon and announced that if her father would not run for governor, she would. Bailey had been all of six years old.

"Very well," said her mother, turning away and slipping out of her brassiere, "but you must agree to my conditions."

Bailey's hands came off her hips. "That depends on your conditions." After several months of benign neglect, Bailey was resentful of any intrusion into her life.

While slipping into a robe, Irene wondered just what

she did want from her daughter, especially this summer. It took another drag off her cigarette before she could finally say, "You can go into Myrtle if you're home before midnight."

"Easily done."

"Don't jump just yet. Myrtle Beach is up that terrible two-lane seventeen, and you're going to have to take it slow. Plan your night accordingly and leave early. I have a meeting of the Pawleys Island Civic Association, and there's a big fight brewing about that developer who wants to fill in the marsh. I have no idea what time it'll break up. Alice Frey will wait up for you."

"I don't think she has anything to worry about."

"Bailey, I'm not finished."

"I'm not surprised."

"Bailey, don't be smart!"

"What else? What else?"

"Someone else drives, and you don't drink or smoke or leave the presence of the others. When one girl goes to the restroom, the whole group goes."

"Mother, that's just plain silly. Not everyone needs to go to the restroom at the same time."

"Well," said Mrs. Gillespie, "you'd better hope they do or you've broken our agreement."

WHERE THE BOYS ARE

Kate didn't think much of Myrtle Beach, but at the moment they were at the southern end of the Strand with its beach houses and smaller motels, and very few cars on either side of the road. The girls were headed for the strip, that part of Ocean Drive where the action was: the rides, the food, and the boys, and they were tooling along in Adelaide Belle's Buick convertible with the top down. The top had been up until the traffic began to back up; then the girls' scarves had come off and the top had come down. And if people were surprised that Adelaide Belle owned a convertible, it was easily explained by residents of Pawleys Island. The convertible had been purchased after the first annual Pawleys Island Fourth of July parade. Addy Belle was not going to let Queen "B" show her up!

Bailey rode in front with Ginny, who was driving; Melanie sat behind Bailey and beside Kate in the backseat, and when the cars began to slow down and the boys began to holler from cars, from the sidewalks, even from motel windows, patios, and porches, Kate realized she'd entered another world.

Cars, pickups, and hotrods jammed the street in both directions. Teenagers crowded in seats, or sat on top of them in convertibles, or rode on the tops of sedans, feinting surfing stances or lying across hoods. On both the left and right appeared a line of motels with porches, piazzas, and swimming pools, finally giving way to the beach on the right, and from the beach came the sound of fireworks. When the ocean breeze caught one of the rockets, it flew straight up, exploding over the strip into a shower of colors.

Teenagers jaywalked or clogged the wide sidewalks. The Buick was forced to slow down; traffic backed up, and then began to inch along. Clusters of balloons floated by on strings, and huge stuffed animals overwhelmed smaller children. Young men drinking beer or Cokes stepped into the street and walked beside the convertible, trying to make time with the girls.

At the heart of the strip was a massive tan building overlooking the beach, and across the street were the swing, the merry-go-round, and Ferris wheel; behind them, the ultimate thrill ride, the roller coaster. Adults attempting to instruct their children found it impossible to keep their kids' attention over the rumble of rides and the screams from riders. All the radios played the same station, so the corridor between the pavilion and the rides became a concert of AM radios, filling the street with "Hello Stranger" sung by Barbara Lewis.

Kate could only stare, bug-eyed. The closest she'd ever come to anything like this was cruising Main Street on Saturday night, where there wasn't this much noise, and certainly no boys trying to climb into your car or screaming that you were the answer to their dreams.

Bailey turned around and smiled from the front seat. "Pretty cool, huh?"

Once again she wore her hair flipped up, and when they'd left Pawleys, Bailey had slipped out of her pedal pushers, revealing a pair of short-shorts that matched her sleeveless blouse. The cardigan sweater draped over her shoulders was worn at the insistence of Alice Frey who thought Bailey might become chilled. Bailey thought the old black woman had lost her mind. It wasn't how you felt, but how you looked.

Kate scooted closer to Melanie. At any moment one of these boys was going to snatch her up and carry her off. And how did she know that? It had happened in the car ahead of them, the girl squealing and laughing and making little protest as she was dragged over the side of the convertible and into the street.

In the adjoining lane someone made smacking noises, and when Kate looked she saw a driver puckering up. Another boy in the same car offered Kate a beer through the back window, and a third sat on the windowsill on the far side, head and shoulders out the window. In his hand was a half-eaten corn-on-a-stick. He offered Kate a bite, extending his arm across the top of the sedan. Kate shook her head. She also shook her head at those asking her to climb out, or go dancing, or share their lives, or the remainder of the night, whichever came first.

From behind the wheel, Ginny said, "Don't let them get to you, Kate. They're harmless, just bold as hell."

Tonight Ginny wore her black hair in a French twist, a pair of walking shorts, and a long-sleeved blouse. Suddenly she stomped on the brakes when a young man leaped on their hood, slid across the surface, and fell to the street in front of them.

The girls shrieked, and then, just as quickly, the boy was back on his feet, making a "ta-da" sound and holding his arms out like any showman. They laughed, Ginny tooted the horn, and the boy threw them kisses as the convertible continued down the street to the sound of "Shoop Shoop (It's in His Kiss)" on all those car radios.

From a Ford Galaxy 500, one of those with a retractable roof that fit into the trunk, the showman was suddenly showered with beer. The showman waved off the foamy shower and then raced down the centerline in pursuit of the Ford.

"Just go with the flow," said Bailey. "You can always pray for forgiveness Sunday morning."

"Bailey, watch your tongue."

"Hell, no, I'm not going to church Sunday."

A young man passed by and commented that the blonde in the Buick looked like a real chippie. Bailey shot him the bird.

"Yes," said Ginny, glancing at her friend in the front seat, "but we know who really needs to go most of all."

"I brought this dress for church," said Kate. She patted down the fabric, pale in color but with plenty of frills. She'd gotten all fancied up to come to town and her curly red hair seemed to reflect the flashing lights, headlights, and the fireworks from the beach. Every once in a while an errant curl fluttering in the breeze had to be forced back into place.

The next time the car slowed to a stop, Ginny turned around and examined Kate's dress. When they'd picked her up, Ginny had wisely kept her counsel, and why not? On the way over Bailey had said plenty of nasty things about picking up someone who lived in a trailer park, calling Kate a foot-washing Baptist. Well, at least Kate had the good sense to wear her circle pin.

"Yes," said Ginny, "we're going to have to do something about your clothes."

"Or we'll be laughed off the Grand Strand," said Bailey with a laugh of her own. "Just tell them you're a Holy Roller and they'll cut you some slack tonight."

"Don't be mean," said Melanie from the backseat. In sympathy with Kate, Melanie wore a shirtwaist dress, and her long brown hair had been plaited down her back, Kate's handiwork.

"Hey, I'm not the one who wanted to bring chickypoo along."

"Yes, you are," said Melanie. "You said she should come up to Myrtle and learn how to shag."

Bailey ignored the comment, slid up on her seat, and held out her arms as the convertible crawled toward the pavilion. "Line up, boys! The dancing queen is on the scene!"

A water balloon flung from an approaching hotrod flew past Bailey and landed in the backseat between the other two girls. Kate and Melanie screamed, and Ginny turned around and told them to clean it up super quick, that she had to return her grandmother's car in tiptop shape or she'd be grounded for the rest of the summer.

Bailey stuck her tongue out at those in the hotrod, which brought another water balloon flying their way. It, too, sailed past Bailey and landed at the feet of the crowd waiting to cross Ocean Boulevard.

"That your best shot?" she hollered.

Ginny tugged on her arm. "Sit down and show a little class."

Wiping off the backseat, Melanie leaned into Kate and whispered, "She used to be the hula-hoop queen before she became the dancing queen."

Kate laughed.

Above them the blond girl stretched out her arms again as they passed Ninth North and Ocean Boulevard, the epicenter of action along the Grand Strand. Again Bailey sang out, "I'm young and free and only seventeen. I'm the dancing—"

The next balloon caught Bailey square across the back and she shrieked and slid down in her seat. Behind her Melanie and Kate squealed as the water splattered them. The Buick stopped and very quickly a line formed behind them, horns honking and people hollering for them to move along. From the boys in the hotrod came more than one catcall as their car continued down the boulevard in the opposite direction.

Bailey was bent over in her seat. "They got me wet! Those bastards got me wet!" Sitting up, she reached behind her. "My hair! How's my hair?"

Ignoring the cars behind her, Ginny kept a foot on the brake, reached over, and brushed water off with her free hand. "Melanie, Kate, can you help us here?"

But Melanie was brushing water off her own dress, and Kate was watching the hotrod disappear, its occupants convulsed with laughter. In the Buick, Bailey continued to have a fit, screaming that there was no way she could go dancing, not looking like this.

That caused Kate to turn around, but when she reached forward, Bailey leaned away. "Get away from me, you redneck!"

"Stay still!" ordered Kate, sliding forward.

"No, you stay away from me!"

Kate looked to Ginny as the congestion drew the attention of a policeman. Oblivious to the traffic, the patrolman crossed Ocean Boulevard in their direction. People on all four corners of the intersection rushed across the street, weaving through the cars.

"Pull off her sweater," said Kate. "That's all that's wet."

Keeping her foot firmly on the brake, Ginny unwrapped the cardigan from around Bailey's shoulders as she leaned forward. Behind them, the horns became louder and several guys stepped off the curb to chat with the girls. Melanie scrunched down and away from everyone. On the radio Chuck Jackson sang "Any Day Now."

"Hello, baby," said a young man with a deep voice on Bailey's side of the car, "this is the Big Bopper here."

Ginny handed the cardigan to Kate, who hung it over the side and shook it out, then laid it on the seat. In the front Bailey scooted forward to get away from the water pooling in her seat. The young man who called himself the Big Bopper took that to mean Bailey would like to climb out of the car, so he took her arm. Bailey shrieked and drew back from him.

"I don't think she wants to go with you, fella."

The cop was on the driver's side between two lanes of traffic, one inching south, the other at a standstill as cars cut through at Ninth North and headed up Ocean Boulevard. The young man released Bailey's arm, stepped up on the curb, and disappeared into the crowd.

"You okay, girls?" asked the policeman.

Ginny did a fast check. "We're fine. Some jerks hit us with a water balloon, that's all."

The cop glanced at the blonde in the front seat. "That's what happens when you give them a target."

"You ought to arrest them," muttered Bailey, who was checking the condition of her hair in the side mirror.

"Sorry," said the policeman, looking down the street, "but I'd have to catch them first."

"I got their tag number," said Kate, rolling up the two used balloons that had landed in the car.

"You did, did you?" The policeman stepped to the rear of the car. "Well then, smart girl like you, if you got the plate, you'd know the make of the car, right?"

"Yes, sir." And Kate gave him the number, which he dutifully wrote down. Kate also told him it was a tan '53 Chevrolet sedan that had been turned into a hotrod with an exposed engine. "My uncle repair cars," she offered in explanation.

"I'll keep an eye out." The cop smiled at her. It was always nice to meet a girl who knew her automobiles. He glanced down the boulevard. "They're bound to come back this way, and I'll give them a hard time when they do." He stepped away from the car and gestured for Ginny to move along.

With both hands on the wheel Ginny accelerated.

"Are we still going dancing?" asked Kate, leaning forward as they followed a car that had cut through from Ninth North and headed up Ocean Boulevard.

Bailey turned on her. "How can you suggest such a thing?" She faced the dashboard again. "You're such a clod."

"Hey," said Kate, sitting back in her seat, "you're the dancing queen, not me."

Ginny's eyebrows shot up and she turned and looked at Melanie. When their eyes met, the two girls burst into laughter.

"Yes," said Ginny, grinning, "we are definitely going dancing."

"Well, I'm not," said Bailey, hunching down in her seat as the car passed Peaches.

Melanie reached over and touched her shoulder. "Yes, you are. Your hair looks just fine."

"Does not," said Bailey, scooting forward again so her friend couldn't reach her.

"Hey, Bailey," said a young man standing on Peaches'

corner. It was Preston Winthrop, and tonight he wore a pullover that matched only one color of his Madras shorts. His blond hair had grown out, and he wore it down over his forehead and touching his collar. On his feet was a pair of Weejuns with no socks.

"Hey, yourself," said Bailey, perking up, "where've you been, Preston? I've been looking all over for you."

"Well, then," said the young man, opening the door of the convertible, "come dancing."

Ginny slowed to a stop, Bailey stepped out on the street, and Preston closed the door behind her.

"See you later, alligators."

"What about us?" demanded Ginny.

But Bailey had locked her arms straight down beside her body and was shifting her shoulders up and down to the heavy beat of the "Duke of Earl" on the radio.

"Doctor's orders. I'm going dancing."

And she left them, walking arm in arm with Preston in the general direction of The Attic.

The second summer

Scholarship Material

Bailey Gillespie rushed up the steps of the Durant beach house, crossed the screened-in porch, and knocked on the front door. When someone hollered for her to come in, the blond girl opened the door and stepped inside. Bailey was so anxious to see Melanie that it would be a moment before the cool air registered with her, and since Bailey had servants, she paid no attention to the puzzled look given her by the maid closing the door behind her.

"Melanie!"

"In here," said her friend from the living room.

Bailey rushed into the room, and as she did, failed to notice the smile on her friend's face. Or perhaps she thought that smile was meant for her since they'd not seen each other since last summer. Behind her, the maid strolled down the hall, but not too quickly, as there might be some gossip everybody should know. Up and down Pawleys Island, in whatever house had servants, cooks, or creekmen, the Negro grapevine missed nothing.

Her friend lay on the sofa reading *Silent Spring* by Rachel Carson. Melanie Durant was a tobacco heiress from Durham; Bailey, the product of one of the most powerful families in South Carolina. The Baileys and the Gillespies had a good deal to say about who was and who wasn't someone when it came to politics in South Carolina, though at the moment the politicos thought Senator Gillespie's chances could be compared to a sandcastle built on Pawleys Island. Only a few months ago Walter Gillespie had married for a second time, to a woman thirty years his junior, after divorcing Bailey's mom. No one from the Gillespie side of the family attended the wedding, which had been held in Washington to avoid further alarming the voting populace, many of whom were Baptists and considered divorce a sin.

"Have you heard the news?" asked Bailey.

"The Marines have landed in South Vietnam?"

Melanie closed her book and sat up. On the phonograph *Meet the Beatles* played for the umpteenth time, this, according to Melanie's mother, who had closeted herself in an upstairs bedroom and turned the window unit on high.

"Marines?" asked Bailey, stopping at the coffee table. "What are you talking about?"

"Nothing. What's *your* news? And good to see you again."

"Gopher's been accepted to USC."

"Yes?"

"Don't you see, she conned someone into a scholarship, and now that linthead will be in my graduating class, if she graduates."

"Oh, I'm sure Kate can handle the curriculum."

"Oh, sure," said Bailey, taking a seat on the sofa and propping her feet up on the coffee table, "this doesn't bother you, the lowering of standards at Carolina."

"Goodness gracious," said Melanie, placing her book on the coffee table. "Carolina's known as a party school. How much lower can you go?"

"Yes, but—"

"Are you worried Kate will pledge A D Pi. You're a legacy, aren't you? Everyone in your family's A D Pi, aren't they?"

"Kate's not going to pledge. What sorority would have her? A linthead from some mill village?"

"Maybe a sorority looking for new blood?"

"That'll be the day."

Bailey fell back into the sofa and stared at her feet on the coffee table. "I guess it really doesn't matter. Gopher and I don't move in the same circles."

"I'm sure that's a load off your mind."

Bailey rolled her head and looked at her friend. "Is something wrong?" On the turntable the Beatles sang "I Saw Her Standing There."

"Nothing more than Jeb Stuart may be shipped overseas."

"I hadn't heard."

"You didn't see him on the cover of *Life?* Of course not. Everything you learn is by doing, isn't it? But I am curious how you knew Kate had been accepted by Carolina. And how you knew she'd earned a scholarship."

"Oh," said Bailey, sitting up and pulling her feet off the table. "I just heard."

"Bailey, why do you begrudge Kate a scholarship?

That's what they're for, isn't it? Deserving people who can't afford to attend college."

"There's more to college than room and board."

"I was under the impression she had received a full scholarship: room, food, books, tuition, the whole deal."

"Carolina's paying for everything?"

Melanie drew up her feet and wrapped her arms around her legs. "You had someone from your father's office find out who beat you out of that scholarship, didn't you?"

"My father taught me to take advantage of each and every opportunity."

"Last year you hated him."

"I still do, but sometimes I find him useful."

"Good God, but that's harsh."

"Oh, don't give me that. You wish you had a father. I heard you cry yourself to sleep when you didn't have one."

"After my father died, you did." Melanie's arms came from around her knees. "But I got over it. Girls don't always have to have a father. Look at Kate." And Melanie gestured at the hallway.

For a moment Bailey didn't understand, and then she saw Kate Youngblood standing in the hallway door. The redhead was as attractive as Bailey, but without the money, status, or savoir faire, and as she had the previous summer, Kate wore a man's business shirt tied off at the waist, dungarees, and a pair of soiled Keds.

Bailey looked from Kate to Melanie. "What's this?"

"Kate's uncle is remodeling our kitchen."

Oh, my Lord, thought Bailey, I've really stepped in

it. To the redhead, she said, "I'm sorry, Kate."

"You already know?" She walked into the living room.

"Know? Know what?" Bailey looked at Melanie. When Melanie raised her eyebrows and canted her head in the direction of the coffee table where several magazines lay, Bailey quickly added, "Oh, yes. I heard . . . I saw Jeb on the cover of *Life.*" Then something clicked, and Bailey looked at this girl in quite a different way. "You and Jeb . . . ?" She glanced at Melanie, who only smiled.

Kate took a seat on the edge of the coffee table. "I told him I'd write every day. I guess you could say he's my Marine."

"Your Marine?"

"He gave me his ring." She pulled a chain from under her shirt. On it hung a Citadel class ring.

"I—I had no idea you two were serious."

"Yep," said Melanie from her end of the sofa. "He's even been to Greenville and met Kate's family. Unlike some people, Jeb doesn't hold it against Kate that her family lives in a mill village."

"But, Kate, you're only, what? Eighteen?"

"Same as us, and headed to Carolina. I'll be there, too."

"What?" Bailey looked from one girl to the other. Things were moving much too fast, and Bailey was known as a quick study. "I thought you were going to Duke."

"Kate's been to my house, too."

"Been to your house? When?"

"And we had a grand old time."

"Thanksgiving," explained Kate, dropping the ring back inside her shirt and sitting up. "First time I'd been away from home at the holidays."

Bailey couldn't believe what she was hearing, and this redneck was sitting on the Durants' coffee table. It was as if Kate Youngblood had made herself at home. For the first time Bailey noticed the sound of hammering coming from the rear of the house.

What was going on? She'd never been invited to Melanie's place, an estate the size of a small country, but this damned hillbilly had. And she was pledged to a Citadel graduate? Bailey's head spun. Had the whole world turned upside down?

"And what a house it is," said Kate, glowing. "It's got tennis courts, a swimming pool, even a bowling alley."

"Tobacco money," said Melanie, smirking. "It can buy just about anything."

"And your choice of friends, it would appear." Bailey scrambled to her feet and rushed out of the house.

At the Belle beach house Ginny's grandmother snored away in a hammock, a long, low roof sheltering her from the midday sun. Noticing the sleeping woman in her rush up the front steps, Bailey stopped halfway up and her hands went out to balance herself. Keeping an eye on Adelaide Belle, she retraced her steps down the stairs and snuck around the side of the house, the side sheltered by an old oak tree.

The house, really several large rooms, stood on brick stilts. The gaps between the aging floorboards caused Adelaide Belle to insist this was why her house still stood when so many other houses built "tighter than Dick's headband" had been washed out to sea. There were porches at both front and rear, even one on the east side where the family took their meals. An iron triangle was rung to signal the next meal; no bathing suits were allowed at the table, and the last one seated had to say grace.

Electricity had recently been installed, allowing the house to finally have a refrigerator instead of an icebox; still, much of the food came from the creek where Augustus, the house's creekman, caught oysters, clams, and shrimp, and gigged for flounder. Other necessities, such as vegetables, came from the locals, and if you wanted grits, cornbread, or bread, Marlowe's Store would be the place to purchase such ingredients. It was also where Frank Marlowe always kept an extra bottle of sherry on hand for Mrs. Belle. Yet there was no phone in the house, the furniture was discarded mahogany pieces and metal beds with hand-sewn bedcovers, and the building reeked of kerosene whenever someone forgot to open enough windows.

During the summer, the cook came in early and prepared an enormous breakfast, then remained to fix lunch; the family was on its own for dinner. Now the cook opened the screened door at the rear of the house and smiled at the blond girl rushing up the stairs.

"And what can we do for you, young lady?"

"Dropped by to see Ginny."

"Miss Ginny, Miss Bailey's here."

Ginny came down the hall, her twin brothers racing ahead of her. "Oh, hey, Bailey," she said cheerily. "Here we go again. Another summer on Pawleys, and if you're looking for a way to torture yourself, I have a couple of good ideas."

The twins threw their arms around the blond girl's legs. "Ginny's going to drown us! Save us, Bailey!"

"Please, Bailey," pleaded the other twin. "She said she'd drown me first."

"Will not," said the other twin from across Bailey's backside. "She said she'll drown *me* first."

"Will not! Will not!"

And the second twin let go of Bailey and went for his brother. The other twin screamed bloody murder and raced around Bailey, pulling her with him. It took only a few turns before Bailey was dizzy.

Oh, please, why is all this happening to me?

Ginny snatched one boy and the cook grabbed the other, and between the two of them, pulled the two boys off.

"Enough," said Ginny. "Sorry, Bailey, this is no way to start the summer."

Hand on the wall and head down, Bailey was finally able to get out, "If . . . if this isn't a good time . . ." When Bailey no longer thought she might cry, she looked up.

Ginny noticed Bailey's distress and turned her twin over to the cook. "Why don't we walk on the beach?" To the boys, she said, "And if these rugrats follow us, I'll drown them."

The twins squealed with excitement as the cook pulled them into the kitchen.

When Ginny turned to go out the front door, Bailey said, "Your grandmother's asleep out there."

"Well," said Ginny, doing a quick about-face, "we don't want to disturb her, do we?"

"No, we do not," said the cook.

And she forced the twins onto separate barstools. The Belle kitchen was unlike the Durants' and the Gillespies'. It had few amenities, and all the cooking was done on a gas stove fed from a tank on the back porch. None of the cabinet doors closed completely, the floor was stained where the icebox had once stood, and there were no small appliances cluttering the dilapidated counters.

The two teenagers hurried out the door and down the stairs, and by the time they'd crossed the parking lot, the cook had the twins busy with crayons and coloring books featuring Woody Woodpecker, Buzz Buzzard, and Wally Walrus.

As they started down Myrtle Avenue, Bailey couldn't wait to ask Ginny, "Did you know Gopher's going to Carolina? On scholarship?"

"Well, good for her," said Ginny, kicking a rock off the sandy road.

"Good for her! What do you mean 'good for her'?"

Ginny stopped. "Just what I said, good for her."

"Are you taking Gopher's side?"

"Side? What side?"

"Gopher's or mine."

"I didn't know there were sides."

"And you're taking Gopher's."

"And what right do you have to tell Kate Youngblood what to do with her life?"

"Then you're okay with her attending Carolina? Why's that, because you're going to the College of Charleston?"

Ginny stuck her hands in the pockets of her walking

shorts and continued down the road. As she did, the sun burned into the back of her neck. "I really haven't made up my mind."

Bailey caught up with her. "Where else would you go? You're not thinking of going north, are you, not after what happened to your cousin?"

Ginny shook her head. "I don't want anything to do with those people. They made fun of Sissy the whole time she was there. Sissy said she received a marvelous education, but the teasing never let up, just like you're doing with Kate. Why don't you leave her alone?"

A Rambler Ambassador with quad headlights, a toothy chrome grille, and tailfins passed them by. Several boys leaned out and shouted, welcoming the girls to the beach for another summer, but the Rambler didn't stop. Those boys had girls with them.

Ginny squinted and waved, realizing she hadn't brought her sunglasses along.

"Where were you thinking of going?" asked Bailey.

"I'd considered Carolina, but I don't want to be there if you and Melanie are going to fight all the time."

"Carolina! Except for Sissy, everyone in your family has gone to the College of Charleston."

Ginny stuck her hands in the pockets of her walking shorts again, looked down, and swung a foot around, leveling a mound of sand beside the road. "I've been accepted both places, but before I agree to go to Carolina, you're going to have to straighten out your relationship with Mel."

"Me? I haven't done anything. It's all Melanie—"

"And Gopher. What an absolutely horrible nickname for a girl. There's nothing wrong with her teeth, which is sure to be what everyone will fixate on if you keep on calling her that. Just like you believe everyone's fixated on your father's new wife."

"Ginny, how dare you?"

"How dare me? How dare *you?* Last year Kate and several other kids proved there were plenty of people who didn't know about your father and his new wife."

"I don't want to talk about this."

"Well, you're going to have to."

"Why? Because you and Melanie have found someone to fix up? That's your only interest in Kate Youngblood, fixing her up."

"And I thank you for not calling her 'Gopher.'"

Bailey stared at her friend. "You two are ganging up on me."

"We're doing no such thing, and as far as I'm concerned, I'm attending the College of Charleston. It's you that'll have to find another roommate."

"I was always going to have to find a roommate . . ."

"What about Mel?" asked Ginny.

"Mel is serious about attending Carolina?"

"Yes, she is."

"You've been talking behind my back."

"And probably for your own good."

"My own good? What's wrong with me?"

Ginny didn't know how to respond. When there'd been the three of them, she'd always been the peacemaker, but now she was at a loss to understand why Kate Youngblood couldn't be a part of their group. Sure, they'd been snobs before, but they were older, and Ginny had just returned from California, where she'd been the outsider and hadn't liked it one little bit.

"Look," said Ginny, "I didn't want to say anything, but—"

"You were leaving that to Mel?"

"Well, it's good to see her coming out of her shell."

"At the expense of having to suffer Kate Youngblood another summer. She's the one messing this up."

"Messing up what? I'm going to the College of Charleston."

"But you'd attend Carolina . . ."

"If you and Mel would bury the hatchet."

"That's up to Melanie. I didn't take up with some redneck."

"No, you sulked around all last summer and made it uncomfortable for everyone. Remember, I was the one stuck with you, and this year I'm not going to be miserable."

Ginny squinted as she looked over the creek. At the end of a dock a father was teaching his children how to crab, a boat flew by towing more than one skier, and farther down Myrtle Avenue children sold shells from a roadside stand—all scenes that had previously made her feel so welcomed at Pawleys, no matter how much she complained about babysitting.

"California's looking better and better, and don't think I didn't consider staying out there." Ginny always flew out to be with her mother for Memorial Day.

Bailey couldn't believe she might not have had a confidante at the beach this summer, and Ginny was saying *she* was the problem. She wasn't the problem. It was Kate Youngblood. Or her own damn father. Why would anyone in their right mind want to spend the summer in Washington?

"Oh, I hate this!" said Ginny, balling her hands into fists. "We had such a good thing going when it was only the three musketeers."

"Don't blame me. It's Kate Youngblood."

"Oh, right. It's not like the musketeers didn't finally allow D'Artagnan to join their group." Ginny started down the road again. "That's why I didn't want to come to Pawleys. All this whining: you, the twins." And the heat. Such a difference from summer in San Francisco.

Following her friend, Bailey asked, "Ginny, is this something your mother put in your head?"

Her friend turned on her. "My mother has nothing to do with this!" Ginny took a breath and let it out. "Besides, don't you think we're a little too old to be meeting at the beach every summer?"

Another car tooted, and the girls stepped out of the road, waved, and smiled as a former lieutenant governor and his wife drove by; a couple famous for their tans arriving for another summer on Pawleys. Still, little hung on the cord across the backseat, and the rear window of the Fleetwood held few shoeboxes. The two girls watched as the Cadillac trundled down the road. As they did, it occurred to Ginny that only in Haight-Ashbury and on Pawleys Island did you worry so little about clothing.

"Ginny, if you weren't here, I don't think I could bear it."

"And if I wasn't here, maybe you'd get to know Kate better."

"That girl and I have nothing in common."

"You will if we attend Carolina."

"But don't you understand, you just have to go to Carolina. Melanie's rooming with Gopher."

"Would you please stop calling her that?" asked Ginny, glancing over Bailey's shoulder.

"You didn't answer my question."

"I didn't know there was a question in there." This time when she looked over Bailey's shoulder, she smiled. "Oh, hey, Melanie. We were just talking about all of us going to Carolina."

Bailey whirled around and saw the brown-haired girl behind her. Ginny had let Melanie slip up on her. Why was everyone ganging up on her? Again her eyes ached and she knew that tears were only moments away. She'd been crying so much lately . . . What was wrong with her? It wasn't even close to that time of month.

Her predicament wasn't made any easier when Melanie said, "Bailey, you and I need to talk."

"Well, I'm not interested in talking about your new roommate."

"Roommate? How'd you know Kate was staying with me instead of in the trailer this summer?"

"Oh, God," moaned Bailey, and she rushed down the road toward her house.

A PROPER EDUCATION

When Kate walked out on the front porch of the Durant beach house, she was surprised to find Adelaide Belle sitting in one of the wicker chairs. The chairs were large and roomy and had thick cushions, one tied across the back. A small wicker table sat between the sets of chairs, which were white with the exception of worn spots where arms and legs had rubbed the paint off. Screening surrounded the large porch.

"Come out here, girl," said Mrs. Belle. "Don't be afraid of me as are all the other children."

Kate glanced toward the interior of the house, one hand holding open the screened door, the other the door to the house. From inside came the sound of Perry Como on the phonograph, a concession to Melanie's mom.

"I should be getting back to my uncle."

"Then why are you out here? Slacking off?"

"Er—no, ma'am."

"Always move with a purpose, I say."

"Er—yes, ma'am."

"And stop stuttering."

"Er—yes, I mean, yes, ma'am."

"And close that door. You're letting the air conditioning out."

Kate closed the door and stepped onto the screened porch.

"Have a seat there." Mrs. Belle gestured with her glass at the wicker chair across from her. The glass was of simple teardrop shape, slightly shorter than a wine glass, without trim or etching. But when Kate started for the chair, Mrs. Belle said, "No, no, you love the ocean, and they certainly don't have one of those in Greenville. Sit over here next to me."

Instead, Kate took the original seat facing Mrs. Belle, putting her back to the water. "It's all very nice wherever you sit."

The old woman stared at her with those crystal clear blue eyes that the Belle family was famous for. "Don't patronize me, young lady." Today, Mrs. Belle wore a blue jumper over a white long-sleeved blouse. In one hand was the sherry glass; in the other, the cigarette holder.

Kate didn't reply.

"You don't know what the word means, do you?"

"Er—no, ma'am, I do not."

"And I told you to stop stuttering."

"Ah . . . yes, ma'am."

Adelaide thrust her glass at Kate.

Kate took the glass and said, "I'm sorry, but I don't drink."

But Mrs. Belle had disappeared inside, leaving Kate holding a nearly full glass of sherry. Kate didn't know what to do, so she sat there and stared at the amber liquid, then glanced next door at Ginny's house. What *was* Mrs. Belle doing over here?

Adelaide returned with a dictionary. "Don't know how people can stand it." She shivered, and then closed both the front door and the screened door. She thrust the dictionary at Kate and took back her glass when Kate accepted the book.

"You didn't drink any of this, did you?" asked Mrs. Belle, returning to her chair.

"No, ma'am. Like I said, I don't drink."

"Well, at least we cured you of stuttering." After sitting down and taking a sip, Adelaide used the cigarette holder to gesture at the book in Kate's lap. "You know what that's for, don't you?"

"Yes, ma'am." And Kate began to thumb through the pages until she found the word 'patronize.' Once she understood the meaning she looked up. "I won't ever do that again, Mrs. Belle."

"Very well. Now that we have that behind us, you can come over here and sit where you can see this ocean you love so much."

Kate took the chair beside Mrs. Belle. Through the screening she could see men whipping their fishing lines into the ocean, a mother running through the surf, chasing a baby who had lost its diaper, and the Belle twins pouring wet sand from buckets to form a grotesque sandcastle. Seagulls soared overhead, the occasional pelican circled and dived-bombed its prey, and the beach was cluttered with sandpipers, digging here, digging there, then scurrying away with the arrival of the next wave.

"I'm glad Uncle Johnny needed my help again this summer."

"Did he, or did you pester him into bringing you along so you could visit with my granddaughter and her friends?"

"Well, I did pester him an awful lot . . ."

"All year, I would imagine. But if you plan to socialize with my granddaughter, you'll have to do something about that accent."

Kate looked at her.

"It's not just the forming of the words, but you must learn to lower your voice and force the sound from your chest. That will remove the nasal quality. Once you've mastered that, concentrate on sharpening your words."

Kate didn't know what to say.

"I'm not trying to be disagreeable, but people will talk."

"Yes, ma'am, and would you happen to be one of the people talking?"

Adelaide opened her mouth to say something, then realized she was not on her own porch. "Just speak slowly, and force your voice down into your chest. Try 'how now, brown cow.'"

When Kate realized Mrs. Belle was serious, she repeated, "How now, brown cow." After a couple of tries, Adelaide nodded. "And remember to form your words distinctly, like Katharine Hepburn."

Kate appeared puzzled.

"She's a famous movie star. *Desk Set, The African Queen, Pat and Mike* . . . anyway, Katharine Hepburn is from New England and has a rather distinct voice."

"A Yankee?"

"Yes, dear, but not all Yankees are disagreeable. You don't know this, and neither do most young people who come to this island, but if it weren't for Yankees, this part of the county wouldn't have any hospitals, schools, or year-round employment. But to my granddaughter and her set, it's just a place to frolic in the sun. Did you know they used to produce salt on this island? Since you're a cabinetmaker, you should be interested in this."

Mrs. Belle gestured with her cigarette holder where her grandchildren were building their sandcastle. "On this very beach windmills were used to draw the water from the ocean, and then the saltwater was emptied into shallow wooden tubs about ten- or twelve-feet square, standing a yard tall. The vats had covers that could be swung over them in the event of rain, and the saltwater lay in the sun until the water evaporated. Have you heard of Francis Marion? He received a good bit of salt from Pawleys during the Revolutionary War."

"Yes, ma'am. *The Swamp Fox* was one of the first programs I ever saw in color."

"My Lord," said Mrs. Belle, sitting up and spilling sherry on her hand, "that's just what I was talking about."

"Ma'am? I thought we were talking about salt."

Mrs. Belle wiped her hand on her jumper. "No, it's the larger issue: how you children receive your education these days, and much of it comes from that idiot box. I don't think one child out of ten knows that Lafayette, the Frenchman who so ably assisted our country during the Revolution, first slipped ashore at North Island, just south of here, another of South Carolina's barrier islands."

"I don't understand."

"No, I don't imagine you would. Newton Minow said if you had to watch one of the three channels from sign on to sign off, that you'd have to agree you were observing a vast wasteland. Because of this my granddaughter knows little about Pawleys."

Kate returned to silence. Like her grandmother, Mrs. Belle rambled on and set her own agenda for any conversation.

Mrs. Belle took a drag off her cigarette and used it and its holder to gesture at the dictionary. "Always look up words you don't understand. That's the way to master them."

"Yes, ma'am. I always do."

Again those blue eyes focused on her. "Now are you patronizing me again, young lady?"

"No, ma'am. I promised I'd never do that again."

"So what would you've done to learn the meaning of the word 'patronize'? Look up the word once you had returned to Greenville?"

"No, ma'am. I'd look it up today. I carry a dictionary in my purse."

By the look on Mrs. Belle's face it was plain that she did not believe the girl. "Then go get it."

Kate closed the larger book, placed it on the wicker table, and got to her feet.

"No, no, I believe you," said Mrs. Belle, waving Kate back to her chair.

Kate returned to her seat, puzzled but smart enough to keep her mouth shut; that is, until she had something to add to the conversation. If there was one thing she'd learned about Pawleys, the people living here valued good conversation. Well, good food, too, because of all the fishing, crabbing, and gigging.

After Mrs. Belle finished her cigarette and settled back in her chair, she asked, "Well, Kate, what do you think of our little island?"

"Oh, it's very lovely, but to tell the truth, I expected the ocean to be bluer."

"You did? And just what color would you say the waters off Pawleys are, my dear?"

"No offense intended, but it looks a lot like pea soup."

Mrs. Belle laughed and took another sip of sherry. The cigarette had been snubbed out in an ashtray on the railing, one of many two-by-fours supporting the screening. Overhead a fan slowly turned.

"You're exactly right. Pawleys is one of many barrier islands along the Atlantic seaboard, and though we like to think of Pawleys as being special, its ecology has much in common with other barrier islands."

"Barrier islands?" asked Kate. "Like land standing between the ocean and the real coastline?"

"Or floating." Seeing the look on the girl's face, she quickly added, "That was a joke, my dear."

Kate smiled rather weakly. She'd been told on more than one occasion that she had little in the way of a sense of humor.

"During the summer the ocean becomes full of microscopic, one-celled plants, and their numbers increase as the water temperature rises. Their chlorophyll-rich bodies are what give the ocean its greenish tint. Decaying plants and animals from the leeside marshes contribute the brownish color. Leeside is the side protected from the wind, which would be the marsh side of Pawleys. Then, along with the green cells and the decaying plants and animals—"

"Flora and fauna," interjected Kate.

"Correct, but there are also the rivers, bringing silt from inland and dumping it into the estuaries. That's where the river meets the incoming tide. All very nutritious, for the planet, that is."

Kate looked at the beach once again. Children ran in and out of the surf, others sat in pools created by the outgoing tide, and the Belle twins seemed to be arguing over their grotesque sandcastle. Mothers lay on towels, each with one eye on their brood, and small clouds drifted by, so light and fluffy and low you felt like you could hook them and fly them like kites.

How wonderful it'd be to live here, thought Kate. That's why she *had* hassled Uncle Johnny to come to Pawleys this summer so she could have more time to spend with Melanie and to explore, not only the beach but the creek, an absolutely amazing place. She didn't need any book to tell her that.

Uncle Johnny had cut her some slack, only calling on her when he needed another pair of hands. Truth be known, she was becoming quite a fisherman and had cooked several meals her uncle really enjoyed.

"Blue, brown, or green," said Kate with another sigh, "I still think it's beautiful."

"We all do, my dear, and now all you have to do is marry a young man who can afford it."

Her comment made Kate consider her chances and they were not good. Jeb couldn't afford such a place, not on an officer's salary, and none of the Stuart family had any interest in owning property. Jeb's family was into sailing, though Kate had yet to be invited aboard one of the family's many boats.

Mrs. Belle broke into her thoughts with, "I suppose you're wondering why I'm on the Durants' porch instead of my own."

Kate looked at her but said nothing.

"Those grandchildren of mine . . ." Adelaide gestured at the twins, who were viciously stomping each other's half of the castle into the sand. "They've returned for the summer, and with a vengeance."

"They can be a handful . . ." Kate's voice trailed off as she saw Mrs. Belle give her the evil eye. "I meant to say sometimes they're so noisy a person can't think straight, and you have to get away from them."

Now the boys were throwing sand at each other. Mrs. Belle shook her head and sighed. Offshore, dolphins broke the surface, one fin after another.

"My granddaughter said you know the names of all

the flora and fauna along our beach."

"I know a few."

"Please, Kate, no false modesty." Again the gesture at the beach, this time with the sherry glass. "What about those gulls?"

Kate looked at the birds pecking where the twins had destroyed their sandcastle. "Gulls belong to the genus *Larus*, and most gulls, particularly the *Larus* species, are ground-nesting omnivores who eat live food or scavenge whatever they can find."

"'That,' my dear," said Mrs. Belle.

"Excuse me?"

"And say 'pardon' if you don't understand." Adelaide shifted around, the better to put her grandchildren out of her line of sight. "You only excuse yourself when you've made an error."

Kate sat there, processing this. "I think I've got it."

"And try not to overuse the word 'got.' Sometimes it's impossible, but in that particular case you might've substituted 'I understand.'" Mrs. Belle smiled. *"Comprendez-vous?"*

Again Kate was puzzled.

"Sorry," said Mrs. Belle, smiling, "I was pulling your leg."

"But when do I use 'that'?"

"Oh, very good. You remembered the original line of thought even when I took you around Robin Hood's barn. Do you understand what that phrase means?"

"Sort of like chasing rabbits, but with a purpose. Robin Hood's barn was Sherwood Forest, and not even the sheriff wanted to go into Sherwood Forest, so he'd go around Robin Hood's barn to avoid being ambushed."

"Very good, and to answer your question: When referring to an object, use 'that.' 'Who' applies to people, and a seagull is definitely a 'thing,' but tell me, where did you learn all this about gulls?"

"From a book I read. I didn't know if Uncle Johnny would bring me along, but I didn't think it could hurt, you know, recognizing the birds, if someone asked."

Adelaide nodded and then stared at Kate's chest. "May I ask you a personal question?"

"Of course, Mrs. Belle."

"Is that a ring on a chain under your shirt?"

"Yes, it is," said Kate, rather proudly. She hooked the chain under her finger, ran the finger under the chain, and produced the ring from inside her shirt.

"And whose ring is that, if I might be so bold as to ask?"

"Oh, Mrs. Belle," said Kate with a laugh, "are you patronizing me now? It's my boyfriend's class ring."

"Is that so?" Adelaide did not smile but continued to peer at the ring. "It appears to be from the Citadel."

"Yes, ma'am. It's Jeb's. He graduated last semester."

"Jeb Stuart? One of the Stuarts of Charleston?"

"Yes, ma'am. He's being sent to South Vietnam."

"Vietnam? Oh, yes, Indochina."

Kate nodded and beamed. She was proud of her Marine.

Adelaide sat up and thrust the sherry glass at her again. "Have the maid refill this. I don't want to go inside. I might catch my death."

Kate took the glass, got to her feet, and went through both doors, where she met her uncle coming down the hallway.

"I'm gonna need your help hauling out the larger pieces. Got a minute?" He glanced at the empty sherry glass. "You're not drinking, are you, Kate?"

"No, sir. Mrs. Belle asked me to get . . . to have this refilled."

Her uncle glanced toward the porch. "You do want to learn how to be a carpenter, don't you? I don't want to be wasting my time if you're not interested."

"Oh, no, Uncle Johnny, I want to learn everything you can teach me."

"You'd better, or you're gonna end up in Judson Mill like everybody else in our family."

Kate grinned. "Everybody but you and Daddy."

"Kate, what's holding up that refill?" called Mrs. Belle from the front porch and through the front door Kate had failed to close.

Her uncle started for the porch. "I'll have to speak to that old biddy."

Kate grabbed his arm, stopping him and lowering her voice. "Please don't. She's teaching me stuff."

"Teaching you what?" asked her uncle. "How to hold a teacup?"

Kate let go of his arm. "She's teaching me how to use words properly."

"Words? What kind of words?"

Again Kate lowered her voice. "Like you wouldn't say 'old biddy' but just 'biddy.' 'Old biddy' would be what they call redundant."

Uncle Johnny shook his head as he headed for the kitchen. "Words ain't gonna help you make a living, Kate, but being good with your hands always will."

SHOP 'TIL YOU DROP

Georgetown was the capital of Georgetown County and the only place to shop between Myrtle Beach and Charleston, so when the girls went shopping, it was in Georgetown. Alice Frey went along, as there were bags to carry, not to mention she had a list of items Bailey's mother wanted from the A & P.

Georgetown had once been the aristocratic center of not only the South but the whole country, and had once rivaled Charleston when rice planters could compete with upcountry cotton planters. The War Between the States put an end to that when a short-sighted federal government ignored the South to promote grander opportunities out West. Now the backbone of the economy was a paper mill, and children on Pawleys were sometimes heard to say "Eww, I smell Georgetown." The steel mill would not join the economic landscape until 1969.

Still, there was a bustling downtown filled with shops in buildings that would later become part of the National Register, and Front Street was where the girls strolled, flirted with the occasional boy, and window-shopped. From time to time Kate was seen to stoop down and look under buildings at the Front Street docks. As they passed Kaminski's Hardware, Alice Frey fell farther and farther behind.

At the time, the best way to induce customers to pur-chase a television was to place a set in a window, and this was where Alice Frey slowed to a stop, stared, and then shrieked and collapsed on the sidewalk, dropping her bundles. Horrified by the sound the girls stopped discussing the latest fashions and turned around to see Bailey's servant lying on the sidewalk.

Melanie, Ginny, and Kate hung back under the tower clock, but Bailey rushed to her side. "Alice Frey, what's wrong?" The woman lay on the street, face slack, eyes blank.

"Alice Frey, talk to me."

Pedestrians stopped and gawked, and as they did, the other girls wandered over, Ginny in the lead, and as usual, Melanie hanging back. A doctor was summoned, and he and his nurse appeared moments later.

"Is this woman with you?" asked the doctor, noticing the teenager holding the Negro's hand.

"Yes—yes."

"What happened?"

"I—I don't know." Bailey was close to tears.

Ginny bent down and wrapped an arm around her. To the doctor, she said, "We heard a scream and turned around and saw Alice Frey just lying here."

"The Negro screamed?" asked the doctor, kneeling beside the woman. He looked up at the growing number of faces peering at the unconscious woman. "What could've possibly frightened her?"

"I—I don't know," said Ginny, looking for her friends who had been shouldered out of the way.

"Alice Frey's been awfully worried about Wilma lately," said Bailey.

"That's her daughter," filled in Ginny.

"Worried about what?" asked the doctor.

"Wilma ran off up north."

The doctor nodded as if understanding, and did a preliminary check of Alice's limbs, her heart, her pulse, and looked into the woman's eyes. "She's catatonic. We need to get her to the hospital." He looked up at the white faces. "Give us a hand here."

Two men in seersucker suits bent down and slipped their hands under Alice Frey while the doctor held her head.

"Over here!" shouted a man who wore a pair of suspenders and had the sleeves of his business shirt rolled up. The man was opening the rear of an Oldsmobile Vista-Cruiser.

The two men, along with the doctor, carried Alice over to the station wagon, and Bailey followed them. Alice Frey was slid into the wagon, her head held by the owner who steadied it until the doctor climbed inside.

After rolling down the window, the doctor spoke to the nurse. "Call the hospital and tell them we're bringing in someone who appears to have had some sort of seizure."

The nurse nodded and went inside Kaminski's to use their telephone.

Bailey climbed in on the far side of the station wagon to sit beside Alice Frey. As the Oldsmobile backed out of its space, motioned into the street by a policeman, a thought struck Ginny and she ran into the street.

"Bailey, give me your keys."

The car stopped, and moments later the doctor flung the keys out the window. "Meet us at the hospital." And he gave orders for the car to move out.

Ginny tried to field the keys, but they eluded her grasp and ended up on the street. When she bent over to pick them up, the street spun around and she almost pitched forward.

One of the men wearing a seersucker suit grabbed her around the waist and held her upright. "Miss, I don't think you'd best be driving. Wait here while I bring my car around."

Ginny nodded and took a seat on the curb.

A middle-aged woman bent down to her. "Don't you worry, hon, your colored gal's going to be okay."

"She's not . . . mine. She's Bailey's."

"Well, don't you worry about a thing."

The policeman who had directed the station wagon into the street walked over. The girls had put on dresses to come to town and Ginny was brushing hers down.

"Do you need someone to take you to the hospital?" asked the policeman.

"No, no," said Ginny, turning around and looking for the other girls. When she did, the street spun again and she had to steady herself on the sidewalk. For a moment she wondered if it could be something they'd eaten. But that couldn't be. Alice Frey hadn't eaten in the same restaurant. It wasn't allowed.

"Where's Melanie?" asked Ginny, looking around.

"She went in the car with your colored gal," offered the middle-aged woman.

No, no, that couldn't be right. So Ginny held onto the curb and looked around until she saw her other two friends standing in front of the hardware store. Behind them, in the window, a screen was filled with a jumble of black-and-white images.

"Kate . . ." called out Ginny.

Kate nodded, took Melanie by both arms, and stood in front of her. "Mel, are you going to be all right?"

Melanie nodded. In her world, any emergencies were

taken care of by the family doctor who always came out to the estate. "What happened to Alice?" she asked.

"She seemed to have some sort of seizure. Let me check on Ginny. Will you be okay?" Out of the corner of her eye, Kate saw movement on the TV. "Why don't you stay here and watch TV?"

On television Negroes assembling to march from Selma to Montgomery were being set upon by a horde of Alabama state troopers swinging billy clubs, but to Kate it was merely something to keep Melanie occupied. Kate had no idea that Wilma had joined the civil rights march instead of running off up north as everyone believed. But Alice Frey knew.

Several women drawn to the incident now made their presence felt. One of them asked, "Does your friend need to go to the hospital, too?"

"No, she just needs a distraction." And Kate knew very well the meaning of the word "distraction," as people had been saying for years that "someone needs to play with Kate" or "someone needs to distract Kate, her father's not coming again."

Leaving Melanie facing the TV, she joined Ginny at the curb as a Mercury coupe pulled up. Kate and the middle-aged woman were helping Ginny to her feet when the man in the seersucker suit got out and came around the front of his car.

"How many of your friends are going to need a ride to the hospital?"

"I'm—I'm okay. Just a little overwhelmed." In her hands Ginny gripped her purse and the key to Bailey's car.

"I would be, too," said the woman holding Ginny's

arm. "Someone in your family passes out in the middle of the street; it's enough to upset anyone."

Ginny looked around. "Where's Mel?"

Kate pointed at the store window. Neither woman with Mel was watching the screen; they were both watching what was happening on the curb. Kate and Ginny went over to the window, took Melanie's arms, and walked her over to the curb.

"I've got room for all of you," said the man with the car.

"I can drive," said Kate, taking the keys from Ginny.

And she could, too, but only once she remembered where the car was parked and brought it around to where her friends waited. The car was a straight drive, but Kate drove it effortlessly. She'd been taught how to use a stick as soon as her feet could reach the clutch. Her uncles had said, "A girl should be able to drive, especially when she starts dating."

Kate leaned out the window as her friends were helped into the backseat. "I don't know where the hospital is."

"Follow me," said the man driving the Mercury.

"I know where the hospital is," said Melanie from the backseat. "My brother had his appendix taken out there."

But the man in the Mercury wasn't taking any chances and led them over to Georgetown Memorial.

Back at the scene of Alice Frey's collapse the crowd was being dispersed by the policeman. Many of the people had gone to school with him and did not want to move along. Neither did the policeman, once he saw what was happening in Selma, via the television in the window of the hardware store. The policeman took off his hat and scratched his head. What the devil was wrong with the Negroes in Alabama?

THE SLUMBER PARTY

"Okay," said Bailey, "since you two believe we should do this thing, get a knife."

Melanie rolled off her bed and headed for the bedroom door, the same bed she and two of these girls had jumped on years earlier until being silenced by her parents.

"Just a couple more nails," said Ginny, and she put the finishing touches on her toes. For tonight's slumber party she wore baby-doll pajamas.

"I have a pocketknife," volunteered Kate, her hair up in pink rollers, still wearing her bra and a pair of blue jeans.

"You would," said Bailey, rather sourly. She wore, as usual, an old pair of her father's pajamas.

Melanie, too, had her hair in rollers, and she wore an oversized T-shirt and underwear. Hearing there was already a knife in the room, she returned to the bed. From a tan record player that could be packed and taken anywhere—anywhere there was electricity—played a stack of forty-fives, including "Blue Velvet" by Bobby Vinton; "I'm Going to Knock on Your Door," sung by a very high-pitched Eddie Hodges; "Our Day Will Come," by Ruby and the Romantics; and Bobby Vee singing "Take Good Care of My Baby." There was also the song "I Can't Stay Mad at You" by Skeeter

Davis; "It's My Party," by Lesley Gore; and one song guaranteed to draw the girls off the bed and start them to jitterbugging, "Sweet Little Sixteen," this version by Jerry Lee Lewis.

Kate rolled over on her side and fished the pocket-knife out of her jeans. As she held out the knife to the blond girl, she asked, "Is this a good idea?"

"I've been against it all week."

"I meant letting you have my knife."

"That," said Bailey, taking the knife, "remains to be seen."

"Lighten up," said Melanie, now back on the bed.

Bailey opened the pocketknife, and holding the knife with both hands, flashed a maniacal grin across the open blade. "The doctor is in." She glanced at Melanie. "That light enough for you?"

From the dresser Ginny giggled and Kate fell back on the bed in mock horror.

"You know I have a weak stomach," said Melanie.

"Yeah, I remember. You almost fainted last time."

"Probably because of the way you botched the operation, Doctor Kildare."

"Oh, Richard Chamberlain!" cooed Kate, clutching her hands in front of her. "*Sooo* cute!"

Ginny put the nail polish on Melanie's dresser. On top of the dresser lay a copy of *Sex and the Single Girl*, and this amused Ginny no end. Giving Melanie Durant a copy of *Sex and the Single Girl* was like putting a loaded pistol in her friend's hand. A starter's pistol, that is.

"This is a blood brother ceremony, not an operation," said Ginny, crawling on the bed and taking her place in the circle.

"Blood sisters," corrected Melanie.

The talk of blood was enough to stop Kate from swooning over Richard Chamberlain and she sat up, eager to play.

"Who goes first?" asked Bailey.

"Wait a minute." And Melanie was off the bed again and out the door and down the hall.

"Where you going?"

"I need a drink before we do this."

"You didn't drink last time," called out Ginny.

"Yes," came the voice from down the hall, "and last time I almost fainted."

The other girls laughed and looked at each other, nervously.

Ginny patted Kate's knee. "Everything's going to be okay."

"Oh," said Kate, returning her smile, "I'm not worried. I've hit my thumb with a hammer before."

"Ouch," said Ginny, grimacing.

"Boy, but that has to be tough on a girl's nails."

"Well, it sure made me a lot more cautious."

The other two girls rocked back in laughter. Moments later, Melanie appeared at the bedroom door with a bottle of wine. She put the bottle to her lips and gulped down a long swallow. Drops of wine spilled on her T-shirt, but she ignored them and joined the others on the bed. The bottle was quickly passed around, with Kate being the only one who made a face after swallowing.

"Think the knife should be sterilized?" asked Melanie.

"Yeah," said Ginny, "that's what we did last time."

"I'll take care of that." Bailey hopped off the bed, and

taking the knife and the wine with her, she went over to the hamper in Melanie's walk-in closet and stuck the knife down in the bottle, all the time holding it over the hamper.

Finished, she returned to the bed. "That's in case I spilled any, the maid will just think it's that time of month."

"Kate, the way this works," said Ginny, "is that you have to share a deep, dark secret with the group."

"Yeah," said Bailey, "something from your past nobody else knows about."

"Well," said Melanie, clarifying their points, "others might know, but not many."

"I don't think we want to rehash the same old stuff," said Ginny.

"It's been a while," said Melanie, smiling. "I'm sure we all have new secrets; otherwise, what kind of teenagers would we be?"

"Oh, good," said Ginny, rubbing her hands and smiling lasciviously, "we're finally old enough to deal with sex."

"That's not what I meant," said Melanie, flushing. The girls weren't supposed to even think about sex, but sometimes that's all they talked about.

"Hey, you two," said Bailey, "I'm trying to explain the ritual to the new girl. Anyway, if you lie to us, Kate, we kick you out of the club."

"Does this club have a name?" asked the redhead.

The other girls looked at each other. They had never gotten around to naming their club, never even thought about it.

"You have to have a name. I'm not joining just any old club."

"The Three Musketeers," said Melanie.

"So," said Kate, looking around the circle, "we're now the Four Musketeers."

"Well," said Ginny, with a sigh, "might as well be."

"Yeah," cut in Bailey, "otherwise I'll never hear any decent gossip."

Ginny took the bottle from Melanie and held it out. "Then on with the show!"

"You know," said Melanie, "it bothers me that we never named the club."

Bailey rolled her eyes.

"Oh, yeah," said Ginny, downing the last of the chardonnay, "like this is such an exclusive group."

"Hey," said Bailey, sitting up, "this is supposed to be a special group. We're blood brothers."

"Blood sisters," corrected Melanie again.

"Yes, yes." Ginny smiled as the wine went down. Like her mother said, wine was cool. Only seriously screwed-up people drank the hard stuff.

Melanie slid off the bed, went to the door, and closed it.

"You're stalling," said Bailey.

"I'm closing this door."

Actually, Melanie *was* stalling, as the girls were the only ones in the house, the servants having been given the night off and Melanie's mom playing bridge next door at the Gillespies'.

It was to be a night of bloodletting. They would notch each other's fingers, place them together, and become blood sisters. Three years ago Melanie, Ginny, and Bailey had performed this same ceremony and pledged their everlasting loyalty to each other. Nothing would ever come between them. Now the new girl would join the group, much to the annoyance of Bailey. They would bleed once again.

"So what do you have to confess, Kate?" asked Bailey, locking her arms around her knees and rocking back and forth.

"No," said Melanie, rejoining them on the bed, "that's not how we did this last time."

"She's right," said Ginny. "You make this sound like some kind of gossip club."

"I don't mind," said Kate, smiling all around. "And I do have a secret nobody knows."

"Oh, goody." Bailey stopped rocking. "Tell all!"

"Oh, shut up and stop acting like a fool." Ginny slid off the bed and walked over to the dresser and dug through her friend's plastic coin purse until she came up with some quarters. "Only three. Jeez, Melanie, I thought your family had money."

This was a common complaint. Whenever the girls were out on the town, Melanie never seemed to have any money. Affliction of the rich, Ginny usually said, and Bailey would add, "Tax the rich, I say."

"Does anyone else have any quarters?" asked Ginny.

"You don't need another quarter, not if I'm not going last."

The other three girls looked at Kate. Once again, the new girl made perfectly good sense.

"She's right." Melanie extended a hand. "Give me one of those."

Ginny did, and while she was passing a quarter to Bailey, Melanie flipped hers and slapped it on top of her wrist. The other two stared at her.

"What?" asked Melanie, looking at them.

"I thought we were doing this together."

"Okay," said Melanie, taking the quarter off the back of her hand.

They did it again. Melanie and Ginny came up heads; Bailey had tails.

"Oh, damn," muttered the blonde.

"Sore loser," said Melanie. "Flip, Ginny. I'll call it."

"Now?"

"Sure. We're just establishing the order." Melanie inclined her head at Kate. "Kate goes last so she can see how serious we are about our confessions."

"Oh, boy," said Kate, "true confessions!"

"Makes sense to me." Ginny flipped the coin and Melanie called "tails."

It was tails.

"I'm third." Melanie turned to the blond girl. "Okay, Bailey, let's hear it, and we don't want any of that jazz about stealing from your father's wallet."

"That's right," said Ginny, laughing, "because he's not around enough for you to have done that."

"Just like Nixon said 'You won't have Dick Nixon to kick around anymore,'" said Melanie.

"Checkers speech," Ginny explained to Kate.

"Nah," said Melanie, "you've got that mixed up with Nixon's concession speech when he ran for governor of California."

Ginny shook her head. "The girl reads too many books."

"What you mean too many books? I have to know how to invest all that money I'm coming into."

"Nobody in the world could know enough about that much damn money."

"Wonder what happened to that dog?" asked Bailey.

"Now you're the one who's stalling."

"Okay, but you've got to promise you won't get mad."

"Us?" said the two friends, looking at each other.

"Your secret has something to do with us?" asked Melanie.

Bailey nodded.

"Well," said Ginny, glancing at the pocketknife lying next to her friend, "I guess so. You're the one with the knife."

"I sneak out at night."

"So do we," said Ginny, "and you're usually with us."

"And when I'm out, I steal stuff."

The other girls stopped smiling.

"What?"

"How long have you been doing this?" asked Melanie.

"What's it matter," said Ginny. She leaned forward, held out her hands, and wiggled her fingers. "Details. We want details."

"A couple of years."

"Where?"

"At the beach. I couldn't do it at home. We live out in the country. Well, we did live out in the country. I don't know where we're going to live now. Mama says the house brings back—"

"Wait a minute," asked Ginny, sitting up, "who do you steal from?"

"People's houses."

"Here at the beach?" asked Melanie.

"Jesus!" shouted Ginny, straightening up.

"Keep your voice down," said Melanie, unnecessarily, since there was no one in the house and each room had its own air conditioner. They might not even hear any boys who came around.

"I know what you took," said Ginny, nodding. "My hairbrush, the one passed down through generations of Belles."

Bailey only stared at the bed.

"I ought to smack you for that."

The blond head jerked up. "Hey, you said you weren't going to get mad."

"You're right. I did. Where is it?"

"In my closet."

"Okay, but I want it back."

"What did you take from me?" asked Melanie.

"Not you. Your mother."

Melanie considered this. "Oh, I know. Her new reading glasses. We turned the house upside down looking for them. She had to go into Georgetown for a new prescription."

Bailey stared at the bed again.

"Just our families?" asked Ginny.

"Nope." This time Bailey did not look up. "You know nobody really locks up their place on the beach."

Melanie grabbed a pillow from a stack of throw pillows and clutched it to her chest. "We weren't at home when you did this?"

Bailey looked up and smiled. "Now that wouldn't be much fun, would it?"

"My God," said Kate, her hand rising to her mouth.

"You slipped inside their houses while they were asleep?"

Bailey nodded again.

"Jiminy Cricket, that took nerve. I don't do it like that."

All three girls turned on the redhead. "What are you saying? You sneak out at night and steal stuff?"

Kate looked from Melanie to Ginny. "Okay if I cut in line?"

"Please do," said Ginny. "And I need to find a weapon to defend myself. There appears to be no honor among girlfriends."

"I'm going to tell my mom," said Melanie, laughing and holding up the pillow between them.

"No fair!" said Bailey, swatting the pillow away. It ended up at the base of Melanie's desk. Melanie Durant was the only kid at Pawleys with a desk, and sitting on it was a portable typewriter. That wasn't all. In the bathroom she had an electric toothbrush.

"You said you wouldn't tell!"

"Lighten up, girl," said Ginny.

"Yeah," said Melanie, "we were just kidding."

Another thought crossed Ginny's mind. "Just our houses?"

Bailey shook her head, and reeled off a list of homes, some of them rentals where the summer crowd vacationed on Pawleys.

"Oh, my," said Melanie. "Did you ever get caught?"

"Twice."

"Oh," said Ginny, laughing again, "then you weren't really sleepwalking after all?"

Melanie explained to Kate that Bailey had been found

in people's homes twice last season, and the reason for her being in someone's home had been blamed on sleepwalking, probably brought on by problems at home.

"Yeah," said Bailey, wistfully, "my life has really been messed up lately."

Ginny reached over and gave her friend a hug. Melanie leaned over, too, but instead produced a pillow and crowned Bailey with it. The blonde screamed and grabbed at her rollers.

"You know," said Mel, "I should be mad. I had a date who wouldn't wait around while we were searching for my mother's glasses."

"No great loss," said Bailey, adjusting her curlers. "None of your boyfriends ever work out."

"Gee, thanks."

"Don't be mean," said Kate.

"The truth hurts," said Ginny, "and that's what this little séance is all about."

"You mean 'session,'" said Melanie. "A séance is when the dead speak to the living."

"Bailey's going to be dead if she doesn't return my hairbrush. That hairbrush belonged to Rachel Belle. She brought it all the way from Massachusetts when she married into the family."

"Ginny has Yankees in her family tree," explained Melanie.

That caused Kate's eyebrows to go up. She'd rarely met a Yankee, and certainly not one who'd dare marry a Southerner.

"You really want to go ahead of me and Mel?" asked the pale-faced brunette.

Kate nodded, and then smiled at Bailey. "Because I do something like you do."

"Sneak out at night?"

"Oh, no. Not in Judson Mill. There's always someone getting off their shift."

"Then what do you do?"

"Shoot out people's windows with a pellet gun."

"What?" asked the other three girls, who had hardly ever held a weapon.

"But if you don't go outside, how do you do it?"

"From the second story windows of my house after Grandma goes to bed." Kate smiled. "I've even done it from Grandma's room while she's been asleep. She's a real heavy sleeper."

"And never been caught."

"I've come close. Someone said they saw a light from my window, but I'm not stupid. They sent a deputy over to check it out."

"And?"

"Oh," said Kate with a smile. "I came downstairs all right." She giggled. "Wearing a shortie nightgown and with my hair in pigtails, bangs down in my face. My grandmother almost fainted and ran me back upstairs but quick."

"Oh, my lord," said Melanie, clutching the throw pillow again. "My mother saw that look in *Seventeen* and canceled my subscription."

"You can have my old copies," said Ginny. "You read too many books anyway."

"How many windows have you shot out?" asked Bailey.

"What? Oh, nine at last count."

"How long have you been doing this?"

"Since I was sixteen."

"Good God," said Melanie, "you need help."

"No more than I do," said Bailey, looking across their tight circle. She and Kate locked eyes for a moment, and then the moment passed. "Well, Ginny, what's your story?"

Ginny put her hands behind her, leaned back on the bed, and said, "Well, you know how I go to visit my mother the first of each summer and each Thanksgiving?"

"Oh, God," said Melanie, "don't tell me you're not a virgin. They tell me those California boys are wild."

"Who'd you do the dirty deed with?" asked Bailey, grinning. "Jan or Dean, or all the Beach Boys?"

"Nothing like that. When I'm in California I smoke dope."

"What?" asked Kate.

"With who?" asked Bailey.

"With my mother and whatever guy she's living with."

"Your mother lives with different men?" asked Melanie. "Wow! How cool."

"I thought your parents were still married," said Bailey.

"They are, but my mother's what they call a 'free spirit.'"

"But what's this dope stuff?" repeated Kate.

"Drugs," explained Melanie.

Kate still didn't understand and said so.

"Jeez Louise," said Bailey, "we'll have to give you an education before you embarrass us all to death at Carolina."

"I've heard of dope," said Kate with a shrug. "I just didn't know you could smoke it."

"Grass," confirmed Ginny. "Marijuana. Everyone in California smokes grass."

A whole state that smoked grass? Now that was hard to believe, thought Kate, but these girls seemed to know what they were talking about.

"So whose secret is this?" asked Melanie, grinning maliciously. "Yours or your mom's?"

"My mom's? Why would it be my mother's?"

"Well, I heard of this family in Raleigh. They were taken to court for letting their kid drink with them, and I don't mean cutting the wine at dinner. The court called it 'child endangerment.'"

"My mother's not at fault here," said Ginny, her voice rising.

"Hey," said Kate, "I thought this was about us."

"That's mean," said Ginny, "what you're saying about my mom."

"Cool it, Gin. I was just asking."

"Well, keep your damn questions about my mom to yourself."

"Hey, hey," said Bailey, looking from one girlfriend to another, "what's this all about?"

"Oh, Ginny's mad at her mother for deserting the family," said Melanie. "She's never—"

And with a shriek the brunette lunged across the bed.

Melanie screamed and ducked, but Kate and Bailey grabbed Ginny and pinned her arms back, especially her hands. Ginny had a great set of nails, and they hurt when they cut into you.

"Is that someone downstairs?" asked Kate, looking at the door.

Everyone stopped, they let go of Ginny, and Melanie hid the empty wine bottle under a pillow. Bailey slid off the bed, went to the door, and opened it. Hearing nothing, the blond girl walked to the end of the hall and returned moments later to find Melanie adjusting her rollers and Ginny looking anywhere but at Mel.

"Nobody down there." Bailey closed the door and rejoined them on the bed. "You okay?" she asked the two combatants.

Ginny crossed her legs but would not look at Mel. "They call them 'issues' in California."

"Issues?" asked Bailey.

"When you have problems, it's called 'issues.'" She looked at Bailey and Kate. "Like y'all's problem with authority."

"What are you talking about?" asked Bailey.

"Authority?" asked Kate.

"Like the cops," explained Melanie.

"Like the pigs!"

"Oh, Ginny, don't be such an ass."

"Pigs?" asked Kate.

"She means the cops." Bailey rolled her eyes. "And I gave up a night of dancing for this."

"Stealing stuff and shooting out windows," said Ginny. "You don't think you two have a problem?"

"No," said Bailey. "It was kinda fun. Certainly more fun than what this evening has turned out to be."

"Cops are there to protect you," added Melanie.

"Protect the property of the rich," said Ginny. "And that would be you and your family, Mel."

"Oh, and the Belles of Charleston don't have money?"

"Not like the Durants."

"Oh, so I'm guilty by association."

"And by degree, it would appear," said Bailey, snorting.

Kate sat there, thinking. Finally, she asked, "So, if I do something bad, I have issues with somebody?"

"Both of you do. With authority, with your fathers, and one of these days it's going to catch up with you."

"What if someone does something to you?" asked Kate in a voice so low no one heard her.

"Oh, and smoking dope isn't a problem?" asked Bailey.

The brunette was silent, staring at the bedcovers.

"Yeah, right," said Bailey. "I thought so. Okay, we need to get this show on the road or I'm going to have to call Preston and ask him to take *me* to the submarine races."

Bailey's hand came up to her mouth. She didn't know where that came from. She didn't want anyone getting the idea she and Preston were more than enthusiastic dance partners, but sometimes, when the two of them could slip away, she and Preston would kiss until they couldn't think straight.

The other girls hadn't appeared to notice. Kate seemed to be off in her own world, and Melanie was glaring at Ginny, who returned her look in spades.

Finally, Melanie broke off the stare and returned the pillow to the stack behind her. "I'm tired of this game. I don't want to play anymore."

"Nobody's playing," said Bailey. "This is serious business to us."

"I have nothing to say." Melanie crawled off the bed behind Kate. "Go home, especially you, Ginny."

"Wait a minute," said Bailey, "you have to share a secret. We did."

"I don't care," said Melanie from the dresser and with her back to the bed.

Kate swung her feet around, off the bed, and went to her friend. Melanie flinched when the redhead put a hand on her shoulder. Bailey and Ginny simply watched from the bed.

"Come on, Mel," said Kate, "what's the problem?"

Melanie was crying now. "All three of you, go away. You, too, Kate. Spend the night with someone else."

"Hey," said Bailey, crawling across the bed where she ended up on her stomach, "we're not going anywhere. You're telling us a secret. I did, Kate did, and so did Ginny, though I think what Ginny had to say was pretty silly."

"Being corrupted by your own mother is not silly," said Ginny, and she sat there, thinking.

Kate put both hands on Melanie's shoulders. "It's okay, Mel. Everything's going to be all right."

Melanie shivered and continued to cry.

"Hey," said Bailey, "don't make it easy on her. She's got all that money and thinks she can get away with anything."

"Come on, Bailey," said Kate without turning around, "give her a break."

"What's fair is fair. Everyone told a secret and Mel has to tell one, too."

"Uh-huh," said Ginny, as she slid off the bed. "All of us have secrets, and all our secrets, we could stop doing them right now, couldn't we?" She looked at Kate and Bailey. "Smoking dope, breaking windows, stealing stuff? We could stop right now, if we wanted to."

"I guess that's right," said Bailey. "If we wanted to."

Kate nodded in agreement, her hands still on Melanie's shoulders.

"Well," said Ginny, "Melanie has something being done to her that she can't stop, isn't that right, Mel?"

It was a long moment before the brown-haired girl nodded.

"But you've wanted to tell us, haven't you?"

Another nod.

"She wants to tell us what?" asked Bailey, now sitting on the edge of the bed.

"Oh, Bailey," said Kate, "you are so out of it."

"I'm out of it. What am I out of?"

"And you want to run for governor."

"Hey," said Bailey, coming off the bed, "I don't need to be lectured by some linthead."

"I'm not a linthead. People in my family are."

Bailey shrugged. "Same difference."

"No, there's a big difference. I'm getting out of Judson Mill."

"Would you two please shut up?" demanded Ginny. "Melanie has something she wants to tell us."

"Oh," said Bailey, sarcastically, "she has issues?"

"Matter of fact, you've wanted to tell us this for quite a while, haven't you, Mel?"

Melanie nodded. She also whimpered.

Ginny bit her lip. "Does it have anything to do with your stepfather?"

143

Melanie lowered her chin to her chest and began to sob. Kate's hands slid off her friend's shoulders and she backed away, unsure of what to do, certainly not wanting to be touching anyone at this particular moment.

Ginny said, "Daddy warns me every time I go visit my mother that a father will never touch his daughter in the . . . the wrong places, but you have to watch out for . . ."

When Ginny stopped there was only silence in the room. A girl's laughter carried up to them from the beach, even over the hum of the air conditioner.

Melanie finished what Ginny had started. "But you have to watch out for your mother's boyfriends . . . and stepfathers."

In a low voice, Kate asked, "What did he do to you, Mel?"

"She doesn't have to talk about it," said Ginny, putting her hands on Melanie's shoulders. Slowly, she began to massage her friend's shoulders.

Bailey had slid off the bed. Now she stood there, dumbstruck.

"I have someone who puts his hands on me," said Kate. "He shouldn't touch me, but he does."

Ginny's hands fell away as Melanie turned around.

The brown-haired girl wiped her tears away. "Your Uncle Johnny?"

Kate nodded.

"Oh, sweet Jesus," cried out Ginny, and she bent over and clutched her stomach.

Bailey stared at Kate. After a long moment she walked over and put her arm around her, and then opened her

144

other arm to Melanie. All three of them stood there, hugging and crying until Ginny finally joined them. There would be no need for the knife tonight.

The Neighborhood Watch

The man in the dark business suit came through the back door of the Gillespie beach house, noticed the new kitchen, and said to the maid that it must be tough to work in such a dump. Alice Frey did not smile. Actually, she appeared rather sad.

Joshua Simms Belle, called "Simms," noticed this, as white people are accustomed to doing, being severely outnumbered in the Low Country. Still, he said nothing but proceeded down the hall, past the stairs, and to the living room. There, three women waited for him: his mother drinking sherry and smoking a cigarette fitted into its holder, a grim-faced woman simply smoking, and a third, with neither cigarette nor drink, twisting her hands in her lap.

Simms shrugged out of his suit coat—his tie was already loosened—and hung it on a peg in the hallway. "Good evening, ladies," he said, walking into the living room.

Dutifully, he kissed his mother on the cheek, and then bent down and gave each of the other two women a peck on the cheek. Contrary to what people might think, even after a long day at the office in Charleston, and the drive up to Pawleys, Simms Belle was not put out. The father of Virginia Lynne and the twin boys was distinctly aware that he should keep these women happy; otherwise, he'd be hip-deep in children all summer, and the associates at his law firm might end up in as much of a funk as Alice Frey.

His mother thrust out her glass. "Refill, please."

Simms took the glass over to the bar and poured more sherry. It was evident that he'd been dragged up here to be the bad guy. God knows why these three couldn't handle the problem. They certainly had the tongues for the job.

Once he returned the glass to his mother, she said, "Pour a drink and sit down, son."

Simms did, noticing the open windows and the breeze off the ocean. An ocean breeze was always best. An inland breeze carried the threat of mosquitoes from the marsh.

"And make yourself at home," said Irene, smiling, smiling like a barracuda.

Irene Gillespie favored her daughter, tall, regal, and with a great figure. Irene had first come to Pawleys as a child and eventually persuaded her husband to purchase a home here. While her husband had been governor, Irene had spent most summers on Pawleys, her husband commuting into Columbia for legislative sessions and other political chores. Many fathers did that during the summer, arriving late Friday evenings and rising early, usually around 4:00 a.m., to commute back to work Monday morning. And only time would tell if the voters of South Carolina would accept a divorced senator remarried to a much younger woman. Oh, well, there were four more years for Walter to work his political magic, and from what Simms had heard, there wasn't anything Senator Gillespie wouldn't do for his constituents. Still, it did mean that Walter's political ambitions effectively ended at the state line.

Simms took a seat in a rocking chair, the women on the other side of the coffee table, and sipped from his drink. Whatever he learned tonight wouldn't come from the small woman sitting between the other two. Though she had more money than God, Carolynn Hamby was terribly insecure, and like her daughter, small chested, with thin arms and legs, brown hair and eyes, the eyes of an animal abroad in some unknown land.

He and Carolynn had played together, danced at Pawleys pavilion, and even shared a summer romance. And when Simms had been fighting in the South Pacific, wallowing in the mud and being eaten by insects, when-ever he thought of home, it was of Carolynn Durant. He often wondered if she'd returned to Pawleys that sum-mer. And Simms promised, if he survived that damn war, he'd return to the States and learn what Carolynn had been up to.

But that had never happened. In San Francisco Simms had taken a wrong turn and run into a woman who could be both fire and ice, sometimes both at the same time. After a whirlwind romance this California girl agreed to his proposal of marriage and moved to Charleston where she could paint a different type of vista. But once there, like so many other outsiders, his bride became preoccupied with the treatment of the Negro in the American South, though Simms had yet to meet a Yankee who associated with Negroes, even in the army.

"And to what do I owe the pleasure of the company of so many attractive women?" he asked with a broad smile.

"Simms, don't be silly," said his mother. "We didn't

call you up here on some fool's errand."

"Oh, Addy," said Irene, "he's just arrived. Give him a moment to enjoy his drink." And the barracuda smiled again.

"If you'd been with me today, you'd have to agree y'all are the most attractive women I've been with all day."

"Knowing that," said his mother, after another drag off her cigarette, "I'm not sure it was a compliment after all."

"It was meant to be," said Simms, noticing the edge that crept into his voice whenever he spent more than thirty seconds in the same room with his mother. Simms gulped down his drink, stared at the floor, and most of all tried to keep his mouth shut. Being a lawyer, that was nearly impossible.

Carolynn Hamby glanced at her watch and smiled. "It's not even seven, so you made good time."

"Probably drove much too fast," said his mother after sipping from her sherry.

"Alice Frey is making sandwiches."

"Thanks, Irene. There aren't many restaurants between here and Charleston." Simms glanced toward the hallway. "Is Alice Frey ill? She didn't look at all well."

Irene opened her mouth to explain, but at that moment her servant walked into the room with a sandwich, potato chips, several sweet gherkins, and a glass of iced tea on a silver serving tray.

She placed the tray on the coffee table. "Anything else, Miss Irene?"

"No, thank you, Alice. Why don't you call it a night?"

"There's still the kitchen to clean up."

"I'm sure it can wait until tomorrow."

"Thank you." And the sad-looking woman left the room.

Simms looked at the sandwich. "For me?"

"Of course. We may have rushed you up here, but we are not going to starve you to death."

The women chuckled as Simms picked up the sandwich, swaddled it in a napkin so the crumbs wouldn't end up in his lap, and bit into it.

When the screened door at the rear of the house slammed shut, Irene said, "Alice Frey's daughter has run off up north."

"Good riddance," said his mother, after taking another drag off her cigarette.

Simms chewed up a mouthful of sandwich, followed by a pickle, and some potato chips. "This Wilma we're talking about?"

"Simms, don't talk with your mouth full."

Carolynn Hamby smiled in sympathy. She knew why Simms never spent the night on Pawleys, and it was a shame. Sometimes Carolynn needed someone to talk to, but how did you let a man know you just wanted to talk? For men it never ended there, and if you thought about it, and Carolynn *had* thought about it, Simms Belle had yet to divorce his wife.

Irene said, "Wilma appears to have taken up with radicals."

"Communists," stated his mother.

"Now, we don't know that," said Carolynn, who never thought the worst of anyone, and in truth had never been exposed to the nasty side of life, except in her personal life.

"Think what you wish," said Addy Belle, "but I've been around this world four times and spoken with quite a few world leaders, and these civil rights people smell of communists to me."

The others let that go, especially her son. In the past he'd come home and found his mother arguing with Joe Pyne on the radio.

Simms returned to his sandwich, and the women allowed him to eat; after all, arguing with a man couldn't help his digestion. Several potato chips went down with the remainder of his sandwich, a couple more pickles, and then Simms finished his drink.

"Well," he asked, "what have the girls gotten themselves into this time?"

"What makes you think it's the girls' fault?" asked Irene, a pinched look coming into her face.

"Well, last time we had a meeting of this sort was when the girls stayed out all night. I believe they were thirteen."

"This is much more serious," said his mother, "and has ramifications that will reverberate through their lives."

"Oh," said Simms, not knowing what that meant, unless the girls had decided to do some serious drinking. Underage drinking always concerned Simms, as Charleston was known as a place where you could always find a drink, even during South Carolina's many prohibitions.

Simms heaved himself out of the rocker and went over to the bar and fixed another drink. Looking up, he asked, "Anyone want anything?"

Only his mother did, and after refilling her sherry

glass, Simms returned to the bar, had second thoughts about his own drink, and mixed his bourbon with plenty of water. He wasn't going to get snookered into spending the night on Pawleys.

Irene lit another cigarette but waited until he was seated before saying, "Simms, we need to do something about who the girls are associating with."

"Sure. Who's the boy? I'll have a talk with him."

"No, no," said his mother, tapping ash from her holder and into an ashtray in her lap. "It's a girl, and since I'm only Virginia Lynne's grandmother, she won't listen to me."

"Well, she should, and for that very reason: you're her grandmother." He looked at the other two women. "But I don't understand, you say the girls are hanging around with the wrong element, but if it's not boys, who is it?"

Irene gestured toward the rear of the house. "You saw my new kitchen?"

"Sure, and it looks terrific."

"I'm not talking about the remodeling, but the carpenter."

"The . . . carpenter? Your carpenter's been hanging around the girls? How old is he, and why haven't you fired him? Hell, why haven't you had the sheriff pick him up? There has to be more than one carpenter in Georgetown County."

And with that, his mother and Irene Gillespie started in on him, Irene defending herself; his mother, as usual, lecturing *him.*

Simms didn't understand a word, and when there was a pause, he pointed at the woman sitting in the middle. "Why are you here, Carolynn? Do you have an interest in this?"

"She does!" said both his mother and Irene.

Simms said nothing, just sipped from his drink and waited.

Finally, Carolynn sat up and cleared her throat. "I do have an interest in this, Simms. My daughter's involved, too."

"Involved in what?"

Amazingly, the other two women let her speak. "Last summer when Irene had her kitchen remodeled, the carpenter brought along his niece as his assistant. Though the work was being done here, at Irene's, my daughter and the carpenter's niece hit it off. They're the same age."

"Bailey appears to be the only one who stood up to this girl," interjected Irene.

Carolynn turned her head ever so slowly and stared at her neighbor. Irene Gillespie quickly returned to her cigarette.

"What's the problem? Is this girl smoking, encouraging the girls to stay out late, borrowing money?"

"She's not our type," spit out his mother.

"If that's so, isn't this similar to a summer romance? When the girls go off to school, she'll return home."

"That's what you don't understand," said Irene, leaning forward, "this girl is going to the same school as our daughters."

"This carpenter's daughter—"

"Niece," corrected his mother.

"Fine. This carpenter's niece is attending school with the girls next . . . but how can this be?"

"Because," said Irene, stubbing out her cigarette in an ashtray on the arm of the sofa, "she's talked them all into attending Carolina."

"We don't know that," said Melanie's mom.

"The carpenter's niece is attending Carolina?"

"Somehow she wrangled a scholarship," said Irene.

"Yes," said his mother, "just who does she think she is, Sarah Bernhardt?"

Since everyone else in the room was a little fuzzy as to who exactly Sarah Bernhardt was, the room went silent until Simms said to Carolynn, "I thought Melanie was going to Duke."

"Well, so did I," said the thin woman, shoulders slumped, hands slack in her lap.

"And Virginia Lynne's attending the College of Charleston."

"No, she's not," contradicted his mother. "Haven't you heard anything we've said?"

Simms suddenly realized this was one of those times when you simply sat there and took it. These women's thoughts might not be organized, hell, whatever they said might not make any sense, but the only way he was going to have any chance of returning to Charleston at a reasonable hour was to shut up.

Still, with Melanie's mom looking so glum, he just had to ask, "What would you like me to do, Carolynn?"

"Oh, Simms," said his mother, "don't be so opaque. We're having this meeting to thrash out how we're going to handle this."

"And," added Irene, "to make sure you'll support us in our decision."

"Of course I'll support you. Why wouldn't I?"

153

"We need some way to rid ourselves of this girl," said his mother. "My Lord, she even listens to Elvis Presley."

And that's when Simms stopped chasing rabbits and focused on his mother. "When did Virginia Lynne decide to attend Carolina?"

"You don't know?" asked his mother, coyly.

"This is the first I've heard about it." And if there was one thing he was going to get to the bottom of before leaving Pawleys, it was why his daughter wasn't planning on attending the same school the other women in their family had attended.

"It's that girl," said Carolynn Hamby. "And now she's working in my house."

"Your house?"

"I decided to have the kitchen remodeled."

"And this carpenter's daughter works there?"

"Carpenter's niece," said his mother.

"And this carpenter's niece is responsible for Virginia Lynne switching schools?"

"Son, you're not paying attention. The girl is a menace. We must do something about her, and we must do it now."

"Melanie was all set to attend Duke," said Carolynn, "but now she's going to Carolina with Kate."

"Kate?" asked Simms.

"Don't be such a ninny, son. Kate is the carpenter's niece."

"But Virginia Lynne has been accepted at the College of Charleston."

"Haven't you heard a word I've said?" asked his mother. "She's attending Carolina."

"If she does, it'll be on her own dime."

"You'd do that to your own daughter?" asked Carolynn, her face showing real concern.

"Impossible," said his mother. "That girl has him wrapped around her finger."

"Where's Virginia Lynne now?" asked Simms, rising from his chair.

His mother gestured toward the beach with her cigarette holder. "Out there with the others, and the girl."

Simms put down his glass. "Then I'll speak with her right now."

"You'll just embarrass her," said Carolynn, looking up from between the other two women. "Do you even understand why we're having this meeting?"

Actually, Simms was still rather confused on that point.

"Because of this." Carolynn pulled a letter from a pocket of her walking shorts and handed it across the coffee table.

Simms noticed Carolynn still had a pair of great-looking legs, a little on the thin side, but still well formed and tanned. He also remembered to take the letter from her, an acceptance letter for Melanie Fielding Durant to attend the University of South Carolina.

He looked up. "I don't understand."

"And I was just as puzzled as you are."

Well, thought Simms, you and I are both puzzled, but over what I have no idea.

"I told Melanie she was, under no circumstances, to attend the University of South Carolina, and then this comes in the mail." And suddenly Carolynn began to cry.

Simms wanted to go to her and to comfort her. It

wasn't right for someone as kind as Carolynn Hamby to suffer as she did.

"Melanie comes into her majority soon," said Carolynn, as if that was the answer to Simms's questions. "She . . . she went to the bank and they advanced her money against her inheritance. It's that damned tobacco money again. My daughter can do as she likes. She doesn't have to listen to me." And the small woman bent over, clutched her face in her hands, and sobbed.

The other two women put their arms around her. Simms's mother looked at him as if he was the cause of Carolynn's distress.

All he could think to say was, "I'm sure Melanie will meet some nice girls at school and they'll take her under their wing when she joins a sorority."

Evidently that was the wrong thing to say. Carolynn gave a startled cry, rose, and fought her way out of the embrace of the other two women. Struggling off the sofa, she stumbled across the room, into the hallway, and out of the house.

"Now see what you've done," said his mother.

The barracuda was firing daggers at him.

Simms heard footsteps going down the front steps and glanced out the front window to see Carolynn stumbling through the sand and in the direction of her house. Simms glanced at the bar, thought better of it, and then stepped into the hall. After taking down his suit jacket, he followed Carolynn out of the house, across the porch, and down the front steps.

"Leave her alone," cautioned his mother as her son went out the door.

"You can't do anything for her, Simms," said Irene.

"I don't know what he thinks he can accomplish," added his mother. This he heard through the window.

And as he went down the steps, Irene asked, "Do you think Simms has a soft spot in his heart for Carolynn?"

"Simms has always had a soft spot for Carolynn."

But Simms wasn't headed to the Durants' but on his way to the source of these women's unhappiness. He found his daughter and her friends sitting around a campfire with several young men. Some of the boys he recognized, even Jeb Stuart, who had recently graduated from the Citadel. Sitting on a blanket beside Jeb Stuart was a red-headed girl Simms didn't recognize.

Jeb was immediately on his feet, shaking his hand. "Mister Belle, good to see you again, sir." He pulled the redhead to her feet. "And this, sir, is Kate Youngblood. A friend of ours."

The redhead was a tall one, and she, too, extended her hand and shook his firmly. But when she spoke it jarred him. All the words came out through her nose.

"Nice to meet you, sir."

The other teenagers were on their feet now. Simms spoke to them all, shook hands with most, gave Bailey a hug, shook hands with Jeb Stuart's younger brother, James, and Preston Winthrop, son of a neighbor in Charleston. As usual Melanie Durant said not a word and hung back.

"Daddy, I didn't know you were coming."

"I missed you and the twins." He gave his daughter a hug. "Walk on the beach with your old man?"

"Well," said Ginny, glancing at the others, "we were

157

about to go down to the pier."

"All right. If you need me, I'll be with the twins, but I don't have much time." He gestured at the Gillespie beach house. "Your grandmother held me up in there."

"Then I'll walk with you."

Simms told everyone how it was nice to see them again, how nice it was to meet Kate, and he and his daughter strolled down the beach together.

When they were out of earshot, his daughter said, "This is about my going to Carolina, isn't it?"

"Yes, it is."

"I just changed my mind, that's all."

"When were you going to tell me?"

"I would've gotten around to it sooner or later."

"Well, it's tough duty to hear it from your grandmother. I thought you'd been accepted at the College of Charleston."

"And UC-Berkeley."

He stopped and turned on her. "Berkeley? You'd go to California for your education?"

Ginny grabbed his arm, forcing him to continue down the beach. After they stepped over one of the groins, and with a sudden lightness in her voice, she said, "I'm sure you'll be able to find another babysitter."

"But Berkeley, I never thought—"

"Mother lives out there, if you've forgotten."

"Virginia Lynne, do you really think you could live out there with those people?"

Ginny let go his arm. "Why not? Are people in California so different from the ones living in Charleston?" She realized what she'd said and laughed.

They continued down the beach arm in arm. From one house came the sound of laughter, from another creaking rockers, and at a third "Help Me Rhonda" was being sung by the Beach Boys.

"So it's either Carolina or Berkeley?"

"I think so."

"Would this have anything to do with the twins?"

"Daddy, I wasn't born to babysit."

"You didn't answer my question."

Ginny became quiet as they trudged along, and the Beach Boys were left behind. No problem. The same song could be heard from other houses as teenagers began to take over the radios on Pawleys Island. Ginny and her dad passed couples walking hand in hand. Many smiled and nodded. Their children waved and greeted them.

"Well, Virginia Lynne?"

"I don't want to lie to you."

He pulled her to a stop and faced her. "And I wouldn't want you to. Remember what we agreed when your mother left, that it was going to be tough enough without the lies."

"Yes, sir, and you've always been a good father."

"That remains to be seen, especially if I don't allow you to go to school in California. What is it you want out of life, pumpkin?"

"I don't know, but I think I'll have more options at Carolina."

"No, you'd have more options at Berkeley. It is, as your mother always said, 'a part of the modern world,' but you must have a plan. You must not let life simply happen, and this is one of those important junctures in your life."

"To tell you the truth, I may have had enough of Charleston."

"More likely you've had enough of your family."

"Daddy, that is so wrong!"

But he only stood there, and that's what drove Ginny nuts. Her father always made sense, always insisted on his children being straightforward and forthright, and to always have a plan. Short term, long term, what were you going to do with your life?

And that was the problem. She had no plan. After her last trip to the West Coast she'd become conflicted. That and the fact she could never lie to this man. As far as she knew her father had never lied to her, and she trusted him implicitly.

"I think I want to go to school with the other girls."

"And this would include Melanie?"

"And others."

"Let's take the others later."

Oh, God, thought Ginny. He's in his cross-examination mode, but Carolina was a decent compromise. The other girls would be there to help her sort out her life.

"If Melanie goes to Carolina instead of Duke, then her mother will have little or no contact with her."

"Oh, I don't know about that."

Simms raised his hand and waited until a couple passed by. Teenagers in love, it would appear, and as Simms stood there, he reflected on his summer romance with Carolynn Hamby. When Virginia Lynne fell in love, he'd be damned if he'd allow it to happen in California and lose her as he had the girl's mother.

After the teenagers had disappeared in the darkness,

he said, "You can spin all the yarns you want about how much you'll miss me and the twins, but fact is, and I've seen this happen with others, once a child leaves home, whether they go to school or take a job, you hardly see them again."

"Oh, Daddy, I don't think—"

Simms raised his hand again. "Please let me finish."

Again Ginny closed her mouth.

"When children leave home, that's when *they* control how much time they spend with their parents, and you can really tell. It's as though they put their parents in a box, on one of those really high shelves in their closet, and when they're feeling guilty, they pull down the box and take their parents out—in other words, go visit them."

Ginny couldn't help but laugh. My God, where did he come up with these metaphors?

"So if Melanie doesn't go to school close to home, what does that leave for her mother? Robert dropped out of Duke and roams the country like Jack Kerouac. Melanie's sister, Jo Anne, had to be locked away for her own good. And since Mrs. Hamby shot her last husband, all that family history will give pause to any man interested in courting her, or her money."

Ginny nodded. "I see what you mean."

"I'm not sure you do. I just spoke with Mrs. Hamby and she's very upset with Melanie's decision to attend Carolina."

Ginny nodded. "We saw her rush out of the house."

"And Melanie didn't go to her, but that's an argument for another day. I still have the twins and the hope that your mother may someday return to Charleston.

Besides, by the time the twins leave, you'll have children of your own and need *me* to babysit for *you*."

"Oh, Daddy!" And she slapped him playfully on the arm.

He took her arm again and they continued down the beach. As they walked along, they passed more couples and small children climbing over groins which they, too, had to step over. The breeze had picked up, making for pleasant strolling, and most people nodded or said good evening. They could tell there was a serious discussion going on between father and daughter.

"Tell me about this new friend of yours, Kate Youngblood. Who are her people?"

"Oh, she's really cool. She's become one of our gang."

"Your grandmother doesn't see it that way."

"Oh, Nana's so square."

"Virginia Lynne, please. She's your grandmother."

"But why shouldn't Kate be part of our crowd?"

"Well, for one thing, she talks through her nose."

"Daddy, she was just nervous. Her accent's a lot better than it was last summer."

"You don't think she'll be nervous at Carolina? She's certainly not going to be rushed."

"Oh, we don't care. If they won't take the four of us, we'll rush again when we're sophomores. That'll prove we're serious about staying together."

Simms stopped. "Are you serious?"

Ginny set her jaw. "Absolutely."

"Virginia Lynne, being in a sorority is a very important part of collegiate life, whether at Carolina or the College of Charleston, and to put this off a year—"

"Sorry, Daddy, but we're sticking together."

"Are you sure Kate can even afford to be rushed?"

"She has a full scholarship and plans on working for any extra money she needs. She has a job in the cafeteria."

Simms glanced down the beach. "Is she working this summer?"

"Yes, sir, with her uncle."

"What's her uncle like?"

Ginny shivered.

Her father saw this. "Are you cold?"

"No," said his daughter, flashing a nervous smile, "the breeze just caught me wrong. That's all."

"You were telling me about Kate's uncle."

"He works all the time."

"And he wants Kate to be with him."

"Yes, but he's learned that's not going to happen."

Her father regarded her. "I'm not sure I like the way that sounded, children giving ultimatums to adults."

"Daddy, her uncle goes barhopping, and Kate's left in that dingy old trailer all by herself."

"So, you've adopted her, and the rest of your group goes along?"

"They do," she said firmly.

"I have to say I've never seen you accept anyone into your circle, not at Ashley Hall, certainly not here at Pawleys."

"I've changed. I've grown up. We've all changed."

"Nothing wrong with that, but you're telling me that Bailey Gillespie has bought into this?"

"It took a while, but she finally came around."

"Uh-huh, and what brought her around?"

Ginny looked out to sea, remembering the ceremony

in the bedroom that had shed no blood. "They're a lot alike, and that's what put Bailey off at first."

"You're telling me that Kate Youngblood is as driven as Bailey Gillespie?"

"Yes, sir, but a lot more low key. You don't really notice it, or realize what she's capable of. It sort of surprises you, and as I said, last year they didn't see eye to eye."

"Because of the Gillespies' divorce."

Ginny nodded and shivered again.

Her father shrugged out of his suit jacket. "And I imagine you were able to help in that regard."

"Yes, sir, I've been through some of that."

Simms fitted his coat over his daughter's shoulders and turned her around. "Let's walk back to your friends." On the return trip, he asked, "You sure this Kate Youngblood doesn't just bring out the mother hen in you?"

"Sorry, but I'm not like that at all."

"You don't think so?" said her father, chuckling. "I beg to disagree." He smiled at her. "You're going to make a terrific mother, Virginia Lynne."

"Thank you, Daddy, but I've had my fill of babysitting."

"Uh-huh, and what does Jeb Stuart see in Kate?"

"They're in love."

"Sorry, but they call that puppy love."

When his daughter tried to object, he added, "I don't know what the Stuarts are going to say about this."

"Summer romance."

"And this is not a summer romance, you, your friends, and Kate Youngblood?"

"No, it isn't. Mother gave me a copy of *The Feminine Mystique* last Christmas, and I want to do more with my life, just as Kate is doing with hers."

That caused her father to stop. "For God's sake, don't tell me you believe that claptrap about women being able to make it on their own."

"Mother has."

Simms looked out to sea, staring at a moon low in the sky. That same moon hovered over another city by the sea, San Francisco.

"What, Daddy?"

"Nothing."

"No fair. We promised not to keep things from each other."

"It's not something you want to hear."

His daughter came around to stand in front of him, the surf washing over her bare feet. "I can take it, whatever it is."

"I don't think so."

She pulled the jacket tight and waited him out.

Simms looked at the sand, and in a moment of pique, kicked at a metal bucket washing back and forth in the surf. He missed.

"First, you must understand that I don't make a policy of spying on your mother. One of my associates told me what I'm going to tell you."

Ginny nodded and pulled the coat even tighter.

"When my partner was in San Francisco, he had a weekend free, so his wife joined him and they took in the sights. Haight-Ashbury's where they saw your mother. His wife remembered your mother from her showings in Charleston."

"Do I want to know what she was doing, or is it any of our business?"

"It becomes your business if you're making decisions based on some book your mother gave you." Her father cleared his throat and looked out to sea again. "Your mother lives with men, Virginia Lynne. She can't support herself."

"And how do you know that?"

"After I was told your mother was hawking her paintings on the street, I hired someone, and he spent a couple of weeks photographing your mother's transactions and inquiring as to how much her customers had paid for her work. What he learned was that her paintings don't sell well enough to put food on the table."

"Maybe she was having an off week."

"I hired him for two different weeks, and during the height of the tourist season. I did that in the event you came to believe that your mother could make it on her own."

Now it was Ginny's turn to look out to sea. That wasn't what her mother had told her. Her mother said she and her "friend" shared costs equally, and that she could hold up her end of the deal. But her mother had lied in the past. Could this be just another lie?

"If you have proof she's living with other men, why haven't you divorced her?"

"Is that what you want?"

"No, sir, I want her to come home so we can be a family again."

He reached out, gathered his daughter into his arms, and hugged her. "And that's what I want, too."

"Mother believes you weren't the same man she married once you returned to Charleston." His daughter disengaged herself from her father's arms as more water rushed across her feet. "She said you were more fun out in San Francisco."

"I probably was. I was . . . well, after being overseas I was just happy to be alive, dance, drink, party, whatever anyone wanted to do, I was ready. But as I came to know your mother's friends, I noticed a sense of irresponsibility about them. Still, they presumed to judge me, and they especially liked to rub my nose in my own conformity, daring me to cut loose. My time for cutting loose ended when I returned to Charleston and had to provide for a family, but if you live with someone from California, there's pressure to conform to their sense of . . . well, lack of conformity.

"Really, Virginia Lynne, I don't know what else I can do to make your mother happy other than move out there." He smiled. "And then worry like hell about how my children are being raised."

"You want her to realize the error of her ways and come back to Charleston."

"I'm not the one who walked out on the family."

Ginny didn't know what to say. She was in total agreement with her father. Her mother should come home, and that's what Ginny always spent the first few days of her visit arguing about with her mother, before eventually giving up.

"So Mother gives me a book about how women shouldn't live their lives through their husbands—"

"And I don't think it's realistic because the women who've really done something with their lives have accomplished zilch as far as I'm concerned."

"Because none of those women stayed at home and raised a family?"

"Is that so wrong?"

"Not at all," said Ginny, shaking her head. "I'm going to marry a man who'll meet me halfway."

"That'll be the day," said her father, laughing. "Women will always do the heavy lifting in any marriage, as I was forced to learn when your mother left. I wouldn't wish that on any man."

"Then I'd better have mine thoroughly housebroken before I bring him home to meet you."

THE PAYOFF

"Archie" Archibald was told there was a Negro who wanted to see him, and that he was waiting at the back door of the bar.

Archie was a rangy man with ropy muscles who stood six feet tall and had a beard that caught plenty of sawdust. Archie Archibald was a carpenter who lived along the Waccamaw and preferred hunting and fishing to working. Still, a man had to eat, and over the years, Archie had learned that the folks who owned homes along the beach would pay for style and grace when it came to their carpentry, so Archie had apprenticed himself to a master carpenter. Now he could hunt and fish anytime; that is, if the damned outside contractors would stop soliciting business on Pawleys!

"I don't do business with the colored."

The bartender shrugged. "I'm just telling you what I was told by the cook." Before he moved down the bar, the bartender popped the cap on another Blue Ribbon and placed the long neck in front of Archie.

"I didn't order no beer." He held up the one he was drinking. "I'm not finished with this one."

"Compliments of the fellow waiting to see you." The bartender grinned, exposing several missing teeth. "I suppose it's his way of hurrying you along."

"I don't hurry for no Negroes."

"Don't suppose you do, but you can go out through the kitchen if'n you decide to do this thing."

Archie stood at the bar, thinking. While he did, he finished his Blue Ribbon, then he picked up the new bottle and sauntered down the bar with it, through the kitchen, and out the back door.

It was like the bartender said. A Negro stood, battered fedora in hand, at the back door. As Archie stepped outside he looked both ways.

"Ain't nobody out here but me, Mister Archibald."

Satisfied that he wasn't being set up, the white man turned his attention to the black one. "How you know my name?"

"Oh, I gots a cousin works at the lumberyard down in Georgetown." The Negro broke into a grin. "Says you one strong white man, Mister Archibald."

"Yeah? So what."

"And tough."

"I think that's about all the information you've earned with that free beer, boy." Archie turned to go.

"Yessuh, I understand. I brung you this."

Archie looked. In one hand was the Negro's hat, in the other a folded up dollar bill. No, thought Archie, looking closer. That's not a one dollar bill. That's a hundred dollar bill.

"What's that for?"

The black man rubbed the bill, and Archie realized it had been torn in half. There was only half of a hundred dollar bill in the Negro's hand.

"It's for you, Mister Archibald."

Archie took a long pull off his Blue Ribbon. "Don't figure half a bill is worth much of anything."

"Yes, suh, that's right. My missus has the other half."

"Uh-huh, and does this missus have some work for me, maybe something that involves jumping out of windows in the middle of the night?"

It took a second for the Negro to understand. When he finally did, he laughed. "Oh, no, there's no jumping out of any bedroom windows. You wouldn't want to climb in my missus' window in the first place."

"Watch what you say about white women, boy."

"Yessuh," said the Negro, becoming serious again. "Didn't mean nuthing, jest that my missus is an old lady, that's all."

Archie took another swallow from the beer. "So what's your missus want?"

From inside the battered fedora the Negro took a black-and-white photograph and handed it to Archie. It was a photograph of a white man in blue jeans and a dirty T-shirt doing carpentry work.

"What's your missus' interest in this fellow?" Archie did not recognize the man.

"She says I's to give you half the bill tonight, along with that picture. Then, the day after my missus hears this white man is in the county lockup, I's to meet you back here and give you the other half."

Archie looked at the photograph, turning it over in his hand. There was nothing on the back, just a black-and-white photograph of a short, stocky man who appeared to be in his thirties. Fellow could be a handful; Archie really didn't know, but you always took the measure of a man before you asked him to step outside.

"And where do I find this fellow?"

"He works on Pawleys." And the Negro told him where.

"And if I get tossed in the county jail doing this chore for your missus . . . ?"

This time the black man did not smile. "I don't think that's any of my missus's business."

"Yeah, well, then, there's the rub."

"Yessuh, I understand. I has other white men on my list."

"You have a list?" asked Archie, his eyebrows rising.

"You ain't the only carpenter around these parts"—he gestured at the photograph again—"but that fellow ain't from around here."

"That so?" asked Archie, studying the photograph with growing interest. "Well, in that case, maybe we can work out something. Give me a few days."

"Yessuh." And the black man turned to go.

"Say, boy, what were you gonna do if I picked you up by your heels and shook the other half of the bill out of you."

"Why, Mister Archibald, that ain't possible," said the Negro, smiling again, "not the shaking part, but I jest plain don't have the other half."

"And maybe I don't believe you."

"Can'ts help you there, but I can give you the other

half any day but Sunday."

"And why couldn't you meet me on Sunday?"

"Why, suh, that's the Lord's Day, and I drive my missus to church."

A Phone Call to Daddy

"Daddy, I need your help."

"You're not calling for money, Bailey?"

Walter Gillespie had taken the phone from his wife. The two of them were leaving for a state dinner, and they were late. Arlie was driving them to the White House, and his chief of staff stood at the door with his wife.

"No, sir, I'm not calling for money."

"Well, this is a pleasant surprise."

"Daddy, we don't have much time. I need a bus stopped and you know the people who can do it."

"A bus stopped? I don't understand."

The new Mrs. Gillespie motioned for her husband to come along. The senator raised a finger, asking for a moment. His chief of staff muttered something about taking phone calls, any phone calls when you were about to leave for the White House. Unless that phone call came from the White House.

Bailey read out a number. "This bus is headed for Greenville and I want it stopped. If you can't call, give me the name of someone *I* can call."

"Bailey, I have no idea what you're talking about, but I have a state dinner to attend. You do remember where state dinners are held, don't you?"

"Daddy, I need this done immediately. Kate's uncle was thrown in jail for brawling and she can't stay at the trailer any longer. There are just too many strange men there."

"Trailer, like in trailer park?"

"Yes, sir, so Kate's been put on the bus and sent home since she has no one to stay with."

"This Kate's a friend of yours, a girl who lives in a trailer?"

"I wrote you about her."

"Yes, and if I remember correctly, you did not speak highly of her. You called her a 'linthead.'"

"That's all in the past. I'll explain later."

"Bailey, let me speak with your mother."

"I'm not at home. I'm using a pay phone."

The senator glanced at the grandfather clock in the hallway. "And why's that? It's nearly suppertime on Pawleys."

"Mother wouldn't have allowed me to call."

"And why is that?"

"She doesn't approve of Kate."

"Well, you haven't said anything to convince me, and contrary to what you might believe, young lady, I support your mother—"

"Daddy, we're wasting time!"

"Bailey, what you're asking doesn't make sense, and I need to go. Can we talk tomorrow?"

"Daddy, if you don't do this, we are going to have a serious problem."

The senator sighed. "Do I get to know anything more than what you've told me, I mean, if I stop this bus?"

At the door his wife was pointing at her watch, a jeweled beauty that shone whenever light hit it.

"Not if you want to make that state dinner. Just give

me Arlie and tell him to do exactly what I ask."

"And what's in this for me?"

There was a pause on the other end of the line, and then his daughter said, "Thanksgiving or Christmas. It can't be both."

"Christmas. Can you do Christmas? Marybeth is beginning to get a complex."

"I'll be there just as soon as school breaks."

"Thank you, Bailey."

"I should be back in time for New Year's."

"It's a deal. I'll put you on the plane the day after Christmas."

The senator motioned for his chief of staff to reenter the house. The dumpy man did not look pleased. He, too, was gesturing at his watch, a Timex that would never shine under any circumstances.

The Trailways bus driver had no idea what was going on. First, the state trooper had come up on his rear like a bat out of hell, and then ridden beside him on the two-lane, flashing his lights and motioning for him to pull over. He did, but only after coming upon a Union 76, one of the few service stations on Highway 178.

The state trooper ushered the redhead into the Greenwood police station. With one hand he guided the teenager toward the desk; with the other he carried her suitcase.

"What's this?" asked the dispatcher, looking up from a stack of paperwork.

The girl was terrified; anyone could see that, and the dispatcher was soon to learn why.

"I was told to bring her to the closest station and to report where I dropped her off. I've already called my dispatcher. She's all yours." And he put the suitcase down on the other side of the railing.

"What do I do with her?" asked the local dispatcher, getting to his feet.

"I was told someone would be along to pick her up."

"Who?"

"Well, if the highway patrol was called out for this, I wouldn't be surprised if SLED shows up." SLED, the State Law Enforcement Division, was the state's equivalent of the FBI.

"What's the problem, girl?" asked the dispatcher.

The redhead was incoherent. She babbled, cried, and wrung her hands. This was too much for the dispatcher and he pushed his way through the railing and put an arm around her. But try as he might, he could not get the girl to stop crying.

The trooper headed out the door.

"Wait a minute. When will they be here?"

The trooper shrugged. "I have no idea."

"But is she to be locked up or what?"

"Suit yourself, but my dispatcher said this came all the way down from DC."

"Washington, DC?"

"That's right, and if I were you, I would cover my butt." That said, the state trooper was out the door.

The dispatcher picked up the suitcase and walked the girl through the railing and around to his chair. "Well, I guess it's just you and me, honey. Want me to send out for ice cream?"

The girl only continued to bawl.

The dispatcher didn't know what to do. He had no children, and in truth, his wife liked it when he worked late. Then she could get her work done.

He put down the suitcase and sat the girl in his chair and began to show her how to work the radio. That usually did the job, but this redhead seemed out of her mind. Still, she was a pretty young thing: red hair, narrow face, and a tomboyish figure.

"You don't want to learn how to operate the radio?"

The girl shook her head. "I—I just want to go home."

The dispatcher gave the girl his handkerchief and she wiped her eyes, then blew her nose.

"Well, I'm sure they'll be along soon. Who do you know in Washington?"

"Washington? No—nobody."

"You don't?" And keeping a hand on the girl's shoulder as he would to calm any frightened animal, he asked, "Then why do you think the people in Washington wanted you taken off that bus?"

"I—I don't know. I haven't done anything. It was Uncle Johnny they put in jail."

"Your Uncle Johnny was put in jail?"

"Yes—yes, sir."

Now they were getting down to it. "Why was Uncle Johnny put in jail?"

"Fighting again." The girl snorted and blew into the handkerchief. "Drinking, too, I'd imagine."

"Uh-huh. And where are your folks?"

"I have family in . . ." Kate almost said "Greenville," but what had happened today proved that she'd never escape Judson Mill, and that's where she told the dispatcher her family lived.

"Why that's little over fifty miles away. Why'd they pull you off here?"

The redhead shook her head. "I—I don't know."

The dispatcher put both hands on the table, leaned down, and looked her in the eye. "Girl, are you being truthful with me?"

She nodded several times.

"What's your name?"

Kate told him.

"And you're not in trouble with the law, here in South Carolina or in Washington?"

"No, sir!"

"You wouldn't be"—the dispatcher glanced away—"in the family way, would you?"

Kate drew back, gripping the handkerchief with both hands. "No, sir, that would be a sin."

And the way she said it, he believed her.

"I think those women just wanted me off Pawleys."

"Pawleys Island?" A lot of influential people had homes on Pawleys. "What did you do down there?"

"I was remodeling a house."

He straightened up. A girl remodeling a house. Now that made no sense at all. "Come on, Kate, you have to have done something for all this fuss to be made. It's not every day somebody is taken off a bus."

"No, sir," she said, shaking her head. "I promise I didn't."

The dispatcher considered what she'd said. "Kate, I want to make a few phone calls, but I can't make those calls with you around. There are questions I'd have to ask, and they might embarrass you." He smiled down at the girl in his chair. "Or me."

"Yes, sir." The teenager got to her feet and picked up her suitcase. "You want me to wait outside?"

"No, honey, you're going to have to wait in the back."

Kate looked in the direction of the holding cells. "You're going to lock me up?"

"Well, I can't have you running around while I'm on the phone. Besides, if you took off, it'd be my job."

Kate shook her head. "I won't do that. Promise."

"I'm sorry, but I've still got to do it until I sort this out."

"Yes, sir." And holding her head up, Kate marched back into the lockup.

The dispatcher brought along the keys. "I have to warn you that there's a drunk back there. You won't be in the same cell, but if he wakes up—"

"I'll quote him poetry."

"You'll quote . . . poetry?"

"I learned a lot of poetry my senior year at Parker. I'm going to Carolina this fall. I got a full scholarship."

Which was enough for the dispatcher to conclude that he was dealing with a stark raving lunatic. Nobody who talked with such an accent was going to the University of South Carolina, certainly nobody from Parker High School, and never on full scholarship. So, as quickly as he could, he put the girl in the cell next to the sleeping drunk and locked the door behind her.

Several hours later the dispatcher looked up at the commotion coming through the stationhouse door.

Two middle-aged women and three bobby-soxers were coming through that door, and the two middle-aged women were lookers. The bobby-soxers were certainly cute but showing a bit too much skin for his taste.

"May I help you ladies?"

It was the tall, blond woman with the hard look who answered. "We're here for Kate Youngblood."

"Pardon me?"

"I mean, officer, we were told the highway patrolman left her with you after taking her off the bus, and we're here to pick her up and return her to Pawleys."

"Sorry," said the dispatcher, glancing at his watch, "but she should be home right about now."

What had happened was the dispatcher had a friend in the sheriff's department of Greenville County, and the friend knew a firefighter who had attended Parker High School with one of Kate's uncles, and Kate's uncle knew damn well not to call his mother, meaning Kate's grandmother. After confirming that his niece was, indeed, being held in the Greenwood city jail, he set out for Judson Mill, where he told the supervisor he needed to speak to his older brother. From there, the two brothers hit the road, and an hour later, they were at the Greenwood police station where they found their niece quoting poetry to a drunk who sat mesmerized in the next cell. Only after Kate finished reciting "The Rime of the Ancient Mariner" did the drunk finally agree to their niece's release.

In the Dodge on the way home, things got a bit noisy, with considerable emphasis on whether Kate was still a "nice girl." Only after returning to Judson Mill did the two uncles shut up, but not for long. There, Kate's grandmother took over and things got louder still. Finally, one of the neighbors came over and beat on the door, reminding them that people had to work in the morning.

Having been chewed out by their mother for not knowing what had happened down on Pawleys, the brothers kicked their neighbor off the porch and set to flattening the man. It was only when the neighbor's wife stepped on her porch and jacked a round into the family shotgun that the Youngblood brothers picked up their neighbor and carried him into his house. It appeared their neighbor was going to be laid up for quite a while. A couple of hours later, more visitors arrived, two middle-aged women and three teenage girls, trooping up to the front door of the Youngblood house and demanding to speak to Kate.

The third summer

KATE'S SECRET PAST

A skinny young Negro was ushered into the office of Simms Belle, and it made everyone in this lily-white law firm rather nervous. Belle's secretary, a no-nonsense matronly type, remained at the door, clutching the doorknob after announcing that Mr. Belle's visitor was Melvin Ott. Ott had been sent to see Simms Belle by Harry Hartner of the Columbia law firm of Fox, Massingale, and Rembert. Behind Simms's secretary, one of the senior partners stood, looking through the doorway from the lobby.

Ott's clothing was nondescript: brown suit, tan shirt and orange tie. His head bald. He wore a cheery smile and held a manila envelope in his hand. Crossing the room, Simms saw the young Negro take the measure of the office, the paneling, the windows overlooking Broad Street. Simms was sure he'd taken in the plush carpet—if only through his shoes—felt the tingle of the air conditioning on this unusually hot spring day, and heard the phonograph playing Piano Sonata No. 16 by Mozart. The music made it easier for Simms to concentrate on his work, drowning out the noise from Broad Street.

An adjoining door opened and Simms's uncle appeared. The elder Mr. Belle noticed not only the young Negro but also the secretary standing at the door and clutching the doorknob.

"Everything all right in here?" asked the senior Belle. Simms's uncle was named for one of the more famous Belles, the one who had had the unfortunate grace to fight on the wrong side of the Civil War.

Simms, who up to this moment had remained calm and detached, probably what the young people would call "cool," sat up in his chair. "Everything *is* going to be all right, isn't it, Ott?"

"Yes, sir," said the young man, handing the manila envelope across a desk littered with contracts and law books. To the senior Belle in the adjoining doorway, Ott smiled and said, "I'm a courier from Fox, Massingale, and Rembert in Columbia."

"We know who Fox, Massingale, and Rembert is," said Simms. He had put down his ballpoint pen to take the envelope.

"Er—yes, sir."

"Fox, Massingale, and Rembert is hiring Negroes as couriers these days?" asked Franklin Belle from the adjoining door.

"Well, sir, I'm sort of a special case."

"Yes. I imagine you are." The elder Belle gestured at the manila envelope. "You could've left that with any one of the secretaries."

"Actually, I was told to give this envelope directly to Mister Belle."

At that, Uncle Franklin raised an eyebrow but did not inquire as to the contents of the envelope. Still, both uncle and secretary waited until Simms was satisfied that the envelope contained only photographs and a credit report on one Raymond Youngblood, who, at first glance, appeared to be worth a great deal of money, most of his holdings in real estate in Greenville County.

"Everything's fine, Uncle Franklin."

That did not satisfy his uncle. "Young man," said the senior Belle, speaking to Ott, "I want you and your kind to know that this law firm will do whatever it takes to maintain the peace and good order in Charleston."

Ott smiled. "Yes, sir, but I'm from Columbia."

"Are you being impertinent, boy?"

"Oh, no, sir." Ott's face immediately lost its smile. "I have relatives here in Charleston. I'll make sure they get the message."

"See that they do."

"Harry Hartner sent him to see me, Uncle Franklin."

"That may be so, Simms, but Harry Hartner is a Republican."

"Yes, sir, and now Senator Gillespie has become one, too."

"Well, we'll see how long that lasts," said his uncle, turning away. "Hiring the colored. Next they'll be bringing in women."

From the other doorway Simms's secretary asked, "Will there be anything else, Mister Belle?"

"I don't think so." Glancing at the young man standing before his desk, Simms added, "Why don't you take an early lunch, Evelyn? I'll see you when I return from the courthouse."

The woman's relief was palpable. "Yes, sir. Thank you, sir." And with a glance at Ott, she left, closing the door behind her.

Ott watched her go. "Bad times coming for both white and black folks again this summer."

Simms put down the envelope. "You wouldn't happen to have any information about where the next riots will break out, would you? I have a daughter who visits her . . . relatives in San Francisco each summer."

"Yes, sir, I understand, and it might be better if her mother visited her at Pawleys this summer."

Simms placed his arms on his desk and leaned forward. "Just who are you to come in here and threaten my family? I might call the police, no matter who you know in Columbia."

"Oh, no, sir. I thought you were asking my opinion. From now on I'll keep my opinions to myself."

"See that you do." Simms leaned back in his chair and regarded him. "Harry Hartner said I should make some time to speak with you." Harry Hartner had come off a farm in Edgefield County and clawed his way up the legal ladder using a steel trap for a mind and a reputation for knowing where all the bodies were buried around the state capital.

Simms gestured at the paperwork covering his desk. On it he had laid the manila folder, the photographs, and the Dun & Bradstreet. "As you can see, I'm a very busy man."

"Yes, sir. I'll make it quick."

"See that you do."

There were two straight-back chairs in front of the desk. Still, Simms did not offer the Negro a seat, but simply leaned back and listened to what Ott had to say.

"Well, sir, one day Mister Harry calls me into his office and says a woman he does legal work for has some concerns about her daughter. Her daughter attends the University of South Carolina."

Now Ott had Simms's attention. Virginia Lynne attended USC. Chalk up one for the home team, even if the home team had to settle for a tie, meaning his daughter had not chosen the College of Charleston but the University of South Carolina. Still, Virginia Lynne was not attending UC-Berkeley.

"Are you permitted to tell me who this woman is, the one whose daughter is attending USC?"

"Oh, yes, sir. The girl's mother is Carolynn Hamby, formerly Carolynn Durant, of the Durant Tobacco—"

"I know who Carolynn Hamby is, Ott."

"Yes, sir. Anyway, I was hired to keep an eye on Miss Melanie while she's in Columbia."

"And you learned Melanie Durant rooms with my daughter in Simms Hall, and they're in the same sorority."

"Yes, sir, I found that out."

"So you've come to tell me what about my daughter?"

"Oh, no, sir," said Ott, shaking his head, "I'm not here about Miss Ginny—"

"Virginia Lynne."

"Yes, sir, Virginia Lynne. I'm here about another roommate, Kate Youngblood."

Simms glanced at the Dun & Bradstreet. Could this Raymond Youngblood be related to the girl who had finagled her way into the good graces of his daughter?

"Pardon me for saying this, Mister Belle, but it's

pretty well known your mother wanted Kate Youngblood off Pawleys Island last summer."

"We all did, Ott."

"Yes, sir, and I can see where people would think she doesn't fit in, but she just might . . . fit in, that is."

"Kate Youngblood fits in at a sorority at South Carolina—Harry Hartner sent you all the way down here to tell me that?"

"Yes, sir, he did, when I learned Kate Youngblood's father owns a sizable piece of real estate in Greenville County."

"I thought her father was out of the picture."

"He is, but Raymond Youngblood puts all his extra money into buying property around his plant in Greenville. Have you ever heard of Mobile Looms?"

Simms had to think. The Belle family owned interests in several textile mills, but try as he may, Simms could not place Mobile Looms. Certainly not some operation large enough to churn out enough money to purchase acreage in the fastest growing county in the Upstate.

People had predicted when Donaldson Air Force Base closed, that would be the end of Greenville, but Greenville had diversified long before the base closing, and at its economic core was a strong and prosperous textile industry. It was often said that when Greenville sneezed, the rest of the state caught a cold.

"Can't say that I've ever heard of Mobile Looms."

"It's owned by Miss Youngblood's father and he has a fleet of trucks servicing looms in the Upstate; that is, everybody but Deering Milliken."

The Upstate was north of the Midlands, and the

reason Mobile Looms, or few others, did little or no business with Deering Milliken had to do with Roger Milliken's penchant for privacy. Begun in Portland, Maine, after the Civil War, Deering Milliken invested in a new facility in Pacolet and changed the history of South Carolina forever.

Gesturing at the Dun & Bradstreet report, Simms said, "Tell me more about the Youngblood family."

"Yes, sir. Mister Raymond's daddy began his loom-re-pairing business in a garage out behind his house and he traveled from one plant to another repairing looms, the really hard-to-fix stuff. He did all his traveling in a mule-drawn machine shop, and then later worked out of an army surplus truck. When his sons were old enough, they joined their daddy visiting his plants, and when the senior Mister Youngblood passed, the oldest brother, Raymond, took over the business. None of the other brothers, and there were three of them, was inter-ested in doing all that traveling, which is a shame, seeing Raymond don't travel all that much these days. Anyway, the brothers allowed Raymond to buy them out—"

The intercom buzzed on Simms's desk and when Simms answered it, he told his uncle, no, they wouldn't be lunching at their club today.

"You sure about that?" asked Franklin Belle over the intercom.

"Yes, sir," said Simms, glancing at the Negro. "Mister Ott and I haven't finished our business yet."

"Mister Ott . . ."

"But thanks for the invitation." Simms released his button on the intercom. "Take a seat. You said your name was Melvin?"

"Yes, sir," said Ott with a larger smile. "Thank you kindly, Mister Belle."

"Would you like some coffee or a Coke?"

"No, sir. There's not a lot of restrooms in Charleston, so I'd better not."

Simms leaned back in his chair and asked, "Where did Harry Hartner come across you, Melvin?"

"Oh, my mother used to clean Mister Harry's house, and when I got in trouble with the law, Mister Harry had the sentence reduced."

"Sentence?"

"I killed a white man and had to go to prison for a while. Mister Harry got me an early release."

Simms glanced at the Dun & Bradstreet. "So you're not licensed to investigate."

"No, sir. I just run errands for Mister Harry."

"I see. And all this information about the Youngbloods, you dug that up yourself?"

"Yes, sir," said Ott, grinning from his chair. "I'm proud to say that I did."

"Then tell me what you've learned, Melvin."

"Yes, sir," said Ott, settling into his chair. "Well, Mobile Looms' carding machines are supposed to be the best in the world, which is where the money comes from that Raymond Youngblood is using to buy up property in Greenville County. He owns land along that new I-385 into Greenville."

"But Kate hasn't seen a dime?"

"Not so's I found out. Raymond is, like white folks say, the black sheep of the family. He never goes home, never sees his family, even on holidays. I don't think he ever leaves the property."

"A real recluse?"

"Yes, sir. Miss Kate went to see him one time, but the security people wouldn't let her in. So she got some poster paper and a felt marker and made up a sign saying 'I'm Raymond Youngblood's daughter' and stood outside the gate of Mobile Looms all day."

Simms couldn't help but laugh. "What happened?"

"Nothing, as long as she stayed off the property. After three days of that she never went back, and as far as I know, she's never seen her daddy again."

By now, Simms had this Youngblood character figured for a real jerk, but it wouldn't do for one white man to call another a 'jerk,' not in the presence of a Negro. "Quite an eccentric."

"Yes, sir, that he is."

"What happened to the girl's mother?"

"Died from TB."

"Tuberculosis? How long ago was this?"

"1949."

"1949?"

That was hard to believe, but South Carolina's senior senator, Tad Billings, had recently toured the most rundown and dilapidated neighborhood in the state and found more than one case of tuberculosis and God knows what else. And Billings' tour had taken place in the state capital! His tour had made the powers-that-be hopping mad. Still, when you had one senator who'd gone over to the Republicans, how could you correct the other, especially if you wanted to hang onto your seniority?

"So Kate has no brothers or sisters?"

"No, sir, just those uncles."

"What are those brothers doing now? I guess what I'm really asking is what did those three brothers do with their share of the money from the sale of Mobile Looms?"

"Oh, not much money changed hands. The business was still being run out of a couple of old army surplus trucks when they sold out. One of the brothers is a fixer at Judson Mill. A fixer is someone who goes from one machine to another—"

"Fixing machinery. I know what a fixer is, Melvin."

"Yes, sir." Ott grinned again. "Mister Harry says I have a bad habit of offering information when I'm not asked."

"And probably what makes you so valuable."

"I hope so. Anyway, one Youngblood brother's got a garage and a used car lot out on White Horse Road. That's business highway 25 on the west side of Greenville."

"And the third brother?"

"Well, sir, that would be the carpenter who did the work on Pawleys Island, and that's why I'm here."

"This sounds like it has something to do with my mother."

"Yes, sir, I'm afraid it does. While I was finding out all this for Mister Harry, meaning whether Miss Kate was a gold digger or not . . ." Ott cleared his throat. "I come across what concerns Mrs. Belle. Your mother has a Negro working for her—"

"Augustus."

"Yes, sir, and Augustus was told to find a carpenter who wouldn't like it if Miss Kate's uncle took any more remodeling jobs on Pawleys Island."

"This would be the Uncle Johnny who was thrown

into jail for public intoxication and brawling."

"Yes, sir, but he didn't pick no fight. It was the other carpenter done it. Archie Archibald said he called out Johnny Youngblood for taking business away from the locals."

"How'd Uncle Johnny come across the Gillespie remodeling work in the first place?"

"Johnny Youngblood built cabinets for Senator Gillespie and some of his friends over in Fraser County. Word got around—"

"Yes, yes. How's my mother involved, Melvin?"

Ott looked at the floor. "She paid this Archie Archibald, through Augustus, a hundred dollars to get Miss Kate's uncle thrown in jail."

To Simms the whole idea sounded rather Machiavellian, and just like his mother. Simms remembered dating a girl his mother didn't approve of, and when he told his mother they might get married, the girl suddenly left town to go live with relatives in Tennessee. He never heard from the girl again.

"So," said Simms, "without a chaperone at the beach, Kate had to go back home. None of the other families would take her in."

Ott looked pained but nodded.

"Melvin," said Simms, sitting up, "this is the first I've heard about this. I'll speak to my mother and find some way to make it up to Miss Youngblood."

"Well, Mister Belle," said Ott, growing another smile, "Mister Harry was thinking there might be a way to make this right by Miss Kate and allow me to keep an eye on Miss Melanie at the same time."

CALIFORNIA DREAMING

"You all right, young lady?" asked the limo driver, looking in his mirror at the pale face, black hair, and pale blue eyes of the girl in the backseat.

Ginny came out of her trance and looked at him. Only minutes before she'd gotten off a plane, flashed some traveler's checks, and was on her way up the Coastal Highway, heading for Pawleys.

"I'm—I'm fine." Ginny looked around and realized where they were. "You might want to slow down around here. There's more than one speed trap along this road."

The limo immediately slowed down.

"Thank you, Miss."

With the kind of money this chubby girl had flashed, and where the limo was headed, it meant she was the daughter of someone of means, and there might be other trips, and tips, if he ingratiated himself to her. Of course, he'd had to call dispatch for permission to take his limo out of Charleston County, and boy, oh, boy, with three lanes all the way to Mount Pleasant on the new Pearman Bridge, it made for a spectacular ride across the Cooper River.

He glanced in the rearview mirror again. "You need to stop to get something for your stomach, a Coke or Bromo-Seltzer?"

"Oh, no," said Ginny, forcing a smile, "I'm fine, really. I flew back in one of the new passenger jets."

"Where from?"

"San Francisco."

The driver nodded into the mirror. "I landed there

194

when I returned from Korea, and if I hadn't been wounded, I wouldn't have rated such treatment. We took the train out to the West Coast going overseas, you know, playing cards, drinking, sleeping. Time passed pretty slow, but, man, flying back, all I could do was hang on and pray." He laughed. "Lord, that was some trip, the roar of the props, all that up and down . . . Yeah," he said with a sigh, "I can't say I'm sad to see those prop planes go."

Ginny almost confided in him that San Francisco was where her parents had met but knew this would only encourage the driver to continue to talk, so she sat back and stared at the loblolly pines lining Kings Highway, the original post road between Charleston, New York, and Boston.

Ginny knew she should've gone home to the town-house on the Battery, but she couldn't face her father, not yet, so she'd headed to Pawleys. If her grandmother got on her nerves, she'd spend the night with Bailey or Melanie, and tell Nana that she wanted to catch up with all the goings-on.

Each summer, once school let out, Ginny spent a week with her mother, a week without the twins. Her father would arrive later, bringing along the boys, and leave them until her mother felt the twins were hampering her lifestyle. Then her father would fly out, police up the twins—his words, and right on the money—and return to the East Coast, dropping them off at Pawleys.

"Lifestyle" was a word Ginny heard again and again in California. It meant how you lived. There were other words like "free love," and in Haight-Ashbury, where everyone dressed casually, "free love" was all anyone talked about. A person wasn't supposed to be "hung up" on anything, especially their sexuality. Nothing bugged you if you were "cool," even having sex with whoever might come along, and with all the worries teenagers had these days—fodder for every teen magazine!—Ginny found it exceedingly tempting to live a life with few cares.

Her mother told her it was all those prudes along the Battery who had caused Ginny to become "hung-up," and unless Ginny learned to enjoy having sex, she'd be "dysfunctional." All this was explained in Alfred Kinsey's *Sexual Behavior in the Human Female*, which Ginny read with her mouth hanging open. And the pages her mother had turned down the corners of, oh, my Lord . . .

Dr. Kinsey said most people didn't remain faithful to one person their whole lives, and even "going all the way" with a member of the same sex was normal.

Having sex with a girl! That'd been as far as Ginny had been able to read. Still, after constant whining by the boy she was dating on the West Coast, Ginny *had* gone all the way, and it hadn't been any treat; worse, she never saw the boy again, though that might be a bit unfair since she'd left a few days later.

So she wasn't a virgin, and it bothered her. She stayed up nights worrying about it, even though she'd been assured by the boy that if it was her first time there was no way she could get pregnant. Actually, what bothered her was what her father would think. Her mother just laughed, and when her mother wouldn't promise to keep her secret, Ginny had booked a flight east and packed her suitcase with a bunch of T-shirts and jeans because her mother had thrown out all her dresses!

As far as her father knew, she was still in California, and Ginny didn't think her mother would snitch on her. Long distance calls were terribly expensive, and whenever her mother did call, it was on Sunday nights when the rates were much lower.

The other reason Ginny couldn't face her father was because he'd been right: her mother *was* living with a man, actually, living off a man, which seemed to go against everything in *The Feminine Mystique.* What her father had said was true. Her mother lived in a world of little responsibility. Not only that, her mother believed that everything Ginny cherished—the house on High Battery, her clothing, the car given to her at graduation—all that "stuff" caused you to become "hung up."

The next thing Ginny knew the limo was turning off Kings Highway and heading for Pawleys.

"Have a good nap?" asked the driver, smiling in the rearview mirror again.

"Just what I needed."

"Miss Belle, I'm sorry I had to ask you for your last traveler's checks, but my boss only accepts Diners Club and American Express. He hasn't heard of anything called MasterCharge."

"Nothing to worry about," said Ginny. Nothing to be hung up about, and as the limo crossed the causeway, Ginny felt like she was really home.

KATE'S SUMMER JOB

"What are you doing here?" asked Bailey Gillespie as she came through the back door of the Belle beach house.

Kate Youngblood was down on her hands and knees, using a hammer to pry nails from the kitchen floor. She wore a red bandana around her forehead, perspiration ran down her face, and there was sawdust in her red hair. With the sawdust, Kate appeared to have freckles instead of a peachy tan.

Tools were scattered everywhere, empty soda bottles sat here and there, and every window was open to allow in whatever breeze might pass by. Kate would need it. People were saying this would be one of the hottest summers on record, and they weren't talking about the number of inner cities that might burn, ignited by black rage.

Kate looked up from the floor and smiled. "I work here."

Behind Bailey, a young Negro opened the screened door, startling her as he followed her into the kitchen. When Bailey stepped out of his way, the young man walked over to a series of cabinets, lifting one end from the floor.

"Here, Melvin," said Kate, leaving her hammer behind and scrambling to her feet, "let me give you a hand."

"No, ma'am, Miss Kate, we've got it."

Another Negro followed Melvin through the door, Augustus, the house's creekman. The older Negro smiled, spoke to Bailey, and then picked up the other end of the cabinets, actually, planking nailed together with plywood doors jury-rigged in front. Together, the two men hauled the framed piece out of the kitchen, past the screened door held open by Kate, down the steps, and across the parking lot. There it was maneuvered onto a stack of broken-up lumber and a pile of linoleum stacked in the bed of an old Ford pickup. A rope was thrown across the load and tied down and the two Negroes climbed in and drove out of the crushed shell parking lot.

When Kate returned to the kitchen, Bailey asked, "What's going on here?"

The redhead grinned. "Just a little surprise for you and the other girls."

The blond girl looked around again. Not only had the old cabinets been removed, but the linoleum was torn up, leaving only bare floor. The cedar flooring, which looked like the original planking, was stained from when the icebox had occasionally leaked. Adelaide Belle had been one of the last holdouts to be hooked up for electricity.

"I don't understand . . ."

Kate unwound her bandana and wiped her face as she walked over to the refrigerator that stood in the hallway with an extension on its electrical cord. There she took a couple of bottles of Miller High Life from the refrigerator and passed one to Bailey.

Bailey glanced down the hall. "You're drinking the Belles' beer?"

"It's mine. Mrs. Belle has her work cut out for her just trying to drink enough sherry to float the *Titanic*."

Kate popped the top with a church key secured by string to a belt loop in her jeans and did the same for Bailey. Kate's cap had dropped to the bare wooden floor, but Bailey caught her cap and placed it on the surface of a gas stove fed by a tank on the back porch. They toasted to "another great summer on Pawleys" and clunked their bottles together.

Leaning against a frame that had once held the sink, Kate explained. "Ginny's father called me before last semester ended and asked if I'd meet him for lunch. He said he'd seen the cabinets in your house and he wanted to know if I could remodel the kitchen here. When I showed up at Five Points, Mister Belle had a general contractor with him."

Kate took another swig as a transistor radio played Dobie Gray singing that he was in with the in crowd.

"Over lunch the man asked me a bunch of questions about woodworking and a few simple ones about plumbing and wiring—you know, to see if I was smart enough to call in a professional or risk doing the job myself."

Bailey didn't remember Ginny's dad ever visiting her beach house, before or after the remodeling. For some reason Simms Belle and her mother did not get along.

But when was her mother ever home? If a girl really wanted to, she could get into some serious trouble if Alice Frey was given the night off. "You can remodel a whole kitchen?" she asked.

"If not," said Mrs. Belle from the hallway, "then we have a serious problem. There are just so many meals I can cadge from your mother and other residents on Pawleys."

Bailey whipped the Miller High Life behind her and said hello to Ginny's grandmother. In Mrs. Belle's hand was a glass of sherry, and she frowned at the sound from the transistor radio: Charlie Brown enjoying flinging spitballs and calling teachers Daddy-O.

"Where is Augustus, if I might ask?" Mrs. Belle did not drive, and believed anything she needed was within walking distance, or a short drive—that is, if Augustus was doing the walking or taking the short drive.

Kate, who had not hidden her beer, but held it out where God and everyone could see, said, "He and Melvin just left to take a load of cabinets out to the dump."

"*To* the dump, my dear. Southerners are the only people who must identify their location relative to whatever they are speaking about." She glanced at Bailey, still hiding the beer behind her. "I suppose we Southerners would lose our sense of identity if we didn't know where we were in relation to the rest of the world."

And she gave her kitchen a mournful look before wandering back down the hall. "Tell Augustus we're out of sherry and he's to go to Marlowe's without fail. The money's on the refrigerator, if you two haven't already spent it."

"Yes, ma'am," said Kate.

"And don't make so much noise when you get up tomorrow morning. Early hours do not impress me."

"Er—yes, ma'am."

Bailey and Kate leaned over and watched Mrs. Belle push her way through the screened door. Once they were sure she had returned to the porch they smiled at each other, then laughed.

"My God," said Bailey, straightening up, "I can't believe it! You're staying here all summer?"

"Sleeping upstairs, like a member of the family."

"I'm surprised Addy doesn't insist on your sleeping in the cabin." Bailey was referring to a small, ramshackle building on the corner of the Belle lot. The cabin had been there for years, home to many a creekman and his family.

"Can't. Augustus sleeps there."

"Then this must be killing her."

"Well," said Kate, after another sip of beer, "it's not any picnic for me."

"I can't believe you're even here, I mean, back on the island."

"Surprised myself. I thought I'd be in summer school."

"Still plan to graduate early?"

"That's the plan."

"We're going to miss you our senior year."

"I don't think so," said Kate, wiping more perspiration away with her bandana. "From what I've heard the rising seniors are considering your plan about our class taking over the sorority."

"They damned well better if they want to be competitive in anything more than the Walk of Shame." Bailey was referring to the early morning stroll when sorority girls returned to Simms dorm from sleeping over at their boyfriends'. On the stove the radio played "Lipstick Traces."

Bailey glanced out the back door. "I was expecting the president and vice president today, but so far they haven't shown."

"You think they'll come all the way down here?"

"Who could resist a free trip to the beach? Anyway, I'll keep them out of your hair."

"Please do if you're discussing politics. Which reminds me, have you seen Melanie?"

Bailey shook her head.

"She's in a foul mood."

"Which boy is it this time?"

"Daniel."

"Bastard," muttered Bailey before sipping from her beer again. "Christ," she said, examining the bottle. "I can't believe we're drinking in broad daylight."

"Oh," said Kate, with a sly smile, "beer tastes better after dark?"

"And you used to be such a Holy Roller."

"Easily explained. I was corrupted by a bunch of sorority girls." After another swallow, Kate asked, "You expecting any of the boys from the campus to drop by?"

"Sorry, but I still don't like men."

"Until the right one comes along."

"Speaking of the right one, where's Jeb?"

"Should see him this weekend. He's driving up from Beaufort." Kate fingered the ring on the chain around her neck. "What about Preston? You were seeing a lot of him last year."

"ROTC summer camp."

"Gosh. Every boy I know wants to go to Vietnam."

"Damn fools."

"Damn fool Southerners," said Melanie Durant as she strode into the kitchen from the front of the house. "Southerners have too much bloodlust."

"I don't know about that," said Bailey, giving her friend a hug. "Elvis Presley served his hitch and came home a sergeant."

"Elvis served in Germany." Then to Kate, "And Jeb's tempting fate. He might come home in a body bag."

"Body bag?" asked Bailey.

"Plastic bags used to ship the dead home from Vietnam."

Kate shivered. "Do we have to talk about this?"

"Of course not," said Melanie. "I apologize, Kate." Noticing what they were drinking, Melanie asked, "Who brought the beer?"

Kate gestured at the fridge. "Help yourself."

"Fine with me, but you do know Mrs. Belle is out there on the front porch?" Still, that didn't stop Melanie from helping herself to a beer.

After popping the cap with Kate's opener and taking a long swig, she surveyed the disaster that had formerly been the Belles' kitchen. "I just had to come down here and take a look. Ginny's father actually hired you to do this?"

Kate nodded.

"I know other sororities borrow you to fix up stuff, but this . . . this is too much. Do you need help moving anything?"

"Nope. Got two boys of my own."

"Afro-Americans," corrected Ginny Belle as she came through the back door. "Negroes are touchy about what you call them these days."

The girls shrieked and rushed her and hugged her and kissed her and had a zillion questions, especially about her blue jeans, tie-dyed T-shirt, and long straight hair.

"Finally gave up struggling with it, did you?" asked Bailey, smiling.

"Nope," said Ginny, fingering several strands. "This is how the girls in California wear it."

"Surfers?" asked Melanie.

"Not surfers, hippies."

"Hippies?" asked Kate.

"Free thinkers." Ginny held out her arms, turning one way, then the other. "This is their uniform. Everyone wears it." Meaning the tie-dyed shirt, jeans, and sandals. "Except the establishment."

"The establishment?" asked Kate, trying to keep up.

"Those who know better," said Ginny's grandmother from the kitchen doorway. Mrs. Belle's sherry glass was almost empty, and once again she frowned at the music coming from the transistor radio. Chuck Berry singing about the virtues of rock and roll. "I thought I heard Augustus return."

"Nope. Just me!" And Ginny crossed the room and gave her grandmother a big hug.

After returning the hug, Mrs. Belle said, "You're early, my dear. Not that I'm not pleased to see you, but does your father know you've returned from the West Coast?"

Ginny lost her smile. "Not yet."

Mrs. Belle arched an eyebrow. "Problems with the smart set in California?"

"I don't think they're so smart." From a fabric purse Ginny pulled a pack of smokes. Her friends stared, horrified, as Ginny lit up in front of her grandmother.

The cabbie appeared at the screened door holding up a suitcase. "Miss," he said, shading his eyes so he could see inside. "You sure you don't want this?"

"Like I said, throw it in the trash," said Ginny, walking toward him.

"Well, Miss Belle, that's just it. I wondered if you'd mind if I took it along."

Ginny laughed. "I don't think they're your size."

"Actually, I was thinking about my daughter."

"Then give them to her with my best wishes."

"Thank you." And the cabbie peered through the screen, trying to make out the others in the kitchen. "Do you need any more business cards?"

"No, what you gave me will do just fine."

"Well, thank you again, Miss Belle." And he went down the steps and returned to the cab.

"What's in the suitcase?" asked her grandmother.

"Nothing but a lot of bad memories." Ginny took another drag off her cigarette and let the smoke out through her nose.

"Smoking now?" asked Mrs. Belle.

"No, smoking and not hiding it. On that point I'm in total agreement with the hippies."

"And would that agreement also include communal living and group sex?" asked her grandmother with a sly smile.

Ginny reddened, even under her T-shirt. Eyebrows rose and looks were shared by the other girls.

Mrs. Belle chuckled and returned to the front of the house. "Well, let me know when Augustus returns."

"Speaking of Negroes," said Ginny, "what's the story on Alice Frey's daughter?"

Bailey shook her head. "Wilma could be institutionalized for the rest of her life or she could come out of it any day."

206

"Jeez," said Melanie. "Alice Frey ought to sue the state of Alabama."

"I didn't know you could sue the government," said Kate.

"You can't," explained Ginny. "If you could, someone would've already stopped this stupid war in Indochina."

Melanie glanced at Kate. "Let's remember who's in the room, if you don't mind."

"Sorry, Kate," said Ginny, heading for the refrigerator. "Whose beer is this you're drinking?"

"Mine, but I have a reputation for sharing, even with hippies."

"I'm no damn hippie."

Bailey laughed. "That remains to be seen."

"Yeah," said Melanie. "We'd have to see some curl in that hair before we accept you as a normal person."

Ginny stuck the cigarette in her mouth and took out a beer. Once again, Kate furnished the church key.

"Still, I am curious," said Melanie. "You don't think we should be helping the South Vietnamese fight the communists?"

Ginny watched her bottle cap hit the floor. "Actually, I think this country's throwing its weight around where we have no business."

"I don't know, Gin. The communists are gobbling up Europe, and if you let them, they'll take over this hemisphere, too. Look at Cuba."

"Cuba's no threat to this country."

"For God's sake," said Bailey, "think about what you're saying. Those missiles could've reached Charleston."

"Do we have to talk about this?" asked Kate, who was visibly shaking.

Bailey gave Kate a hug and called a truce, one of many she'd had to declare whenever Ginny and Melanie squared off over politics.

Bailey bummed a smoke off Ginny and lit up. "You know, I like this, smoking in public."

"Uh-huh," said Melanie. "I'll wait and see if either of you smoke *or* drink in front of your own family."

"Well, I could," said Ginny. "After all, I'm an adult."

"You aren't an adult until you can pay your own way."

"Oh, Kate," said Bailey, "don't give us that working class crap. You're one of us now and have to look down on all those blue collars."

"All my family wear blue collars."

"And look where that got them."

"I think the point Bailey is making," said Melanie, "and making rather indelicately, is that you want more out of life."

Kate nodded and thought of her father. Though she was stone broke at the moment, she'd make him respect her, one damned dollar at a time. "Who's paying for Wilma's stay in the hospital?"

"We are, of course," said Bailey. "She's still part of the family, whether she's institutionalized or not." After another drag off her smoke, Bailey asked, "Who's this Melvin Ott who's helping you?"

"Augustus found him when I said we'd need another pair of hands. The truck came along in the deal. I buy the gas."

"Actually, I pay for the gas," said Mrs. Belle from

the kitchen door again, "and truth be known, my son found him; Ott, that is."

Everyone looked at her.

"Melvin Ott was sent here to spy on me."

"Nana, please," said Ginny, dropping her cigarette to the floor, stubbing it, and leaving a black smear across the planking. "I don't think the government would send an Afro-American to spy on you."

"Afro-American?"

"There are German-Americans, Italian-Americans, and if the Negroes want to celebrate the fact they're from Africa, what's wrong with that?"

"Why aren't white people called "English-Americans?" asked Melanie. She was totally ignored. The show was between Ginny and her grandmother.

"If you want to celebrate your ancestors coming to this country in chains," said Mrs. Belle, "who am I to object?"

"We're the ones who enslaved them."

"Oh, please, Virginia Lynne, let's not have this conversation. I've never owned slaves."

"But the Belle family has in the past."

"And how is that relevant today?"

"Well," said Ginny, placing her hands on her hips. "I think we owe them something."

"Oh," said Mrs. Belle, laughing, "such as an apology? Sorry, my dear, but those weren't white people selling their own people into slavery but their fellow Africans."

"That doesn't excuse us for enslaving them over here."

Mrs. Belle took a drink from her sherry glass before realizing it was empty. "Well then," she said with a frown, "I don't know what you're going to do. You evidently left California in a huff, and if you don't feel comfortable with your own kind, where does that leave you?"

"I just might join the Peace Corps."

That was too much for her friends and they clustered around her, demanding reassurance that Ginny wasn't going to join the Peace Corps.

"Yes," said Kate with a laugh, "at least not until I finish this kitchen."

Ginny surveyed the damage. "My father told me that he'd hired you, but this looks like it could take forever."

"That's right," said Bailey. "The sooner Gopher's finished, the more time we'll have for lying in the sun, hanging out with boys"—the blonde held up her bottle—"and drinking beer."

"Let's all pitch in," volunteered Melanie.

"Yeah," said Ginny, "why not?"

From the doorway Mrs. Belle moaned. "My lord, what did I do to deserve this?"

On the transistor radio Elvis Presley sang "Don't Be Cruel."

THE SORORITY MEETING

After a short meal and long day at the beach, Ginny, Bailey, and Mel sat down with representatives of the sorority, three blond girls, two of whom were the president and the vice president. The meeting was held in Bailey's living room while the girls' mothers and Ginny's grandmother were having evening cocktails over at the Belles' house. It was also early enough for the blondes to return to Columbia if things didn't work out. After all, they'd had their day in the sun, and what a day it had been! All three girls were burned to a crisp, and none of them would be doing much sleeping tonight, whether at the beach or on the return trip home. Where Kate Youngblood was, no one had any idea, but these days the redhead had a tendency to disappear whenever Lieutenant Jeb Stuart was around, because he was shipping out soon.

Most of the girls in the sorority were blond, beautiful, and tramps, in Bailey's opinion, and Bailey, like most Southern women, did not suffer fools easily. For this reason their visitors had been given little encouragement to apply lotion and now wore as little clothing as possible; their sunburn itched like crazy, and there was nothing more they wanted to do but take another cold shower.

As cigarettes were passed around, the president said, "Bailey, we were pleasantly surprised to have you and the other girls pledge our sorority."

"But," said the vice president, "then we learned you weren't looking for a sorority to take Kate Youngblood, but were looking to take over one." She tsk-tsked. "Poor form."

"Yes," said Bailey, lighting up her smoke, "a regime change usually happens at the end of the fall semester. We're just speeding up the process."

"Yeah," said Ginny from where she sat on the floor next to an ottoman, "about a year and a half."

"Regime change?" asked the blonde who was just along for the ride. "What's that?"

"Actually," said Bailey, "when we return to school there's lots of work to be done."

The sorority president grinned. She could take a joke as well as the next girl. "Well, what's in it for us, the rising seniors?"

"You get to party," said Ginny, shaking out the match she'd used to light her cigarette, "drag down the grade point average for another year, and concentrate on having your rings by spring."

Two of the blondes gave her a dirty look, but the vice president extended her hand and smiled. "I'm already engaged."

"But sophomores running a sorority," said the president. "I don't think that's ever been done before."

"Well, this is your chance to make history."

The rising seniors shot Ginny a dirty look, and the vice president withdrew her hand. She said, "I don't remember the last time a Belle from Charleston ever attended USC; that is, with the exception of the law school."

The president was silent. She hadn't gotten where she was without knowing the score, and that's what she was trying to figure: the score. "Don't y'all realize you'll have to do all the work of the sorority?"

"Has to be done," said Bailey, letting out a breath full of smoke. "We're going to give A D Pi some serious competition."

"But why?" asked the blonde along for the ride. "College is for having fun." She giggled. "And finding a husband."

"I really don't think you could understand," said Bailey.

"Give us a try," said the president, feeling the heat, so to speak.

"Just think of it as our community service project," said Ginny, grinning from her seat on the floor.

"We want to take the sorority in a different direction," said Bailey in a more serious tone.

"To repeat: why bother?" asked the vice president.

"Yes," asked the third blonde. "What's wrong with how things are done now?"

"Hey, listen," said Bailey, leaning forward, cigarette ash dropping to the floor, "what's wrong is that we rank at the bottom of every category, with the exception of sports where we show up somewhere in the middle."

From a chair near the hallway door, Melanie cleared her throat. She rarely attended these meetings. They could turn rather nasty.

"Ah," said the vice president, "the mouse speaks."

"God," said Ginny, shaking her head, "you people make me wish I'd stayed in California."

"I don't think you'd be missed if you went back out there."

"Girls, please," said the president.

Ginny glared at the vice president, and from her chair near the hallway, Melanie said, "You people don't know how to listen, so how could you make a rational decision?"

Mouths fell open, including Ginny's and Bailey's.

"My family didn't send me to Carolina to listen to a bunch of self-centered girls whine, and that's all you're capable of. You need to learn to listen and then form opinions."

"Shut up, mouse," said the vice president. "You never said anything on the hall, so why should we listen to you now?"

"No," said Bailey, jabbing her cigarette at the vice president, "you shut up. Melanie has the floor."

"But you're not the president," said the third blonde. "You can't say who speaks and who doesn't."

"That's right," said the vice president. "We didn't come all the way down here to be lectured to."

"Oh, but you did," said Ginny. "Now shut up and listen."

"Now, girls," said the president, smiling all around and trying to ignore her sunburn, "there's no reason to be rude. Go ahead, Melanie."

Standing, Melanie said, "All three of us made sacrifices to join your crowd, and then we learn what everyone told us was true. You're all dumber than posts." And the thin girl stalked out of the house, across the porch, and disappeared in the darkness of the beachfront.

After watching her go, the president said, "Well, I guess she doesn't mind whose feelings she hurts."

Ginny's laugh turned into a snort and she leaned into the ottoman to cover her face. Once she had composed herself, she looked up at Bailey and said in a startling East European accent, "Well, Boris, I guess it's just . . ."

"Yes, of course, Natasha," replied Bailey in the same funny accent, "moose and squirrel, once again."

All the three blondes could do was stare from the other side of the coffee table, and rub, scrape, or scratch their sunburn.

"You know," said the vice president, touching her sunburn, "I do believe Bailey wants to run for president of the sorority council."

"Oh," said Bailey, "you can count on it."

"But why can't you wait your turn?" asked the third blonde.

"Yeah, it's not like we're a weak class," said the vice president. "Our sorority has always elected leaders from the rising class."

"From members who love to party," said Ginny. "And in this group there are plenty of party animals."

"Look," said the president, sitting up to break her skin's contact with the back of the sofa, "we need to get on with this. My sunburn's pretty bad."

"Yes," said the third blonde, scratching in a very unladylike manner, "I'd even settle for some vinegar."

"That's an old wives' tale," said the vice president.

"No," said Ginny, "it's an old wives' remedy."

"Well," said the vice president, smiling, "it takes one to know one."

Ginny glared at those on the other side of the coffee table, then got to her feet and left the room.

"There are no 'turns,'" said Bailey, watching Ginny go. "We're not our mothers. We plan on doing something with our lives."

The third blonde turned to the president again. "What do they mean 'do something with their lives'?"

"Don't give us that career woman crap . . ." The vice president reddened even more than her burn. "I'm sorry. I didn't mean to be vulgar."

Bailey leaned forward again. "Listen, this is the way it's going to be, and you three are going to sell it to the rest of the girls."

"I don't think you'll make any friends with that tone," said the vice president.

"Yes," said the president, "it's not very conciliatory." She lifted her blouse, breaking its contact with her skin.

"Think what you may, but I have access to the levers of power at Carolina."

"Bailey," said the president, dropping her blouse, "don't brag about your family's political connections. It's unseemly."

Ginny returned to the room with a bottle of white vinegar.

"And I'm going to start using that power," said Bailey, glancing at Ginny. "Now, I invited you down here for a nice little visit, but what I get instead is a bunch of high-handed fools who don't know their time has come and gone."

"Yeah," said Ginny, twisting off the cap, "you want to organize socials, we don't care. Just leave the serious stuff to us."

"Well, thank you, too," said the vice president, eyeing the vinegar bottle.

The third blonde turned to the president again. "What are they talking about? What's more important than organizing socials?"

Bailey fell back in her chair and let out a long sigh. "I don't know why I even try."

Ginny offered the bottle of vinegar to the girl on the end of the couch. The blonde shook her head and held her nose. The president passed, too. The vice president sat up, waved off the bottle, and tried to loosen her blouse. She wanted to go somewhere and strip naked but what good would that do? She'd still itch. God, how was she ever going to get to sleep tonight?

What had she wanted to say? Oh, yes. "What makes you think you can talk to us like this?"

Bailey leaned over and stubbed out her smoke in an ashtray on the coffee table. "That's easy. I'm going to be the new president. You'll be working for me."

The third blonde looked at the others. "She's kidding, right?"

The president knew better than to underestimate anyone who was politically connected. In a way, she, too, had been politically connected or she wouldn't have her job. "I understand why you, Ginny, and Melanie joined, but how does it further your agenda to induct someone like Kate Youngblood?"

"Yeah," said the vice president, touching her sunburn again, "what does she bring to the table, so to speak?"

"That's a perfect example of groupthink from a bunch of stuck-up phonies," said Ginny, putting the top back on the vinegar and placing the bottle on the coffee table. "Kate's the only member with a four point oh. But how would you know? You always pledge a bunch of Playboy bunnies who have trouble keeping their legs together."

"What a tacky thing to say."

"How rude."

"You can't talk like that to us."

"We will," said Bailey, sitting up again, "and you'll take it. I've been to our sponsor and laid out a plan. She'll back me one hundred percent. We're going to stop being the laughing stock of the sorority council. Don't forget, I've been to those meetings—"

"Yes, what were you doing there?" demanded the president.

"Spying on us, that's what," said the vice president.

"I just wanted to learn what the other sororities thought of us, and it didn't take two trips. We've been on academic and social probation the last three years. Three years before that, before someone did some creative work with the numbers, we would've been on probation then."

"How do you know that?" demanded the president, forgetting about her sunburn for the moment.

"Anyway, our advisor realizes it's going to take a lot longer than a year to turn things around, and we need to get started now."

"You think you can induct a better class?" asked the vice president, shaking her hand. Her cigarette had burned to a stub without her ever taking a drag. She found an ashtray, put it out, and shook her fingers, then sucked them. Now they, too, were burned.

"It'll be a snap with you people out of the picture. No more pledging down."

"But you can't do that," said the president. "We've just been elected."

"That vote will be thrown out, and once an emergency vote has been taken, I'll be sworn in as the new president."

The blondes looked at each other. They were in the right, they were in control, but Bailey Gillespie didn't act like she understood any of that.

"You can't do this to us," said more than one of them.

"We're doing it." Bailey turned to Ginny. "Would you get the phone, please?"

"I didn't hear the phone ring," said the third blonde, looking puzzled.

Ginny went into the hall, and with a cord that allowed the phone to be taken into the living room, dining room, or even on the front porch, she handed the instrument to Bailey.

"Yes, operator," said Bailey, "please place that call now."

The operator did, and when the sorority advisor came on the line, she asked, "Okay, which dumb blonde am I talking to?"

ALL YOU NEED IS LOVE

One hot, sunshiny day, when all four girls were lying on the beach, and after Melanie had gone into her house to use the bathroom, Kate sat up, put on her sunglasses, and looked to make sure Mel had actually gone inside.

"What are we going to do about Mel?" she asked.

Lathered with lotion, Ginny, who was practically unconscious from too much sun, turned her head. "What?"

The fair-skinned girl lay facedown on a plain white towel, and the straps from the top of her two-piece lay at her sides so there would be no tan lines. On the radio which leaned against a metal red-and-white Coca-Cola cooler, the Drifters sang "Up on the Roof."

"What about Mel?" asked Bailey. The tanned blonde lay on a blue-striped towel between Kate and Ginny, but instead of using suntan lotion, she used baby oil with iodine. Bailey pulled a leg up, squinted, and pushed a finger into her skin. A white spot appeared where she'd applied pressure. "I hate to say it, Gopher, but you're the one closest to Mel these days."

"I'm not sure I'm the closest . . ."

"Don't deny it, Kate. You stole her away from us."

"What?" asked Ginny, trying to move, trying to think. "Did I fall asleep? This sun is frying me like an egg."

"With your skin, you couldn't get a tan if someone offered you money," said Bailey.

"How much money?"

"Wrong analogy. You *have* money. You couldn't tan if you were promised a date with Tab Hunter."

"Tab Hunter?" Ginny gripped the front of her two-piece and rose up on her arms. "Tab Hunter is coming to Myrtle Beach?"

"No, you ninny, all I was saying—"

"Hey," said Kate, glancing at the Durant beach house, "I don't know how long we have before Melanie comes back."

"Probably that time of month," said Ginny, "and for a small girl, she really gets it heavy." Menstruation was heavy on Ginny's mind, too. She'd missed her period for the second month in a row.

"Nah," said Bailey, "she's expecting a call from Daniel, but he'll never call. He's got her number."

"Well," said Ginny, refastening the strap behind her back and sitting up, "if he's got her number, he'll call."

"I didn't mean that kind of number."

"Then what are we talking about?" asked Ginny, shifting around on her towel and adjusting her ample cleavage.

"Look," said Kate, "we need to do something about the type of boys Melanie dates."

"You mean Daniel?" asked Bailey. She slapped Kate's leg to test for burn. Daniel Caldwell was Melanie's latest flame, and another jerk as far as the girls were concerned. Melanie could really pick them.

"Ouch!" screamed Kate, and she scrambled away, bumping into the cooler. Sunglasses and Coke bottles went flying and she knocked over the radio. "Watch it! I'm burning, too."

"Now that I look back on it," said Bailey, ignoring her friend's distress, "the summer you barged into our lives might've been Melanie's best summer ever."

"Yeah, right," said Ginny, reaching for her sunglasses, "the summer after her mother shot her stepfather."

"No, you jackass, that summer Melanie didn't have a boyfriend. She was too busy fixing up Gopher."

"They're all jerks," said Ginny, putting on her glasses and reaching for the Coppertone. "Even the ones at school."

"How does she do it?" asked Bailey, squinting into the glare off the ocean. Finally, she put on her sunglasses. "Is she some sort of magnet for chumps?"

"Lightning rod would be more accurate."

"There you go again," said Kate as she propped up the radio and readjusted the dial in time for Jerry Butler to sing "He Will Break Your Heart." She put her sunglasses back on.

The other two girls turned and stared at her.

"What?" asked Bailey.

"What?" asked Ginny, opening the bottle of suntan lotion.

"You two have spent so many summers on this island you can't hear an ordinary person speak."

"Kate," said Bailey, "you've made it perfectly clear you don't like us kidding you about your family, but that doesn't mean you can make fun of us"—Bailey straightened her shoulders and puffed out her chest—"the class of Pawleys Island."

"I'm talking about Melanie's boyfriends!"

"Well, so were we."

"Not the way I was." Kate glanced at the house again. "I've been thinking there should be something we can do."

"Like what? Fix her up? That would really tick Daniel off, and if Daniel's mad—"

"Melanie's mad," said Ginny, rubbing lotion into her legs.

"That's what I'm talking about. Mel always ends up with these jerks, and then she comes to me, crying."

"I know what you mean. She used to come to me."

"I wonder why she never came to me?" asked Bailey.

"Yeah, sure," said Ginny, continuing to rub in the lotion, "like you have a sympathetic ear."

"I don't know. I sort of got the idea those guys were Melanie's type."

"Jeez, that's cruel," said Ginny.

"That's just what I mean," said Kate. "What can we do to change Melanie's type?"

"You mean pick her boyfriends?" asked Ginny. "That doesn't seem right."

"I don't know what I mean. I just don't want to see Melanie hurt again."

"But what can we do?"

"How about putting some of that on me." Bailey

scooted around on her towel, turning her back to Ginny and loosening the strap on her bikini. "That sounds like work for a head doctor."

"Shrink," offered Ginny, squirting lotion on Bailey's back.

The blonde shivered. "That's cold."

"What do you mean cold? It's been out in the sun all day."

"I don't care. It's still cold."

"And head doctors are called shrinks."

"Sheesh. I wouldn't want to go see anyone called a shrink. What do they do, shrink your mind?"

"Shrink your troubles away," said Ginny, rubbing the lotion in with both hands.

"Melanie's mom sees a shrink," said Kate, "so that shouldn't be that far off base. I mean, if we're going to suggest something."

"What do they do?" asked Bailey, leaning into her knees.

"Melanie says her mom and the doctor just sit and talk. When the hour's up, he rushes you out the door so he can 'shrink' his next patient."

"But talking, I don't know about that," said Ginny. "That's what friends are for."

"But what if your friend has the same problem?" asked Kate.

"None of my friends have the same problems," said Ginny, continuing to rub the lotion in on Bailey's back. "Each one of you is screwed up in your own special way."

Bailey said nothing. She was too busy mocking Ginny, leaning forward, head over her knees, letting her tongue hang out, and gasping.

"That's what my mother does in coffeehouses," said Ginny.

"Coffeehouses?" asked Bailey, raising up and looking over her shoulder. "What's that?"

"A place where you buy coffee, talk, and listen to music."

Bailey laughed. "Like those holes-in-the-wall in Five Points where the hippies sit around and drink—"

"Kool-Aid," said Ginny. "Most of them are too young to drink. My mother drinks coffee, and she sits around and talks."

"Talks about what?"

"About the war, integration, nuclear proliferation, but mostly they bitch about how their men treat them."

"And run right back to the jerks," said Bailey, laughing. "All those women are kooks."

"Kookie, Kookie, lend me your comb," sang Ginny. She slapped Bailey on the back as a signal she was finished.

Bailey yelped, straightened up, and almost lost her top. As she fitted it back, the Fontane Sisters began to sing "Seventeen."

"God," muttered Ginny, "I remember those days."

"What days?" asked Bailey, retying the strap.

"When we were all young and innocent."

"It's not possible for you to have been innocent, not where you come from. Everyone knows Charleston is the Sodom and Gomorrah of South Carolina."

"I'm sorry, darling," said Ginny in a rather affected voice and lifting her head, "but Charleston has more churches than any other city in the state. That's why we're called the Holy City."

Steve Brown

"Guys, please," said Kate, "I'm trying to make a point here."

"Guys?" asked Bailey, turning on her. "You've been hanging around too many Jersey boys who come down here for their education."

"What point are you trying to make?" asked Ginny.

"Melanie's choice in men. I'm not saying Melanie needs to see a doctor, I was just thinking there should be something *we* could do to help."

"Oh," said Bailey, smiling, "you want to fix her up, like you did our kitchens?"

"I am not a perfectionist!"

"Well," said Bailey, leaning back, "that certainly struck a nerve."

"Bailey's right, Kate. You're the only rising sophomore with a four point oh. I don't know anyone who studies like you do."

"And I know why," said Bailey, chuckling. "Her boyfriend left her for the queen, the Queen of Battle."

"Queen of Battle?" asked Ginny.

"Military jargon for the infantry," explained Bailey.

Ginny nodded as if she understood or cared. "You know, my father will kill me if I don't get my teaching certificate. He doesn't want to see me end up like my mother, and if I didn't know better, I'd think my mother was trying to sabotage my education so I'd be more like her."

"Your mother needs a shrink," said Kate, wrapping her arms around her legs, placing her chin on her knees, and looking out to sea.

"She definitely needs to stay out of coffeehouses," said Bailey, straightening up. "But my course is set, I'm

225

double majoring in poli-sci and history, and along the way, making the right connections. Ginny, your father thinks all the right people attend the Citadel and the College of Charleston, but he's wrong. The movers and shakers go to Carolina and always have."

"And the farmers go to Clemson," said Ginny with a laugh.

"Are you two ever going to listen to me?"

"I'm sorry," said Bailey, "but I don't see what we can do about Melanie's choice of beaux."

"People fall in love with the strangest people," said Ginny, thinking of her father's predicament. She looked off in the distance and saw a couple of shrimp boats, nets spread wide like a pair of extended wings.

Kate shook her head wearily.

"Okay, kiddo, what's your plan?" asked Bailey. Gopher might be the child of lintheads, but she sure came up with some damned good ideas, not that anyone in the sorority would ever give her credit. And she'd lost her accent. Now how had she done that? Bailey suspected it had something to do with watching old black-and-white movies while everyone else was at the ballgames on Saturday afternoons.

Kate glanced over her shoulder and saw Melanie coming down the steps from the Durant beach house. "Well, since the two of you have wasted this opportunity, we'd just better think about it. But I'm telling you Mel deserves better."

Ginny glanced over her shoulder. "Maybe it's all that money. Maybe the good ones are scared off by money."

Bailey looked, too. "From what my mother says,

Melanie's father and stepfather were both jerks. Maybe Melanie inherited her taste in men from her mother."

"Your mother is a gossipmonger," said Ginny.

"Well, your grandmother wears combat boots."

"Oh, God," moaned Kate, "it's not Pawleys Island, it's genetic. You really can't hear me."

"Melanie really loved her dad," said Ginny.

"She didn't know the man." To Kate, Bailey said, "Okay, let me think about it and I'll come up with a plan."

"Pardon me, but have you heard a word I've said?"

"Of course. I was just engaging in some dual-track thinking."

"Dual-track?" asked Ginny.

"What are you talking about?" asked Melanie, rejoining the group, and smiling, albeit nervously. She always imagined the girls were talking behind her back.

"Can't tell you," said Ginny, snickering.

Kate only looked out to sea.

"Sure, we can," said Bailey, smiling. "We were discussing your Christmas gift. How do you feel about eight-tracks?"

VISITORS FROM THE SEA

One evening, when all four girls and three young men were socializing at the Durant beach house, several bricks came flying through the side windows of both the living room and dining room.

Bailey was slow dancing with Preston Winthrop to "Smoke Gets in Your Eyes," Melanie was taking another tongue-lashing from Daniel, and Ginny was sitting on the sofa listening to some nonsense from the latest bronze god to have graced their presence. Kate Youngblood sat in a corner, a pensive look on her face. Her Marine was being sent overseas, and tonight, Jeb was with his family in Charleston. He might not see her again before shipping out for South Vietnam.

Occasionally, Melanie's mother came downstairs and checked to see that the lights were still on and that everyone had both feet on the floor. When she did, Daniel stopped berating Melanie, the motor-mouth bronze god shut up, and Bailey backed off from heating up Preston Winthrop.

When the bricks shattered the glass in the side windows of the living room and the dining room, all four girls screamed. Ginny was so startled that she froze, but the incident seemed to mobilize Bailey into action. She wrestled her way out of Preston's arms and ran for the front porch. She was trailed out the door by the boys as she flung back the screened door and rushed down the steps and onto the beach.

"What was that?" asked Preston.

"It's happened before," said Bailey, "and this time I'm going to catch the bastards."

"What are you talking about?" Preston paused at the bottom of the steps and looked up and down the beach. "Who?"

But anyone they could see wasn't running up or down the beach but swimming for a flickering light out to sea. Joining Bailey at the surf, Preston saw the water being chewed up by several pairs of arms and legs.

"What do we do now?" he asked.

Back at the house, Kate, pale and shaken, paused at

the top of the porch stairs. "What's—what's going on?"

From behind her, Ginny said, "Don't go out there, Kate."

Kate turned around, and as she did, saw a figure out of the corner of her eye. No. Make that two figures.

"There they are!" And she pointed at the figures rounding the side of the house.

Preston, Bailey, and the other two boys left the shallows and raced back to the porch.

"Only caught one," said one of the figures approaching the porch, "but one's good enough." And he shoved the other figure to the sand in front of the steps.

Kate peered into the darkness. It couldn't be who she thought it was. "Jeb?"

"James."

Bailey, Preston, and the other two young men stopped and caught their breath. James Stuart stood over a young man kneeling in the sand.

"What are you doing here?" asked Kate, coming down the steps.

"Happened to be passing by. Sorry, I didn't get here in time." He looked at the porch. "I suppose the screening is the reason they threw the rocks through the side windows instead of the front."

"Bricks," said Ginny. She held a brick in one hand and clutched the screened door with the other.

Preston took the young man by the ear, and the intruder came shrieking to his feet. He wore dark clothing, had a flattop, sunburned features, and square shoulders.

"Tell me who you are, and what the hell you think you were doing."

From the door of the screened-in porch, Melanie said, "He's my cousin."

Everyone looked up at the brown-haired girl.

"My uncle had two wives. The first one he divorced and my cousins never got over it."

"Shut up, Mel!" said the young man below her in the sand.

Preston kicked Mel's cousin behind the legs, and the young man went to his knees again. "You, my boy, are S.O.L."

"Their side of the family was cut out of the will. They do this every year, but we can never catch them."

"I didn't do nothing," muttered the young man.

Melanie's mother appeared on the porch. "I've called the sheriff."

Melanie faced her. "Are you sure we should do that?"

"Yes, dear, I'm afraid we should."

"Do—do I have to talk to the sheriff?"

"Not if you don't want to, dear." Mrs. Hamby looked at the others. "I'm sure there're more than enough people who can tell the sheriff what happened."

Preston shook James's hand. "Good work, cadet."

"It was nothing. Anyone could've done it."

"Yes," said Kate, eyeing the person who might become her future brother-in-law, "if they just happened to be passing by."

FEMALE PROBLEMS

"Arlie, this is Bailey."

"Your father's on the floor of the Senate," said the

chief of staff, "but I can have him call you when he returns to the office."

"I don't want to talk to him. I don't even want him to know I called."

"What is it?"

"I need the name of a good doctor for a rather delicate female operation."

"Bailey, if this is for you, I'm going to have to tell your father about this conversation."

"Arlie, you're a little too bright to be making enemies of the Gillespie family."

"That sounded like a threat, Bailey."

"No, it sounded like my father."

Silence on the Washington end of the line, and then Arlie asked, "What can I do for you, Bailey?"

"Is the door to your office closed?"

"It usually is."

"And no one can listen in?"

"If they do, they'll be out of a job, and nobody in this town wants to be let go by a United States senator. They'd never work in this town again."

"Good. What's the name of the doctor?"

"People usually cross state lines to have this procedure done."

"I can do that. We're still at Pawleys."

"And I ask you again, Bailey, is this operation for you? Because if it is, and I don't report it to the boss, it won't matter how angry you become. This could be my job."

"It's not for me, I can promise you that."

"Then I'll give you the same warning you gave me: you're a little too bright to be lying to someone who

231

could help you become governor someday."

Bailey chuckled. "I knew I'd called the right man."

And Arlie gave her the name of a doctor in a small town outside Savannah.

"This isn't some back-alley abortionist you're sending us to, is it?" asked Bailey.

"Don't believe all the stories you hear. The figures for abortions are highly inflated to soften up the American public to accept legalized abortion."

"Well, I'm not sure abortion shouldn't be legalized and get it out of these back alleys."

"You're not listening. Most abortions are done by trained and licensed physicians, like the one I'm sending you to."

"I've just been elected president of my sorority, Arlie, and I'm going to pledge girls who want to do more with their lives than be wives and mothers. I'll have a small army across the state when I make my first run for public office."

"I wondered how you'd get started."

"I'm starting, believe me, I'm starting."

"And as a woman running for public office, in a state with zero women in public office, it might be time to start doing your homework about issues such as abortion. You may have some minds to change, and the first one may be your own."

"Well, then, send me the material and I'll study it before going back to school."

"I'll send it to Melanie Durant's. Mrs. Durant doesn't have the reputation for being as nosey as some of the other women who summer on Pawleys."

"Thank you, Arlie."

"And you'd better make damn sure no one, especially your parents, sees you reading this stuff. If I was quick to jump to conclusions, your mother and father will make that same leap in record time."

THE RABBIT'S TALE

Simms Belle knocked on his daughter's bedroom door. When she didn't answer, he knocked again.

"Go away, Nana."

"It's not Nana."

"Daddy?"

Simms cracked the door. Seeing that his daughter was decent, he stepped inside, closing the door behind him. He'd seen the twins peering through a crack in their own door, frightened to the point of distraction. Raising teenagers was turning out to be quite a challenge, and Simms couldn't expect his mother to do everything.

When he was growing up nobody called you a teenager. You were either a child or you were an adult. But today there appeared to be a whole industry for teens, one intent on exploiting them and, at the same time, separating them from their parents. You always had the different clothing, but now there were the movies, TV, and music that played constantly. And for the first time music could go anywhere, not just be listened to at home or in your car. It was as if the children of his daughter's generation had been granted possession of an invisible barrier, and a rather loud one.

He'd have to speak to Carolynn Hamby before leaving Pawleys. Carolynn seemed to have her head screwed on better than most. Irene Gillespie was useless. When

Simms called children "kids," Irene would correct him, saying "kids" were baby goats, and Irene had been teaching Bailey since she could talk that her daughter had a vagina, not a "pee-pee."

Simms looked around his daughter's room. He could smell the cigarettes, but there were no empty liquor bottles underfoot; that left his daughter's love life, and it was at these times that Simms really missed his wife.

"Mind if I sit down?" he asked.

Gone were the posters of movie heartthrobs. Those had given way to ones of folk singer Joan Baez; former folk singer Bob Dylan, who had recently plugged in, much to the dismay of his fans; and some damned-fool Negro giving the black power salute.

"I'm sorry," said his daughter, scooting over and making room on the bed. She drew her legs under her and leaned into a stack of pillows. Previously, that stack had been made up of stuffed animals, but the animals had been replaced by throw pillows.

"Nana says you've been locked in here the last three days, that you haven't eaten, and she doesn't think you've bathed."

"I'm fine, Daddy."

"I'm sure you are, but I just wanted to check."

Ginny glanced out the window and saw that the sun was setting. "Nana called you up here for this?"

"Well, she was worried."

"She just wants me to babysit."

"That may be true, but your grandmother still worries about you." Her father smiled. "We all worry about you, Virginia Lynne. You're a teenager." Even the word sounded funny on his tongue.

She smiled, and Simms took this moment to evaluate his daughter. Virginia Lynne was a grown woman, and it wasn't just that she stuck out in all the right places. She had a different attitude, and Simms wondered how much all those trips to California had contributed to her new attitude.

"Come on, pumpkin, tell me what's on your mind."

Ginny stared at him for the longest, and then threw her arms around him, clutching him, and sobbing into his shoulder. "Oh, Daddy, it's so horrible."

Simms put his arms around his daughter. "It's something . . ." He cleared his throat. "It's something you weren't comfortable discussing with Nana?" And suddenly Simms wished he was anywhere but here. His office in Charleston would be nice, maybe even the far side of the moon.

Ginny backed off, wiping her tears away, and in that moment she remembered Bailey had warned her not to say anything about their trip to Georgia or what Melanie Durant's unlimited resources had purchased. Kate had not made the trip. They assumed she was with Jeb. God knows what they were up to, and with Jeb about to go overseas, the two of them were so hot and heavy, you might come upon them anywhere. When Bailey saw them in the clutch once again, she'd say, "For God's sake, get a room!"

"But you can't tell your father about the operation," warned Bailey. No one was comfortable with the actual word.

Melanie nodded in agreement. She revered her dead father and wished things had worked out between her mother and her stepfather. They just couldn't let Ginny lose her father, as everyone else had.

"But I've never lied to my father."

"Don't give us that," said Bailey. "Everyone lies to their parents. Even your parents lied to their own parents."

Ginny shook her head. "Not since my mother left us. I've always told him the truth."

"Then tell him another truth," suggested Melanie.

The other two girls looked at her.

"There's always something else you can tell him."

"That's right," said Bailey, eagerly. "Like the time my mother suggested I'd been sleepwalking when I was caught in those people's houses. I jumped on that faster than a duck on a June bug."

"Come on, Gin, haven't you done something else you could confess to?" asked Melanie.

And Ginny had sat there and wondered what could equal having an abortion. Or justify being locked away in her room for the last three days.

Downstairs, Simms reported their conversation to his mother. "Virginia Lynne says her mother's been encouraging her to call her by her first name, demanding that she smoke dope, and coaxing her to give up any inhibitions she might have about sex. She says she loves her mother, but she's conflicted. Each trip to the West Coast makes her that more anxious."

"Then why did she wait all summer to settle into this funk?" asked Adelaide Belle.

"I asked her that. She said her friends couldn't help her, which I'm pleased to hear, and that she couldn't ask your advice because you've taken sides against her mother."

Steve Brown

"Well, she's right about that." After a sip of her sherry, his mother said, "You're a fool, Simms Belle. You were a fool over that girl's mother, and now you're being a fool over your own daughter. Any woman can see what the problem is."

"Yes, ma'am, but I wouldn't be any woman, would I?"

"No, I don't suppose you would. The truth is Virginia Lynn's pregnant."

"Mother, please be serious."

"Simms, now listen to me. Girls don't remain this upset over a broken heart, not when there are so many potential beaux around, and believe me, son, there have been plenty of boys around your daughter this summer."

Simms glanced at the stairs. "Are you sure about this?"

"Absolutely."

He got to his feet. "Then have Adrian Reynolds check her out. Adrian and I were at the Citadel together."

The doctor stuck his head in the examination room where Ginny was dressing. "You okay, Virginia Lynne?"

"Yes, I am, Doctor Reynolds." Ginny turned away to finish buttoning up her blouse. "What . . . what are you going to tell my grandmother?"

"Very little, since your father called—"

"My father called . . ."

"Your father considers you a minor, and you his ward. I'm not to tell your grandmother anything."

"Nothing about . . . anything?" A flush crept up the

sides of her throat and Ginny turned away. The man was a doctor, but it was still embarrassing to talk to him. Why weren't there any women doctors?

"I'm to tell Mrs. Belle nothing more than, as your father put it, whether the rabbit died or not. All the rabbits die, Virginia Lynne; otherwise we wouldn't know whether a woman was pregnant or not."

Ginny's concerns weren't for any damn rabbit. "So you're going to tell my grandmother . . . what?"

"Nothing more than you aren't pregnant."

"And my father?"

"Why, Virginia Lynne, if I know your father, he'll never ask."

The fourth summer

Home Again, Home Again

"**M**y goodness," said Bailey Gillespie, coming through the back door of the Belle beach house. "It's true. You are here again." And she chuckled at the sight of Kate Youngblood brewing a pot of tea on the new electric stove the redhead had installed only last summer. Plastered on the side of the stove was a gold sticker that read: Live Better Electrically.

The two young women embraced and evaluated each other. Bailey wore walking shorts and a sleeveless blouse and she already had her summer tan. Once again, Kate wore jeans and a man's business shirt tied at the waist, but this summer a new pair of Keds.

"Mister Belle called again," said Kate, returning to the stove. "Right after Ginny told him I'd been kicked out of the sorority."

Bailey followed Kate and put a hand on her friend's shoulder. "I'm sorry about that. I really am."

Kate gave her friend a wan smile. "When you took over the sorority, I guess you never thought one of your first official acts would be kicking me out."

241

Bailey gave her a hug. "You've got that right."

"Still, I did recruit a good number of prospects for the incoming class."

"I still can't believe you went to all those high schools. Where'd you find the time?"

"No love life," said Kate with another weak smile, "and being out of the sorority, no social commitments."

"But how did you know who to contact?"

"Melanie said to search out the status seekers."

"What?"

"The name of a book by Vance Packard. She said all I had to do was ask the girls in sororities who the movers and shakers were at their high schools, and those teachers would know the right candidates. So I charged into those schools and told the teachers I represented *all* the sororities at Carolina, and it turned out Melanie was right. Those teachers told their students to look us up, that we'd make sure every girl learned everything they needed to know about rush."

"And you're out on your ass." Bailey shook her head. "I'm sorry, Kate, but the letter about your marriage wasn't sent to me. That letter was received by the sorority council, so there wasn't anything I could do about it. But if I ever find out who sent it, their daughters will never see the inside of a sorority house at Carolina."

Kate was silent.

"So what do I call you now? Mrs. Stuart? Or do you hyphenate your name?"

"Youngblood-Stuart, now that would be a mouthful."

"Ginny told me you were keeping your own name."

"Ginny's a fool." Kate blushed. "I'm sorry. I shouldn't have said that."

"But I agree. She *has* become a fool, and the only hippie in the whole sorority system."

"Sometimes I wonder why she doesn't just drop out."

"I don't think her father would finance her education if she left Carolina. Most of what Mister Belle seems to do"—Bailey gestured at the tea on the stove—"such as hiring you to work for the Belles, appears to be an attempt to keep balance in Ginny's life. I don't think Ginny's leaving Carolina would fit into Mister Belle's equation.

"Look, Kate, we miss you on the floor, and I'm sure you had to scramble for a place to stay once you left, but I can tell you that no one has the ideas you brought to the table." Bailey smiled. "Actually, if I could get you to read more about politics, I think you'd be useful when I run for governor."

Kate stared out the window overlooking the parking lot. "I never did belong there or here at Pawleys either."

"Kate, what a terrible thing to say. You're the only one with a four-point average, though we do have some very promising freshmen. I'm sure any college would've been proud to have you."

Kate's eyes stung, and for a moment she thought she might cry. "That's very sweet, Bailey." She returned to the pot as it began to whistle. "I need to take this to Mrs. Belle."

"How is she?" Bailey glanced down the hallway. "Ginny tells me next to nothing, and we're roommates. She's always running off at the mouth about how much she hates LBJ, and I find as many excuses as possible to stay away from our room. I don't know if you've heard the latest, but Ginny's decided it's men who're the problem."

"Well," said Kate with a laugh, "that has to play hell with your love life."

Bailey glanced down the hallway again. "How's Addy? Actually, that's why I came over. I wanted to say hello."

Kate took a serving tray from one of the new cabinets and placed a cup and saucer on it. "About the same. They send an LPN over three days a week to work with her."

"Work with her? You mean like exercise?"

Kate nodded.

"But aren't they scared they'll give her another stroke?"

"Mrs. Belle says she won't live as an invalid, and to tell you the truth, the woman acts like she'll recover." Kate took the pot from the stove and poured the boiling water into the cup. Next, she added a tea bag, draping the string over the lip of the cup.

"How long did Mister Belle hire you for?"

"As long as I could stand it, which kind of surprised me. I've never thought of Mister Belle as being a particularly mean person."

"You've never been subjected to his mother."

"I am now."

"So how long do you think *you* can stand it?"

"Until Jeb comes home. Then I'm off. I should be able to finish my teaching degree wherever they station him, unless it's overseas. Marine wives can't travel overseas."

"You can earn a degree even if you're not at school?"

Kate picked up the tray. "The University of Maryland offers degrees for what they call nontraditional students. I can even get my master's."

"I hate that this happened."

"Well," said Kate with a weak smile, "we all had to grow up sooner or later. You can't spend your life on Pawleys Island."

Bailey followed Kate down the hall. "Tell me what to expect."

"Left side of her body is numb and her speech is slurred." Kate glanced over her shoulder and asked, "Will Ginny be stopping by?"

"I have no idea. Like I said, we're hardly speaking. Ginny seems to have figured out a way to rebel against both her parents. She's gone hippie to irritate her father but won't move to San Francisco to satisfy her mom. Lately she's become enamored of Senator Eugene McCarthy."

Slowing down as she approached the front door, Kate said, "You heard Mister Belle finally divorced Ginny's mother?"

Bailey gripped her friend's arm, stopping her. "You're kidding. Does this mean what I think it means?"

"I hope so. If something doesn't click between Melanie's mom and a guy like Mister Belle, Mrs. Hamby will end up letting her ex-husband move back in."

"Her ex-husband has his hooks in that deep?"

"Well, when Melanie's at school, her mom is all alone on that big old estate. And Melanie says her stepfather is being awfully solicitous of her mom."

"Jeez, the things women will put up with to have a warm body in bed with them at night."

"Or not," said Kate, smiling.

"And how is Jeb?"

"Did I tell you we met in Hawaii?" said Kate, lowering her voice again. "It's what they call R&R. Rest and relaxation."

"And was it?" asked Bailey, her eyes widening.

"Too much sex to be relaxing."

"Oh," said Bailey, squeezing her arm again, "tell me all about it. I've heard it's beautiful."

"Didn't see much of the island. Tourism isn't what soldiers just back from combat duty are interested in."

Laughing, the two young women walked onto the front porch where Adelaide Belle sat in a wicker chair, legs propped up on a wicker ottoman.

Bailey could immediately see the difference. Addy's left eyelid drooped and she appeared to be thinner, though Adelaide Belle had always been on the thin side. And there was no sherry glass or cigarette at hand. Sitting across from Mrs. Belle was Melanie's mom.

"Oh, Mrs. Hamby," said Kate. "I didn't know you were here. I can fix a cup of tea for you, too. The water's still hot."

Mrs. Hamby still had her movie star looks and a new tan. "No need. Just popped down to see Addy."

Adelaide said something no one understood; that is, until Kate put the tray on the wicker table, bent down, and had Mrs. Belle repeat what she'd just said.

"No, no," said Kate, straightening up. "I don't think so."

Melanie's mom looked at Kate, puzzled.

"What did she say?" asked Bailey.

246

"She said to give the tea to Mrs. Hamby and to pour some sherry for her."

The three women laughed.

"Well, at least she still has her sense of humor," said Carolynn.

Mrs. Belle said something else, and Kate translated for the others. "No sense of humor, just trying to maintain her vices."

MAKE LOVE, NOT WAR

Late one night, after Mrs. Belle had been put to bed, the girls sat up talking on the porch, enjoying a light breeze off the ocean. "Might as well. Can't dance," Bailey had said, referring to the fact that the pavilion had burned down once again. Lightning lit up the sky far out at sea, the tide rolled in, and most of the lights had been extinguished up and down the shoreline as people turned in for the night.

Ginny, Kate, and Melanie sat in rockers, Bailey lay in the hammock, and the radio was tuned to the Big Ape, WAPE, out of Jacksonville, currently playing "Good Vibrations" by the Beach Boys. All four girls had had too much beer and their tongues became loose, exposing a growing bone of contention, one that had lain dormant or been intentionally ignored. But Ginny had pushed and shoved at them for as long as the other three could take it. Or were willing to ignore it.

"Oh, Ginny, admit it," said Bailey, from the hammock. "You've become radicalized." On the ceiling overhead she could read: Kilroy slept here!

Ginny took a drag off her cigarette as she regarded

girls she considered to be some of her dearest friends: Kate, once again trying to remain above the fray; Melanie, well-read and always a threat; and Bailey, leading the attack.

So Ginny seized the moral high ground. "Someone has to oppose this war. They're bombing civilians."

"Sure this isn't your mother we're hearing?" asked Melanie, finishing off her beer. "I get so annoyed by disciples."

"Don't be such a smart-ass, Mel. This war in Vietnam is evil and immoral, and it's doomed to failure."

"Come on," said Bailey, pulling a string and making the hammock swing, "don't you think we're smarter than a bunch of Frenchmen?"

"Why shouldn't we support our troops?" asked Kate. Being responsible for Mrs. Belle, Kate had stopped drinking earlier than the others.

"You're making this personal, Kate."

"For me, this war is personal. I have a husband over there."

"Come on, Ginny," asked Bailey. "You really think you can accomplish anything? There were only twenty thousand protesters who marched on Washington. That's not a lot of people."

"It's just the beginning. We're going to stop this war."

"Well, I wish you luck."

"We won't need luck. LBJ's poll numbers aren't good enough for renomination."

"Wait a minute," said Kate, sitting up. "You're talking about removing a sitting president during wartime. Is that any way to support our boys?"

Steve Brown

From the rope hammock, Bailey asked, "Has that ever been done before?"

"Actually, no," said Melanie. In her lap lay a copy of *Catch 22*. "I think their chances are somewhere between slim and none."

"And Slim just left town," said Bailey with a laugh. On the transistor radio, Aretha Franklin demanded respect.

"LBJ had his chance, and we supported him against Goldwater to protect LBJ's welfare initiatives. He took us for granted, and now he'll pay."

"And who makes these decisions," asked Kate, "about what the government is supposed to do or not do to protect its citizens?"

"Why, the people, of course."

From the hammock, Bailey said, "Looks like a bunch of cowards scared of supporting their country."

"Yeah," said Melanie, "I don't think I'd take your word for anything. You're a woman and can't be drafted; neither can a lot of the antiwar leaders. They're over thirty-five."

"Women should be drafted," said Ginny, elevating her chin. "No one should be exempt." She finished off her beer and put the empty on the railing next to her.

Bailey sighed. "We didn't have this problem when it was just a bunch of colored boys being sent overseas. It wasn't till the college boys began to be drafted that all these sit-ins and protests started."

"Right," said Melanie, putting her empty on the porch deck. This caused her to remember she had *Catch 22* in her lap. She closed the book and placed it on the floor next to the beer. "That's what's wrong with these hippies: no sense of sacrifice. Look what our parents did against the Nazis. Your father was part of that."

"Hey, I have friends who've been knocked over the head by the pigs."

"Are you calling public servants 'pigs'?" asked Kate, taken aback.

Ginny nodded, took another drag off her cigarette, and tapped the ash onto the floor.

This did not go unnoticed by Kate. She was responsible for how the house looked, and Adelaide Belle could still look.

"Ginny," said Melanie, "I don't believe you've thought this through." And that's not the only thing, thought Melanie. Her friend no longer wore a bra, when she could get away with it. Melanie's mom had told her, not only was it unladylike, but Ginny would regret not wearing a brassiere later when her bosoms began to sag. On the radio The Doors asked for someone to light their fire.

"It's the same old story," said Bailey, pulling on the string and making the hammock swing again. "She's been listening to her mother."

"What is it, Gin? Having to make common cause with your mom? I'll concede the point on civil rights for Negroes; it was well overdue, and Johnson should receive kudos for that legislation." Melanie glanced at Bailey. "And we stood by you when your mother led you down the primrose path about premarital sex. What if she's leading you down the wrong road in regard to this war?"

Ginny shot a look at Kate.

Kate saw the look. "What? What did I miss?"

"Oh, it's nothing," said Bailey. "Last summer when you were spending every single minute with Jeb, Ginny started whining about her mother again."

"Yeah," said Melanie, "Ginny's mom believes girls can go all the way with any number of boys."

Ginny said nothing. Was this an attempt by Melanie and Bailey to blackmail her into supporting an immoral war?

"I think that's called gangbanging," said Bailey with a laugh.

"This is not my mother's idea." Ginny took a final drag off her cigarette, dropped it to the floor, and ground it out with the heel of her sandal.

"Hey," said Kate, "watch what you're doing."

"Hey, yourself. This is my house."

Kate looked past the railing and watched the lightning rip the night apart. On nights like this Kate wished she'd spent the day in the creek with a net or clam rake. That would make it much easier to suffer Ginny's idiocy, and her new friends who dropped by and made a mess of the whole house.

"The boys being drafted don't have a choice," said Ginny. "They're shipped overseas like cattle to the slaughter."

"And," asked Melanie, "if we quit this war, what happens to the South Vietnamese people?"

"The South Vietnam government is corrupt."

"How do you know that?"

"They've sold out to *us!*"

"So it all comes back to the United States," said Melanie. "We're rotten to the core, is that it?"

"I didn't say that."

"That sounds very much like what you're saying."

Being drawn back into the conversation against her will, Kate asked, "You want to abandon those people to the communists?"

"Kate, you don't understand. It's the people of South Vietnam who want their country back, and they're fighting for it. Fighting us."

"And," said Melanie, "if we turn our back on them the communists will take over Cambodia, Thailand, Laos, and finally the West Coast."

Bailey laughed. "That should please her mother, the communists taking over San Francisco."

"Sounds like they already have."

"I didn't say that."

"I'm not sure if you understand what you're saying."

Ginny got to her feet. "And I'm not sure we can still be friends."

"Well," said Bailey, glancing at Kate, "that's going to make it tough on Gopher. She has a job in your house."

"She doesn't have to stay. I can take care of my grandmother."

Kate refused to look at Ginny. Her thoughts were with her husband, overseas and in danger, and this stupid girl didn't give a damn whether he lived or died.

"This house belongs to my family," said Ginny, swaying back and forth from the effects of the beer. "If I wanted to, I could kick you all out."

Now Kate looked up at her. "I'm sorry to break this to you, Ginny, but the terms of my employment exclude you from making decisions about your grandmother.

If there were a medical emergency, I would make all those decisions."

Turning to look at Kate caused Ginny to lose her balance. She grabbed the railing to steady herself and her empty beer can tumbled off and into the sand. "That's ridiculous."

"Talk to your father. He's the one who made the rules."

"This is silly. I have a say in Nana's well-being."

"Maybe your father doesn't think so," said Bailey. "Not until you make sense again."

Ginny gripped the railing tighter. "My opposition to the war has nothing to do with caring for my grandmother."

"Maybe your dad doesn't think you'll be around," offered Melanie.

Kate said nothing. She'd made her point, and she had a legal document to back her up. Simms Belle had drafted it. With health care as primitive as it was in this part of Georgetown County, it wasn't smart to mess around with your mother's life. It was also why a telephone had been installed in the downstairs hallway.

"I think what it is," said Melanie, smiling, "is Ginny wants to sleep with a bunch of guys and this antiwar movement takes her reputation off the hook."

"Yes," said Bailey, laughing, "that makes sense. That way we won't think of her as a hooker, but an idealist who drops her drawers for those in the service of creating a more moral America."

"And I think you two are being perfectly horrible," said Ginny. "Maybe I should leave Pawleys."

Kate looked up again. "Don't be so hasty. These two girls are your dearest friends and only have your best interests at heart. I'm the newcomer and have no say in the matter, but you three have known each other since you were in diapers, and some dumb war shouldn't come between you."

"You think the war is dumb?" asked Ginny, skeptically.

"I think all wars are dumb."

"I agree," said Melanie.

They looked at Bailey, who lay in the hammock, staring at them. She said, "My father made his reputation as a war hero. That's why he was elected governor and senator."

"And the war?" asked Ginny, hopefully.

Bailey swung her legs over the side of the hammock and sat up. "I, too, think all wars are dumb."

THE MARINES LAND

The phone rang as Kate and Augustus were closing up the house. It was Franklin Belle, Adelaide's brother, and senior member of the Belle law firm. Kate carried the phone, and its cord, into the living room and turned away from Augustus, who was running a vacuum over the runner in the hallway.

"Yes, Mister Belle."

"Miss Youngblood, could you come into the city tomorrow?" The city meant Charleston to those living along the coast.

"Yes, sir."

It wasn't all that odd for Kate to be summoned to

Charleston. She'd gotten used to it. Sometimes she got the idea that Adelaide Belle's relatives would rather deal with the old lady at a distance. Now they wouldn't have to deal with her at all.

"Since Ginny's left," said Kate, looking around, "I don't think there's much else for Augustus and me to do. We'll have the house closed up by tomorrow."

"Very well, and have Augustus drive you into town."

"I have my own car, sir."

"Very well."

Franklin Belle gave Kate the address of the Belle law firm as if she'd never been there. Evidently the old codger didn't remember when he'd stuck his head through the adjoining door of his nephew's office the day she'd been hired. And suddenly Kate flashed back to the day on the front porch when she'd been given her first lesson. She could hear Mrs. Belle say, "The 'old' in 'old codger' would be redundant, my dear."

Kate smiled as she hung up, and on her way to return the phone to the hallway table, she heard her name being called.

"Kate?" Melanie Durant and Bailey Gillespie came rushing down the hall, looking left and right.

"Yes?" asked Kate, walking back into the hall and replacing the phone on its table. "What is it?"

Augustus looked up from his vacuuming and stared at the two girls as they hovered around their friend.

"Augustus, could we have a moment?" asked Bailey.

The black man nodded, cut off the vacuum, and headed upstairs to close the last remaining windows. There might be plenty of summer left at Pawleys, but no one was going to be enjoying it in this house. As he went upstairs, he noticed Miss Melanie was crying.

Bailey gripped Kate's arm. "You've got to prepare yourself. It's bad news. Really bad news."

Kate looked from Bailey to Melanie and back to Bailey. Oh, my Lord, please don't let it be Jeb!

Or Ginny. She'd left in a huff, crushed shells spitting from under her tires as she and her hippie friends roared out of the parking lot. Ginny had sworn that she'd never return, not until South Carolina changed its tune; and because of that, she'd missed her grandmother's funeral.

Then Kate saw the men standing in the doorway at the rear of the house, two Marines with grim looks on their faces. A sharp pain stabbed through her chest, and she collapsed in the arms of her friends.

MORE THAN A FUNERAL

Melanie and Bailey flanked Kate at the gravesite with a good number of people, black and white, sitting behind them in folding chairs. Even the Virginia branch of the Stuart family had sent representatives. Jeb's younger brother, James, wearing his Citadel uniform, was there, almost a carbon copy of Jeb; the same dark eyes, dark hair, and deep tan.

This was James's senior year at the Military College of South Carolina, and soon he, too, would receive his orders to go overseas. But instead of joining the Marines, James Stuart had opted for a new unit created by John Kennedy called the Special Forces. James sat on the other side of Melanie, and occasionally reached over and gripped his new sister-in-law's hand, trying to buck her up.

Kate looked grim; eyes red from crying, as were Melanie's. As usual Bailey was the steadfast one, counseling Kate that she was a Stuart now and to model her behavior after that of Jacqueline Kennedy. When her husband had been assassinated, the whole world had been looking on; for Kate it would be the who's who of Charleston.

In fact, Kate had already seen how the Charleston elite handled themselves at funerals, because less than two weeks earlier Adelaide Belle had been put to rest in the French Huguenot cemetery after succumbing to another stroke. Many in her family said it had been expected, that Addy had been murdered by the LPN who had worked the poor dear to death when everyone knew a stroke victim needed plenty of peace and quiet, and especially rest. And there were those at Adelaide's funeral who muttered that if Kate Youngblood hadn't been up to enforcing such rules, she, too, should've been barred from the Belle beach house.

So the body of Adelaide Belle was ferried into Charleston by boat, no less. Kate Youngblood had not gone along but had been hustled into Charleston, where on King Street she was fitted in tailored black; Bailey in charge of the selection, Melanie in charge of the payment.

Kate tried to object, but her friends would not hear of it. It wasn't Kate's fault that she had fallen in love with the son of well-to-do people, and if the Stuarts had any sense they'd take over the grooming of their new daughter-in-law. But that wouldn't happen; Bailey and Melanie could see that by the looks Kate received at the ceremony at St. Michael's, so they stayed close to their friend to protect her, even from her new brother-in-law.

A Marine Corps honor guard folded the flag and the senior member stepped forward and handed the treasured bundle to the widow. Down the row Jeb's mother winced, and her husband gripped his wife's arm and steadied her. The remaining family members only stared at the coffin in front of them.

Arms were presented by the funeral detail, rifles pointed into the air and then fired, not once but three times, a twenty-one-gun salute for a genuine war hero. Seconds later, a group of Hueys from Fort Rucker, Alabama, overflew the ceremony with one helicopter symbolically missing from the formation, but not because Jeb Stuart had been a pilot.

Lieutenant Stuart had been awarded posthumously the Silver Star for valor because he and others of his platoon had held off the enemy attempting to overrun the crash site of a downed Huey. While he and others remained behind, a rescue chopper flew the wounded out of the hostile landing zone, the men on the ground left behind because there wasn't enough room for everyone on the rescue chopper. Children, cousins of Jeb Stuart, wearing their Sunday best, sat with their parents and peered from under the funeral canopy to watch the Hueys fly over. It was enough to drown out the sobs of the women and not a few men.

When presented with the flag that had graced her husband's coffin, Kate finally broke down. The officer in charge had seen this before, and he overlooked the widow's grief, stepped back, and saluted. But Kate saw none of this. Head bent over, she gripped the flag and tried to keep from falling out of her folding chair. All she could think was: I'm pregnant. I'm pregnant and I don't have a husband to help me raise the baby.

At the visitation at the Stuart home on South Battery, Melanie and Bailey anchored Kate as she thanked everyone for coming and spoke with friends and relatives, very few of whom Kate would ever see again. Not only had the family not known of Jeb's marriage, but it had been up to the three girls to travel into Charleston and deliver the bad news.

The whole scene had been a disaster, but Bailey had the good sense to go see Ginny's father, who knew everyone who was anyone in Charleston.

Franklin Belle was there, too, saying in a most disapproving tone, "Miss Youngblood, if I remember correctly you were to be here for the reading of my sister's will. If you did not understand the importance of such a request, you should've asked someone of my nephew's standing. Simms would've explained there was a bequest, which you will still receive, but have now dishonored." And the elderly man turned on his heel and tromped off, slamming the adjoining door behind him.

Simms apologized for his uncle. "He and my mother never saw eye to eye, and Uncle Franklin, as you can see, is taking it out on others. All those missed years . . . and missed opportunities."

Simms noticed that these girls, especially the Youngblood girl, appeared distraught. His throat tightened and he was barely able to get out, "Does this have to do with Virginia Lynne?"

"It has to do with Kate." Bailey slid forward in her chair and laid the telegram from the Defense Department on his desk.

Simms scanned the yellow sheet and his face lost what little color a Belle might normally have, the family being so pale. After staring at the telegram, he shook his head. "We couldn't find Ginny in time for her grandmother's funeral, but I'll make sure the Stuarts know about this."

Bailey pointed to the salutation. "It appears you missed to whom this telegram was addressed, Mister Belle."

Simms peered at the yellow sheet again, and then looked at Kate, who sat, head down, sobbing. "You mean . . . ?" he asked.

"The telegram is not the only surprise the Stuarts are going to receive today and we must prepare them for it."

"Oh, my . . ." Simms Belle collapsed in his chair and stared at this child of lintheads who had wormed her way into not only his confidence but also that of many others on Pawleys Island.

Bailey gestured at her two friends. "There's no way any of us could demand a meeting with Jeb's father. If we did, we'd have to explain why he should see us, and the contents of the telegram would come out, and we certainly aren't going to their home without Mister Stuart being there to console his wife."

"Yes, yes," said Simms, nodding. "You're right."

"Perhaps it would be best if you requested an immediate conference with Jeb's father. I understand his office is just down the street. We'll follow you over, and then on to their house on South Battery."

"Yes," added Melanie, "but we have to hurry. Otherwise they'll hear it from some reporter trying to make a name for himself."

Simms placed a call to Jeb's father, with whom he had served in the South Pacific. Fifteen minutes later the three girls were in a conference room, waiting to be ushered into the elder Stuart's office. Melanie and Bailey stood behind Kate, each with a hand on her shoulder. The two girls glanced at each other. There appeared to be some sort of commotion in the other room; then the elder Stuart threw back the door and stalked into the room.

He thrust the telegram in Kate's face. "Is this some kind of a joke?"

The girl did not raise her head but slowly shook it.

Melanie stepped back, but Bailey gripped Kate's chair and said, "No, sir, it is not."

The elder Stuart regarded the young blonde. "I know you from somewhere, don't I?"

"Yes, sir, I'm Senator Walter Gillespie's daughter, Bailey."

Stuart looked at Kate again, then glanced at Melanie, who was trying to put more chairs between her and this new threat.

The elder Stuart looked at the telegram, and slowly his face and posture began to crumple. Simms Belle slid a chair under his friend. He sat there, legs splayed out, arms resting on the armrests. The yellow sheet slipped from his hand.

It was several moments before he could ask, "You were married to my son?"

Again Kate nodded but did not look up. After so many summers on Pawleys, she knew she'd find no safe harbor here.

"He never told us." Mr. Stuart looked at Simms. "Who else knows?"

Simms looked at Bailey.

"No one but us, sir," said the blonde.

The elder Stuart nodded. "I'll have to tell my wife." He looked at Kate again. "And I'll have to tell her about you, too, young lady."

"Her name is 'Kate,'" said Melanie, in a low voice, and from several chairs away.

Stuart looked past the redhead to the brown-haired heiress who was soon to be richer than anyone in Charleston. Again he looked at his daughter-in-law. "When were you going to tell us?"

Kate looked up. "That was Jeb's decision."

"Well, it was a damn poor decision on his part."

That was too much for Kate and she broke down and began to sob. Melanie came forward and joined Bailey in putting a hand on her friend's shoulder.

"If they'd told you before they married, you would've tried to talk him out of it," said Bailey, a strain appearing in her voice.

"And why is that?"

"Because Kate comes from Judson Mill."

"I'm sorry," said the senior Stuart, puzzled, "but I don't know where that is or why it's relevant."

Simms Belle put a hand on his friend's shoulder. "Careful, counselor, you're not in court now."

"Of course you don't," said Melanie, screwing up her courage. "It's beyond the Neck," meaning north of what was considered proper Charleston.

"Young lady, I'm not sure—"

"It's a mill village outside Greenville."

"Yes, yes," said Mr. Stuart, nodding, "in that case, I would've objected, and so would his mother."

"How do you want to do this?" asked Simms.

Stuart considered the question, and as he did, evaluated Kate. "Miss Youngblood—"

"Mrs. Stuart or Kate," insisted Bailey.

The senior Stuart glanced at Bailey, then smiled at his new daughter-in-law. "Yes, of course. Kate."

He punched an intercom on the conference table and asked for his secretary. When the woman appeared at the far end of the room, he asked her to learn where his wife was; then he quickly changed that to where his wife would be for the remainder of the day.

"All on the q.t.," insisted Stuart. Once his secretary left, Stuart leaned over and tapped Kate's knee.

The redhead had begun sobbing again. That was quickly cut off when she looked up. "Yes . . . sir?"

"You wouldn't happen to be pregnant, would you?"

Kate's reaction was immediate and visceral. She knew this man had the resources to take her baby away from her. "No, sir, I am not."

The first stop was the Citadel, where James Stuart was summoned from class to the office of the commandant. The commandant was gracious enough to give Jeb's brother compassionate leave, after turning his office over to the Stuarts so James could be told about the death of his older brother and meet his new sister-in-law.

"Where were you married?" he asked.

"James, don't be rude."

He turned to his father. "It was merely a question, sir."

Kate told him where in South Georgia she and his brother had exchanged wedding vows. When she named the town, Bailey and Melanie looked at each other, their mouths falling open.

Bailey couldn't help asking, "When was this?"

Kate told them the date and smiled. She was proud of her marriage to Jeb Stuart.

Melanie and Bailey looked at each other again. Kate and Jeb had gotten married the same weekend they'd taken Ginny Belle to Georgia to have her abortion.

Kate saw their looks. "Is there something wrong?"

Melanie didn't know what to say and looked to Bailey.

"No, no, it's nothing. It's just that . . ." And the blond girl tried to think of a different lie she could sell her friend. "Well, it's just that that weekend we . . ." Bailey looked to Melanie.

The thin girl quickly said, "It's just that . . . that's the weekend we had a discussion about whether you and Jeb were serious or if it was a summer romance."

"Meaning you thought one of us was wasting our time and possibly ruining our life?"

"No, no," said Melanie, continuing to sell the lie. "It was more of a discussion of . . ." Melanie looked at Bailey. She had no idea where to go from here.

Bailey gave it a try. "It was more or less speculation as to what would happen if the Stuarts learned you two were serious."

"Well, I guess we found out!" And Kate stormed out of the commandant's office, down the hall, and out of the building.

The girls chased after her, but James Stuart and his father beat them to her, both protesting that there was nothing wrong with Jeb having married Kate.

Simms Belle asked a more pertinent question. "Don't you think we need to be getting on to see Jeb's mother?"

At the visitation, Franklin Belle sidled up to Kate and begged her forgiveness. "I'm sorry, my dear. I had no idea you had suffered a loss equal to mine."

"It's all right, sir. You had no way of knowing."

From beside her, Bailey and Melanie glared at Franklin Belle, and even more so when he drew an envelope from an interior pocket of his suit jacket.

"This, my dear, is for you. It's the bequest left you by my sister."

"My God," exclaimed Bailey, snatching the envelope away, "you think Kate could possibly be interested in money at a time like this?"

Others in the room turned and stared, many frowning at this breach in decorum. James Stuart closed with his sister-in-law, reached over, and took her hand. Kate glanced at her brother-in-law and hung on for dear life.

"I think, Miss Gillespie," said Franklin Belle, "that you should read the letter before you come to such a hasty conclusion."

"I'll do that right now." Nodding to Kate as she ripped open the envelope, Bailey said, "I don't want the son of a bitch to get away if you want to claw his eyes out."

"Young lady, I don't think—"

"Stuff it, old man," said Melanie, and instantly flushed and looked away.

Melanie only looked back when Bailey asked Franklin Belle, "Is this some kind of joke?"

James Stuart, who now had an arm around Kate, took the paperwork from Bailey. He began opening the second envelope.

"Kate, you're not going to believe this," said Bailey, "but it's an apology from Mrs. Belle. Evidently it was Addy who wrote the sorority council about your secret marriage to Jeb."

Melanie couldn't believe what she was hearing. "Mrs. Belle had Kate kicked out of the sorority?"

"Yes," said Bailey, "what a—"

"Watch your tongue, young lady," cautioned Franklin Belle. "Don't speak ill of the dead."

James Stuart held out another sheet, shaking a deed in everyone's face. "That may be why Adelaide Belle left her beach house to my new sister-in-law!"

The fifth summer

A Home for the Ages

Kate Stuart sat on the steps of her new home and looked out to sea. Beyond the waves, as far as she could see, and as far as she was concerned, the blue of the ocean went on forever, finally joining the straight line of a blue horizon. A tanker, farther out, steamed toward Charleston. People celebrating the beginning of summer strolled by, waved, and continued down the beach. On the radio played the Beatles—she had replaced the transistor with a Philco—but the songs couldn't drown out the sound of an infant's cry. Kate quickly got to her feet and went back inside.

When she reappeared, she had both a bottle and a baby. Again she took a seat on the steps and began to feed the child. It didn't take long to draw a crowd, visitors and permanent residents stopping to admire the newborn; even Old Leatherface wanted to know the child's name, and Kate told him.

The chatter from the porch caused a young black woman to peer through the screened door. "Need anything, Miss Kate?"

"No, thank you, Wilma," said the redhead, who had cut her long hair soon after the baby was born. She hadn't been sleeping well and wondered how she'd look when her father arrived later this afternoon.

"Well," said Wilma, looking no worse for wear after being clubbed into submission by Alabama state troopers several years earlier, "I'll put the clothes in the wash."

"And then get on your studies."

"You sure you don't want me to fix some fresh coffee? Your husband can't sleep forever."

"He was up with the baby last night. It'll be a while before we hear from him."

"Your husband was up . . . ?" The black girl clearly didn't believe the white one.

"He was trying to get the baby back to sleep."

"That don't seem right."

Kate chuckled. "That's not the only thing that's going to seem out of plumb around here."

The young Negro stared at her. "You sure you don't need nothing?"

"Anything, Wilma. The proper word is 'anything.'"

"Yes, ma'am."

"Look it up in the dictionary, but only after you put in the wash. No one becomes someone without an education. You should've learned that from your boyfriend. He wants to know everything, even stuff that's none of his business."

"I don't think Melvin's dropping by today."

"Good. You need to concentrate on your studies."

"Yes, ma'am." Wilma started away, then returned to the door. "Oh, I forgot. The senator's wife, I mean his first wife, she done called again about you working for the Community Chest."

"All in good time, Wilma, all in good time."

"Yes, ma'am."

More people passed the house, and since the sun was rising and the beach was heating up, few stopped to talk or admire the baby. Still, it was a while before Kate went back inside the beach house. There she met Bailey Gillespie coming down the hallway.

"Don't you ever use the front door?"

"If I did, you wouldn't know who your friends were." Bailey held out her arms. "May I?"

"Of course. I was getting tired of being a mother anyway."

"Oh, yeah, like I believe that." Bailey carried the child into the living room. She glanced at the bottle in Kate's hand. "I heard you were caught breast-feeding in one of the restrooms before last semester ended."

"That I was." Kate followed her friend into a room where a man's shirt and pants lay across the sofa. She put the bottle on a table next to a new rocker and picked up the clothes. On the coffee table lay a copy of Dr. Benjamin Spock's *Common Sense Book of Baby and Child Care.* "I don't think the girls at Carolina were ready for that."

"I know I'm not." Bailey took a seat in the rocker, a gift from Melanie Durant and herself, and placed a towel over her shoulder.

Kate went into the hall and hung the clothes on a peg. Upstairs, someone was moving around.

Since she had seen Wilma in the kitchen, Bailey shook her head. "Jeez, I can't stand this."

"What?" asked Kate, returning to the living room. "You want a baby, too? Want me to tell you how you can get one, and how you'll feel a month after delivery?" She took a seat on the sofa.

"Oh, I know how to get a baby. I've just got to work up the nerve."

"Preston still leaning on you?"

"Yeah. Take a guy to a wedding and he's all over you to get married." Bailey glanced in the direction of feet trudging across the upstairs hallway. "What's wrong with me? You've already slept with two guys, and I'm still a virgin. Who would have figured?"

Kate shook her head.

"Not yet?"

"He said that wasn't part of the deal. He just wants to be around to help raise the kid."

"God, that is strange."

"Not if you know your nineteenth century history."

Bailey stared at her blankly.

"Back then, when there were epidemics and such, this sort of arrangement wasn't all that uncommon."

"Well, I've never heard of it."

"He says it's happened before, even in his family."

"Well, I guess you have a lot to learn. You know, Kate, people who live in Charleston are really odd."

"Tell me about it."

Kate's husband called downstairs. "Hey, what does a guy have to do to get some coffee around here?"

Bailey held the baby up and away from her so she could shout toward the stairs, "Get it himself?"

"Bailey, that you down there?"

"It is."

"Go home. I don't want my wife corrupted by you liberated broads."

"Don't be so hasty. I'm teaching her how to go braless."

There was a pause, and then Kate's husband said, "Well, stick around. But what about the coffee? Both of you can't be spoiling my son at the same time."

Wilma came hustling down the hall with a steaming mug as Kate got to her feet. "I thought you were studying." said the redhead.

"Yes, ma'am, but I don't want you to lose another husband." And the black girl headed upstairs.

Bailey looked at her friend, who had retaken her seat on the sofa. When Kate looked up, Bailey saw she was no longer smiling. But she had not started crying, and there had been plenty of tears after Jeb Stuart was killed.

Bailey glanced toward the stairs. "Think this is going to work out?"

"Well, we're giving it one hell of a try."

"Honey," said Bailey, chuckling, "before this is over, you're going to need Mrs. Hamby's shrink."

"What do you hear from Melanie?"

"Spending the summer with her mother, wherever that might be." Bailey returned her attention to the baby. "Hey there, kid, remember me? I'm your damn godmother, and I've got lots to teach you, some of it very bad habits."

"Kids are baby goats, or haven't you heard?"

"I don't listen to my mother all that much anymore."

"But Melanie . . . ?"

"I think she's trying to get her mother to listen to *her,* you know, about the value of dating Ginny's dad."

"Gee, but Simms Belle is a nice guy. He talked Melanie's cousins into suing the Durant estate instead of throwing bricks through their windows."

"And probably doesn't stand a chance with Carolynn, being so far from Durham."

"Gosh, but that is sad."

"Still, if Melanie and her mom come to Pawleys . . ."

The baby cried out, and Bailey moved the child to her shoulder and began to pat his back. "Did you know that once Melanie earns her teaching certificate she'll be rich as Croesus?"

"Really?"

"Melanie comes into her majority by earning a teaching certificate. You know, if Melanie's had trouble with boys in the past, she won't be able to beat them off with a stick after she inherits her gazillions."

The room fell silent as Bailey continued to pat the baby. After the baby burped, she returned the child to her lap. "You know, I think I could handle a couple of these myself."

"What about running for office?"

"What about it?" She leaned down and nuzzled the baby. "A couple of these, why would I ever need to be governor?"

"Yeah, right," said Kate, smiling, "but these baby dolls need their diapers changed."

"Then that's when I'll run for office."

They both laughed and Bailey asked, "What do you hear from Ginny?"

"Not much. She did call and tell me she was going to the Democratic Convention in Chicago."

"What do you mean, as a delegate?"

"I don't think so, but she'll be there supporting Eugene McCarthy."

"Which will lead to demonstrations outside the convention center because all those kids won't be able to get inside, and they'll get all worked up, which is going to be a real problem. My father said you don't mess with Mayor Daley. He'll have his cops out in force, and they aren't afraid to bust a few heads."

Kate shrugged. "What can we do?"

"Nothing. If there's anything we learned from our summers at Pawleys, everyone has to find their own way."

"Yes," said Kate with a smile, "but it helps if you have friends, whether they be tobacco heiresses or those who're politically connected, or even radicals; it makes the journey a lot easier. I told Ginny she always has a room here."

They sat there as the phonograph dropped another LP, *Elvis' Golden Records, Vol. 4.*

After the music resumed, Bailey asked, "That Tet offensive back in March, it signaled the end of the war, didn't it?"

"God, but I hope so. I don't need to lose another husband."

"That's what I keep saying," said Wilma as she came downstairs, made the turn, and headed for the kitchen.

Bailey waited until the black girl had disappeared. "You're doing more for her than my family would've ever done."

"But your father's paying for Wilma's education."

"It's the least he could do. After all, she is a member of the family."

"A member of my family now."

"Until she gets some book learning," said Bailey, mimicking Kate's former accent, "then she'll be on the road again."

"I don't think so. I think Wilma wants to find a job. After Doctor King was murdered, I don't think Wilma wants anything to do with protesting."

Bailey looked up from the baby. "Doctor King?"

Kate glanced in the direction of the hallway. "It makes for a smoother running household."

"You know, I think I will run for office. Even if I don't win, there are things that have to be said."

"Then," said Kate with a smile, "that means we'll have to keep you virginal and baby-free."

"What's this talk about virgins?" asked James Stuart, walking into the living room with his coffee. "Someone offering to sacrifice herself to me?"

Bailey flushed and looked at the baby, but Kate smiled and said, "Sorry, soldier, but women are off-limits for you, with the exception of your wife."

Bailey looked up to see James Stuart's eyebrows go up. Then she watched him go over to the sofa and kiss his wife on the cheek. "Well, that is good news." And James stood there, drinking his coffee and watching his son being cooed to and cuddled by Bailey.

Finally, he turned to Kate. "What's she doing with little Jeb?"

"Trying to avoid running for public office."

To learn more about Pawleys:

Chronicles of the South Carolina Sea Islands
Nancy Rhyme

Heaven is a Beautiful Place
Genevieve C. Peterkin & William P. Baldwin

History of Georgetown County
George Rogers

Pawleys Island . . . a living legend
Charlotte Kaminski Prevost

Pawleys . . . as it was
Celina McGregor Vaughan

Pawleys Island, Historically Speaking
Eugene B. Chase Jr. & Katherine H. Richardson

Pawleys Island: Stories from the Porch
Eugene B. Chase & Lee G. Brockington

Potluck from Pawleys
Gladys Hiott

South Carolina: A History
Walter B. Edgar